Please read, review
and pass on...

THE LOST MAN

David Roy

HOBART BOOKS

THE LOST MAN

COPYRIGHT © DAVID ROY 2021

ISBN 978-1-914322-05-1

First Published in 2021
by
Hobart Books, Oxfordshire, England
hobartbooks.com

Printed and bound in Great Britain by Clays Ltd, Elcograf S.p.A.

The Lost Man

By David Roy

1940

'And what's his name again?'

'Ted Dexter, sir.'

'Sounds like an American.'

'He's from Belfast.'

'A fellow countryman of yours.'

Brooke said nothing. He was from Fermanagh, which in terms of Northern Irish geography was the other side of a bucolic galaxy from the 'big smoke' of Belfast. Besides which he had been brought up in France, yet another galaxy away. The old man pulled a face, a sort of pout, and then carried on.

'What he has done is very commendable. I gather that he is something of a reluctant hero?'

'I wouldn't describe him as a reluctant hero so much as an obstructive one. In fact, I am not sure that one can rightly call him a hero of any kind.' Immediately, Brooke wondered if the term 'recalcitrant' would have been more apt. Probably, he decided, but it would also have suited the PM's love of words too much, drawn him into yet another military fantasy. A 'recalcitrant hero' would have been perfect for him. How he saw himself, in fact. He wanted men who displayed the same careless bravado that typified his own early years. Too often derring-do took the place of practical reality, and Brooke knew that if the task of advising the PM ever came to him, it would be his job to rein the great man in, to turn his wild ideas into workable strategies.

'Then so be it. We shall have to take whatever heroes we can find. We might need men like him in the years ahead. Men who are daring and resourceful.' He made a fist and seemed about to pound the table with it but instead he stopped himself as if afraid of waking a sleeping child. His fist came down on the table gently and soundlessly. He looked at the General as if daring him to contradict his appraisal of Dexter and knowing that in Brooke he had one of the few men with the temerity to do exactly that. Brooke gave a tired smile and watched Churchill pace the room like an elderly bear. He constantly wondered how the old man fuelled his restlessness.

As he waited, Brooke recalled his meeting with Lance Corporal Dexter. He was not at all sure that the words daring and resourceful quite fitted, but he kept his counsel, understanding the old man's need to enthuse about the young soldiers who were saving their country from tyranny.

'If, as you say, he is not really a hero, then we shall have to make him into one', stated Churchill, plainly. Brooke, who sometimes despaired of the PM's simplistic attitude, smiled weakly. He wondered if his boss was dangerously naïve.

'The device he has brought us is top secret, sir. If we make too much of the fact that it is now in our possession then we might undo the potential benefits it brings us. In fact, we need to say as little as possible about this.' There was silence for a moment, the PM drawing deeply on his cigar. Brooke looked on, either waiting for his cue to speak, or for the next lightning bolt of impractical genius to strike the earth. He could never be sure which it would be. Brooke cast his glance round the office, taking in the accoutrements that Churchill had gathered, and which formed a tangible part of his personality. His was not the life of the ascetic, even in wartime, a fact evidenced by the decanter and humidor that lay ready like weapons.

'Very well. He shall be our secret hero', he said at last. Churchill beamed, more than happy with the phrase he just invented. 'A secret hero', he repeated. Brooke fought the urge to roll his eyes.

Chapter One

'Corporal Dexter, take your men down the canal bank and find positions where you can hold up the Germans. You are just to delay them while the battalion withdraws.'

'We might be better off on the other bank, sir', said Dexter as he adjusted his chin strap. His tone was matter of fact. He glanced behind him at his little section, to check that they were preparing themselves for the task ahead. He needn't have worried. Dinger gave him a nervous conspiratorial wink. Ted pointed to the far bank for the benefit of the officer.

'Why?' asked Captain Pomeroy, testily. His distaste for the NCO was evident and he sighed. *Why does everyone in the army think they know better than me*, he wondered? He was sick of bloody NCOs who thought they knew more than their officers.

'Well, sir', began the NCO. 'If those refugees on the path over there', he pointed to the village and both men looked in the direction of a small, but oddly biblical exodus, 'arrive at the same time as the Jerries, we're not going to get a clear shot at them.' He puffed out his chest and tilted his chin slightly upwards as he had been taught on the parade square.

As a man determined to die with his boots on, Ted Dexter rarely stood barefoot, but had he done so he would have risen to an altitude of exactly five feet, eight inches.

4

He was not a giant, but nor was he without presence. People tended to listen to him when he spoke – people who ought to have known better in Pomeroy's view. It was a shame for the army but Dexter, for all his failings, was a born leader.

Pomeroy bit his lip as if making a momentous decision. In this instance, he could actually see the NCO's point but would never, and could never, concede. He had principles, one of which was that officers knew better than NCOs – that was the whole point of having them and training them at great length and considerable expense. Officers were commissioned to make decisions whereas NCOs only had to implement them. It was the natural order of things, an incontrovertible law of nature...

'I realise that', he said with forced patience. 'But if you go onto the other bank you are stuck there, aren't you? There's no way to get back across and you'll be captured.'

Pomeroy had become a teacher talking to a dull pupil. As he spoke these words, he realised that Dexter's capture would actually be a good thing as far as he was concerned; killing two birds with one stone so to speak. *Losing Lance Corporal Dexter and his three dunces* represented no great blow for the army. He was sure that they would fight on without them.

'There's a bridge down there, sir', insisted the NCO. Ted could almost feel the loathing, fear and resentment oozing from the officer. He knew that he should have backed off and accepted the officer's instructions. It was not his place to argue and normally he wouldn't have bothered but...

Ted's men looked on, impassively. None of them, apart from Dinger, wanted to be closer to the Germans than was strictly necessary.

'For crying out loud, Dexter! Those are my orders but if you want to be on the other bank, then go ahead. I'll probably never see you or your men again if you do that, so we won't have to bother with a charge sheet, will we?' His exasperation was tempered with relief that he was ridding himself of this idiotic man. 'Now I'm going to leave you to it. This bank, the other bank? I don't care.'

It was all rather abrupt. There was a note of subdued hysteria in his voice, almost as if he was scared. Pomeroy turned on his heel and strode off, impressively collecting a bicycle from a hedgerow as he did so. He made it look like hedges always contained bicycles which could be picked with less effort than that required to pick berries. They watched dumbly as he rode off, the bicycle wheels wobbling on the cobbles.

'Where did he get that bike?', asked Whitey.

'That's his escape bicycle', said Snowball, sagely. 'He always keeps it handy in case he has to retreat unexpectedly.'

'Withdraw', corrected Dinger, the proper soldier. 'The British Army withdraws.' Dinger, had been a soldier since the age of fifteen. He fitted the army like a hand fitted a glove.

'Aye, in case he has to *withdraw* unexpectedly', said Snowball, rolling his eyes disdainfully. Snowball had been in the army for just a year but he was blessed, or possibly cursed, with much common sense, and Ted used him as an unwitting advisor without making it too obvious that he was doing so.

'He might just want us dead, you know', explained Snowball. Ted gave him a withering look; it wasn't an entirely welcome observation. When Ted needed advice – which was rarely – he had plenty on tap. It was usually the

6

middle ground, somewhere between the rashness of Dinger and the caution of Snowball, that Ted used to guide him in his own decision making.

He surveyed his little army, half a section strong, with a mixture of gratitude and bewilderment. Snowball had temporarily lost his impetus and was standing, silent and thoughtful as if the war had no bearing on his immediate future. Ted smiled.

Snowball's surname was so odd that it circumvented the need to invent a nickname for him. Dinger was Dinger Bell, of course. No-one ever used his given name of George. Perhaps his mother. And his father, if he had one.

Ted's third soldier was called Whitey, Fusilier White. A long, gangly youth, he had the palest skin anyone had ever seen on a living body, thus making his moniker even more apt. Whitey made up the numbers, said little but smiled frequently, giving the impression that he was much too gentle to be a soldier… or anything else really. The army, with its idiotic rough and tumble, had become his refuge, a place where he was accepted. Ted worried that this fragile man might break, or just wrinkle up in the sun like an old, worn chamois leather. He felt responsible for him, not like a father for a son but certainly like an older brother for a younger one.

'You shouldn't wind him up so much, Ted', said Snowball. Ted pulled a face.

'Who?', he asked.

'You', said Snowball.

'I know you mean me. *Who* shouldn't I wind up?'

'Pomeroy. You wind him up and he gives us shit to do. Like this.'

'You volunteered for it, mate', said Ted, indignantly.

'We all volunteered. For the army, that is', said Whitey.

'Shut up, Whitey. Who bloody asked you?', spat Ted. Whitey shrugged and looked down at his feet, quietly exasperated that his opinion seemed to carry so little worth. 'In case you hadn't noticed, Pomeroy had already 'selected' us for this little job. Nothing I said actually made the situation any worse. So, let's get ourselves in the undergrowth, wait for the Germans to turn up and then kill them. Okay?' Ted raised his eyebrows, a facial full-stop, to indicate that the matter was closed. Glancing at the sky through squinting eyes, he set off walking towards the bushy area he had picked out for their hideaway.

'You're always being cheeky to him, that's all I'm sayin', Ted.' Ted stopped but didn't turn. He felt like he had suddenly been given charge of three bickering schoolgirls instead of tough, professional soldiers.

'Just do what you're told Snowball, and don't bloody argue with an NCO', said Dinger, pointing a finger at the older man, as if he was Ted's deputy.

'I didn't say I wasn't going to do what I was told.'

'Right! Enough of this! Let's get in position.' Ted looked sternly at his three charges, wondering if, perhaps, Snowball was right. Their argument subsided and, in its place, as if their collective presence abhorred a vacuum, came doubt and self-recrimination. Just supposing Snowball *was* right? What if they now found themselves in a position so bad, so precarious that they could not extract themselves from it? What if the whole thing really was Ted's fault? What then was Ted's defence? What would he present to the judge and jury that sat with increasing frequency, taking up valuable space in his head?

Ted directed the men into their positions, giving the Bren gun the greatest field of fire and checking that each man knew what to do should they spot the German infantry, or indeed the engineers who might be sent ahead. The Belgian refugees were only a few hundred yards away now, moving along the canal bank like a disconsolate snake. Ted had seen similar sights too many times already, had become inured to it and callous. It wasn't that he didn't care, more that the act of caring had become an abstract notion for him. Perhaps he had run out of pity, or that he was storing the pity up for something else, husbanding his finite emotional resources for some greater peril that lay ahead.

These people before them, these refugees, had certainly given up everything, but they were still alive and likely to remain so. The very act of fleeing ensured that this would be the case. Ted and his men had no such guarantee. They couldn't cut and run with impunity. If the army was Ted's home, as he had so often been told, then it was one which offered him little comfort and even less safety. He asked himself if he would have swapped positions with the refugees but couldn't come up with an answer; neither party was in an enviable position.

He looked over at Snowball crawling in behind the gun, with Whitey taking up station next to him ready to pass magazines across as needed. It was all part of Ted's own drill that he had worked out and that they had practised countless times.

He had faith in his men he supposed, but he didn't trust the Germans to arrive only after the refugees had passed. To do so would give Ted and his men a clear field of fire and that would be too neat, too tidy, too… helpful in the chaos of war. Ted's doubts resurfaced from their shallow refuge, skimming the underside of his

9

consciousness like a fish insistent on being caught. He felt the constricting grip of responsibility squeeze the air from his chest. Oppression was a weight on his body and soul. He began to wonder if he *should* have disobeyed Pomeroy's orders and positioned his men on the far bank instead, putting the moving screen of refugees at their backs. *Did that bastard have it in for him?*

They would still be in danger wherever they were. Another disadvantage of their current dispositions occurred to him now. The opposite canal bank was lined with heavy vegetation for the entire length of the path. The Germans, should they appear, would be very close indeed by the time they came into view. However, they couldn't easily storm his position, simply because the canal was in the way.

Ted hunkered down to make sure that they would all have a view of the far bank from where they lay. He shook his head in silent reproach – he should have done this first, before they settled in.

'Do you ever think about death?'

Ted turned to look at Dinger, as if discovering for the first time that he was a lunatic.

'What?', he said curtly.

'Death. Do you ever think about it?'

'Who's death? Yours or mine?'

'Any', said Dinger. He stood there looking small and with an innocence that Ted had never noticed before. He was like a schoolboy preparing to talk his way out of a compromising situation. 'Just death in general.'

Ted gave a small snort of laughter, dismissive but worried too. If Dinger was getting windy then maybe their situation was worse than he thought. He shook his head.

'No Dinger. I don't think about it. This is hardly the time to start either.'

'We are going to be okay, though?', persisted the other man.

'Not if we stand out here in the open discussing death.'

'Right.' Dinger nodded as if satisfied with the precautions in place to prevent their early demise.

'Let's get into those bushes and we can talk about death when we are running like hell from the Krauts.'

Dinger laughed. Ted smiled. He shared his men's apprehension but it was his job to keep them calm, ready for whatever scrap lay ahead. The truth was that he had no more experience of shooting Germans than they had, but it was he who wore the stripe and collected the extra pay, and that tiny embroidered chevron meant that, in the absence of anyone more senior, their fate lay in his hands. It was he who would make the decisions and they would just have to trust him.

He wondered if they really did. Now that it came to the real thing, *did* they trust him? And did he trust *them*? Would they fight?

***

Rain fell lightly, dampness making its slow way to earth through the layered canopy of trees that gave the soldiers cover. It was warm rain and yet it cooled the air. Impossible physics. Ted imagined, but couldn't see, a rainbow, and hankered after the simpler life of a child, remembering any number of stalled childhood missions in which he had set out to find the pot of gold that every ten-year-old knew lay at its end.

Inaction made them weary and he had let them sleep while he kept watch, but they had only dozed, and each of them was now wide awake and observing intently to their front. Each felt his own weight of expectation, tempered with fear. Not just the fear of death, injury or capture but of letting his fellow soldiers down when required to show courage and resilience.

They watched in silence as the refugees traipsed along the path only twenty yards from them. It was obvious that some of them had seen the soldiers as they took up position and they looked at them anxiously, or looked away as if doing so could remove the chances of being caught up in a gun battle between the two sides.

They knew that the British were waiting for the enemy and therefore, unless they were badly informed, that enemy couldn't be far behind. One or two glanced over, mildly interested at best but the rest, the majority, continued on their way, eyes fixed on some point on the ground just a few feet in front of them. Their flight was a postponement of doom, not an escape. Ted thought of his own family and transposed them into this desperate march, and only then could he begin to feel any real sympathy. If his mother and father had been there, in that collection of frightened humanity, what would he do? Nothing, he supposed. He couldn't help them.

There was no rhythm to their steps, no coordination of effort or sense of purpose. The fact that they were headed in one direction was purely because there was only one direction they *could* head, the one which led them away from the Germans. They came from all walks of life, that much was clear, with one group almost entirely missing:

young men, of course. The Belgian Army was fighting, just as it had done in the Great War, and these refugees were the people who had no place in that fight. Ted couldn't imagine where they were going and again he imagined his own family in the terrible drama he was now witnessing.

God forbid that the Germans ever marched on Belfast, he thought, but if they did where would his mum and dad flee to? There was nowhere. His reverie ended abruptly.

'Ted. I think I see someone in those bushes across there.'

Ted looked over at Dinger. He was dubious, almost convinced that they would not yet encounter their enemies.

'Where?'

'Almost straight across but just to the left.'

Ted looked. They all did.

'There's a bench and some sort of tall plant with yellow flowers. See it? Taller than all the others.'

'Okay.' He felt his mouth run dry, felt the tension in the others, a heightened sense of danger.

'Under that. In amongst all those shiny leaves, there's a bit which is sort of oblong, like a letter box – a gap in the leaves. There's someone in there. You can see them move every now and again.'

Ted wasn't sure. He saw the spot that Dinger had described so well but he knew that the mind could play tricks in these circumstances. The more intently you looked for your enemies, the more likely you were to find them... even when they weren't there. It was even worse at night.

'I see where you mean. But I'm not sure. Can anyone else see it?'

'Can't see anyone moving, Ted', said Snowball. 'You'd think that those refugees might see or hear something – they're much closer than us.'

Just then, as if on cue, one of the refugees stopped, hesitated, peered into the bush and then recoiled in alarm. He was an older man, dressed smartly in clothes that had seen better days, a sort of down-on-his-luck gentleman. He had a suitcase and an overcoat slung over his arm. He glanced over at the British soldiers hidden from view and then swiftly looked away again, perhaps angry with himself for having compromised them.

'Well, *he* saw something Ted', said Dinger.

'He did, Ted', confirmed Whitey, breathlessly. Ted looked over at the long pale man, lying prone, hidden from their enemies.

'Still can't see anything myself', said Ted. His mind was alive with possibilities and plans that formed, fell apart and reformed unbidden and nearly useless. He looked at the slow train of newly homeless civilians and decided it would take half an hour for them to pass, or maybe longer than that.

'What do we do, Ted?', asked Snowball.

'Well...' *That was a good question*, he thought. A firefight with the Germans, if they were actually there of course, would be over in seconds. It might provide a delay while they licked their wounds but it would also give them warning of the British Army's proximity. Alternatively, of course, the refugees might cause a longer immediate delay without any shots being fired simply by providing an unintentional obstacle. Ted couldn't order his men to open fire on the Germans when civilians were in the way. That's if there were any Germans there, of course. Besides which, he reasoned, could four British soldiers bring about a delay of the magnitude that Pomeroy hoped for? These thoughts chased each other through his mind like phantom schoolboys playing tag, and none of them stayed still for long enough to be given proper consideration. Ted's mouth was drier than ever, as if he had marched across the desert, and his heart was racing. He realised that he was on the verge of panic.

'Dinger and Snowball. Very slowly crawl out of this bloody bush. Backwards. No sound, no disturbing the branches or leaves. Head back to the road we came in on and wait there unless it's crawling with Krauts, which it shouldn't be. Me and Whitey are going to stay here for a minute and then follow you. Okay?' He saw their faces bob up and down in the green gloom of the bush. 'Go', he ordered, and they backed out like dogs retreating from an unwinnable fight. Ted looked around to check that they did not shake any branches.

'Couple of minutes, and we follow them, Whitey?'

'Aye, Ted', said the pale man, nervously.

Ted didn't know if he was doing the right thing or not, but he felt better for having at least made a decision, having justified the small pay increment he earned. The figures opposite – those Germans crouched and waiting in cover – still eluded him, however. He looked away, resting his eyes before his brain created what he expected to see.

'Can you see anything, Whitey?', he asked, puzzlement in his voice. He was still sceptical.

'No', said Whitey, flatly.

'Do you think he imagined it, Dinger I mean?'

'Dunno', said Whitey with a sigh. 'He doesn't usually flap too much, does he?'

'No, but…' He stopped as another refugee faltered and looked intently in their direction. She was a young woman, perhaps slightly plump, or maybe just wearing every stitch of clothing she owned, pushing a pram piled high with worldly goods. There may have been a baby in it too, but from his vantage point Ted couldn't tell. Other people impatiently pushed past her, one man remonstrating with barely contained ire.

'Bloody hell missus, why don't you sell tickets…'

'Let's just get out of here, Whitey. You go first on your belly and make for the road.' He watched as the other soldier slithered out, his long khaki-clad body a writhing stick creature. It was when he glanced back that he saw it: the glint of binoculars. 'Time to go, Ted', he whispered to himself.

Chapter Two

Clear of the canal bank, they raced across a field, stumbling, getting up and running again. They were both breathless but relieved when their two friends stood to reveal themselves, like Jack-in-a-box soldiers.

'Right, let's get out of here', said Ted, taking deep breaths, forcing himself to appear calm. His responsibilities weighed heavily. 'The battalion went this way', he added pointing down the road. 'You were right Dinger. There were Germans in the undergrowth.'

'Did they see us, d'you think?'

'Maybe but it doesn't matter now.'

'What's Pomeroy going to say?', asked Dinger, breathlessly. They were now walking quickly, putting distance between them and the canal. Dinger ran every now and again to keep up, his legs shorter than those of his mates.

'About what, Dinger? That we didn't shoot any Germans? I'll just explain to him.'

'He won't like it though, Ted', said Snowball.

'Let me worry about it. Besides if he's bothered he can go back and shoot some himself.' Ted didn't let his desperate stab at humour slow his pace. He was intent upon escape, even one which only freed him to fight another day. All thoughts of hunger or discomfort were displaced by the need to move, to put distance between them and their enemies. Ted imagined the Germans on the near side of the canal now jogging after them. It didn't enter his mind that they might simply be taking it easy, unconcerned by the proximity of a few Britishers. These were men who wiped out all opposition without a thought, part of a vast, uncaring steamroller; they had no need to hurry, no need to take risks.

Ted took a moment to assess his handling of their situation. Had he acted correctly, he wondered? And by that he meant, had he been sufficiently courageous and tactically proficient? And then he thought about cowardice, perhaps the ultimate failing for any soldier. Better to be incompetent than cowardly... although some of his acquaintance were undoubtedly both. His thoughts took a detour of their own volition. Pomeroy seemed to take shape before him, drifting just out of reach as he strode through the field. He pictured the officer in his tailored uniform.

Pomeroy was a coward.

Ted couldn't quite explain how he knew this. What arcane mental processes imbued him with this unusual knowledge, especially since he had never seen any actual proof that might substantiate his belief. He *just knew* – an argument that generally sounded specious. He glanced at his little band. Each man was lost in his own thoughts. He smiled, despite his own fear, but soon unbidden mental processes took over control of his mind.

Naturally, he'd known other men who were cowards and perhaps it was this experience which provided him with his redundant gift. Firstly, there was Sammy McClelland, an old school friend who could throw a stone with unerring, almost supernatural accuracy. Indeed, if he had never been called upon to do anything else then

18

Sammy should have been guaranteed some sort of immortality, but as it was, life – just plain old life – had shown up his shortcomings, notably a lack of courage. He was a big lad with a fearless look that disappeared at the merest hint of trouble. He was the sort of friend you thought you wanted when you were in a tight corner, such as being surrounded by a gang of Catholics who you had just been shouting abuse at.

It had happened. They had shouted, 'Fuck the Pope' at the tops of their voices as a gang of older lads from St Malachy's had been passing. Both Ted and Sammy had already worked out their escape route and immediately sprinted for the gate at the other side of the little park wedged into the corner of two streets. One street – the one they would reach via the gate – was Protestant, and the other – currently occupied by the Catholic boys – was, inevitably, Catholic. The communities lived cheek by jowl in some sort of untrusting harmony.

Their escape plan was good in one respect, i.e. that it was simple, but bad in another – the gate was locked. As Ted had metaphorically and actually rolled up his sleeves ready for a scrap, he glanced over at his friend and was shocked at the look of terror that had taken hold of his face. A man staring at certain death couldn't have been more obviously scared. Ted's own confidence wilted like the leaves on a poisoned flower but inexplicably the Catholic boys just laughed, turned on their heels and left them alone with their shame. They – the Catholics – had won the fight without throwing a punch. Ted knew that he'd learned something that day but, like so many of life's lessons, he wasn't sure what.

Another coward he had met more recently. This was a corporal who had bragged incessantly about his (at the time, untested) prowess as a killer. Ted remembered him from the depot where he had been an instructor for the recruits. He looked like a murderer.

Most of the corporals employed to turn Ulster's callow youth into fighting men displayed an odd mix of compassion and sadism, and did so to great effect, becoming near legends in the process. Ted

19

had worshipped his corporal back in 1936, the year in which he had completed his own training, and yet had described him, without malice, as a 'merciless bastard'. He recalled the tiny tremor of laughter that this description elicited from his father, a man who had once been on the receiving end of similar treatment from similar hard men... twenty years previously, of course.

Corporal Flanagan was different. He had the sadism but not the compassion. The recruits of his section became soldiers despite him, not because of him. He knew his job in a technical sense and could teach them the finer points of soldiering, but they worked hard for themselves to prove that they could become British soldiers, and not in order to win his approval. Flanagan had been posted back to the battalion in 1938, expecting to get his sergeant's stripe but the promotion had avoided him as if his weakness was already apparent.

The regiment had landed in France in 1939 and he continued to strut and brag as he had always done, seemingly desperate to kill the enemy. He believed himself to be virtually indestructible, or so it seemed. That had only changed two weeks ago when they had all been subjected to a Stuka attack, their first real deadly encounter with the enemy. It was a terrifying assault on the senses for all those involved. Their casualties had been light, just cuts and bruises, and the men had emerged from their trenches and shell scrapes when it was clear that the dive-bombers had gone. All except Flanagan, who had to be lifted out sobbing and soiled. Not for him the wry grins or dazed shock of his soldiers. Ted hadn't seen him since and no one even bothered to wonder about his fate, much less make any enquiry.

Pomeroy too was a coward of that magnitude but he disguised it better than most. Ted supposed that was what officer training did for you. Pomeroy's cowardice was more difficult to describe, less obvious, almost an indefinable quality, or lack of one. It was a look or a mannerism, like a flinch that a casual observer could easily miss. It was a way of talking, just slightly strained with an edge of deeply hidden incipient panic. Pomeroy was some sort of minor sporting hero, rugby, cricket or both maybe. He had the poise and assurance of the *well-bred man, destined for success, but Ted knew better. He knew — just knew — that Captain Pomeroy was a coward. He just hadn't shown it yet. Worst of all he seemed to sense that the officer knew of Ted's illicit knowledge. A look might pass between them in which a series of unwelcome truths could pass like electronic signals for which the NCO was the only receiver. Pomeroy knew that Ted knew...*

'You okay, Ted?', asked Snowball, ever solicitous. Ted glanced behind him but didn't stop. His three soldiers walked, heads down as if into a bracing wind.

'I'm fine. Just thinking.'

The road was a straight, grey ribbon stretching from where they were now to where they needed to be in two hours. It was tree-lined and peaceful. Ted found it easy to picture it in better times as some sort of highway enjoyed by the wealthy French motorist, taking his family out for a picnic lunch. He imagined their comfortable saloon trundling along until they found a lay-by and pulled in. They stepped out, this happy bunch, feeling the sun on their faces, enjoying great lungfuls of fresh, fragrant air, far away from the cares of the city and its fumes. Father, Papa — whatever he was known as — would take their huge wicker hamper from the boot and lay it on the rug with reverence before opening its creaking lid to reveal a feast of bread, cheeses, wine... At this point Ted couldn't actually think of anything else that these clichéd French folks ate.

His imaginary idyll was further compromised by the voice of Snowball, his broad Ballymena accent, typically Ulster Scots in its intonation, rending the warm summer air. Ted had never known him to crack a joke but he did so now.

'Hey Ted, why do the French have so many tree-lined roads?'

'Don't know. Is this a joke?'

'Yes.' Snowball could barely suppress a chuckle of anticipation at the impending humorous denouement.

'Don't know. Why *do* the French have so many tree-lined roads?'

'So that the German Army can march in the shade.'

Ted smiled. Behind him he heard Dinger begin to cackle and then Snowball cautiously joined him with a series of broken guffaws.

'Oh, I get it', said Whitey a moment later and he too laughed.

'Have you heard that one before?', asked Snowball. The men maintained their brisk pace but Dinger continued to laugh, forcing a bigger smile from Ted.

'Not heard it before, no.'

'It's good isn't it? My dad told me it. He fought in France in the last war.'

'Well, it's nice that that joke is getting a new lease of life, I suppose', said Ted, doubtfully. He suddenly realised that the joke's subject matter was actually a great human tragedy. Powerful images of destruction and mayhem filled his mind. He saw tanks running over children, grinding their tiny bodies to pulp, and bombers high overhead dropping incendiaries and high explosives onto beautiful towns. He wondered where these images had come from, in which despairing corner of his consciousness they had taken shape. He recalled the OC talking to their platoon commander once, discussing the coming conflict and using the phrase 'industrial warfare.' Ted had reached his own conclusions about what that term really meant.

His stomach twisted with fear, something less than pain, and for a moment their pursuit of the battalion seemed pointless, as if their fates were sealed whether contact was ever made or not.

His three soldiers just kept marching, their faith in him unspoken, unquestioning and quite possibly undeserved, or so he told himself. In reality, they had no option but to carry on. Overhead he saw, but did not hear, aircraft flying towards the enemy, each one nothing more than a tiny black speck, carving an incongruously substantial vapour trail from the blue skies, delivering war where there had been peace. Ted felt weary beyond description. It was a weariness born of low expectations. He couldn't always imagine them surviving the war, and when he thought that, he pictured the Germans in close pursuit hunting them down: himself, Dinger, Whitey and Snowball.

Naturally enough, he'd expected to be tired, exhausted perhaps – after all this was the war they had trained for, training which itself was exhausting. He imagined them walking and walking forever, towards some perpetually elusive salvation, a place that never got any closer, a mobile paradise that slipped along like some furtive animal, always out of reach. His mood transcended mere soldier's glumness and for a time he felt trapped. Without any apparent walls or fences he was imprisoned, entombed in misery, and his mind became so clouded that he wanted to shout out with the sheer frustration of not being able to steer a course to safety.

And yet it was more than mere safety that he craved, it was peace. Not an end to the war either but something more personal, tailored just for him. But what was it? Then suddenly he realised – he wanted to be left alone. He didn't want to see anyone or talk to anyone. Just a day to himself would be enough, to clear his mind and then refill it with something more sustaining.

He could picture the place where he would luxuriate in this solitude too: a white room with a simple bed and nothing else. He didn't crave alcohol, or any other form of stimulant, just a clear mind, some calm, and some time.

'Fat chance', he said to himself.

'What, Ted?', said Whitey.

He looked over at the tall, angular man. 'Nothing, Whitey. Nothing.'

He knew that it would have suited Pomeroy never to see him again. His antipathy towards Ted was both obvious and boundless, but the hilltop town of Cassel, the battalion's new home, was there ahead of them like an ancient fortress used for centuries to dominate the surrounding countryside. It was there that they were headed. It was an obvious defensive position – perhaps too obvious, an easy target.

'We'll cut across the fields, I suppose', said Ted pointing to an isolated farm, beyond which lay the hill. 'We can grab some food from there on the way.'

'Do you think they won't feed us when we get back?', joked Snowball.

'I don't take anything for granted', he said as he led the scramble over the fence and into the field. He heard the clank of a mess tin as Whitey hit the ground. It was the sound of a dull bell, muted by layers of fabric, but a tell-tale nevertheless.

'You'd better sort that bloody thing out, Whitey', he scolded.

Whitey said, 'Sorry, Ted.' His cheeks coloured as he fumbled with his webbing, embarrassed at his display of poor fieldcraft. It was the sort of amateurish thing to be expected of recruits, not trained, experienced soldiers. He felt as if he had let them down, let Ted down. The sounds they made, if they made them at all, had to be the sounds of nature or some facsimile thereof. Metal on metal was the sound of man, industrial in nature and a giveaway to the enemy.

Despite his momentary annoyance, Ted's spirits had lifted a little having sighted their new base. He just hoped that there would be an opportunity for rest once they reached it.

'We should try to keep out of Pomeroy's way when we get back, Ted', said Whitey, breathlessly. Ted nodded but didn't falter as he forced the pace across the field. The house was only five hundred yards away, the foot of the hill maybe half a mile beyond that.

'I intend to, Whitey, don't worry.' The men began to stumble-run towards their destination, a subconscious urgency sending them onwards. Ted thought he heard aircraft and turned his head to scan the vast skies above them, slipping in the process, down on one knee, falling into the ploughed dirt. 'Shit', he said and began to stand. Around him the world had begun to change, or maybe just the valley through which they stumbled.

'Get up, you silly bugger', laughed Dinger but his words suddenly became lost in the bigger event that surrounded them, eclipsing anything that went before. They felt a presence, filled with energy and destructive force. The air was replete with noise, a hundred angry demons screaming, bent on some sort of revenge. As Ted pushed himself up from the ground, he saw Whitey and Snowball fall to their faces and the latter turn to Dinger, urging him to do the same. He did so, pushing Ted back to earth in the process, impelled by a harsher form of gravity. Time faltered and slipped. Ted felt his rifle stock smack violently against the rim of his helmet and his unyielding ammunition pouches, filled with rounds, were thrust into his ribs like an uppercut that left him winded and fighting for breath.

Above him torrents of noise assaulted his ears and then the ground began to shake, pounded by the angry fists of a giant child, its brain all but closed down by the intensity of its tantrum. He felt his entire body lift and fall back and the same thing happened again. Granular rain began to fall in bursts as the topsoil was cleaved from the field, separated, dried out and thrown back in sulky handfuls.

Ted risked a glance from beneath the rim of his helmet, hardly believing what he saw. The air was rent by flashes of reds and yellows, jagged shapes that somehow boiled and ripped. His breath was drawn from his body and he felt he was drowning in an airless hell. Through this curtain of destruction, he caught sight of the house, saw figures running to impossible safety, a flash and the body of a young girl torn asunder, scattered in fragments.

He imagined rather than heard the wail of the parents, their hesitancy, as if they could piece their child back together from bloody remnants, and he felt their despair as it matched his own and became one with it. Part of the house crumbled as he watched, just one corner washed away by fire and unbearable waves of pressure, like the temporary wall of a sandcastle taken by the tide.

Acrid smoke laced with dust and grit assaulted his nostrils, a smell so bad it became a taste that took hold of his throat.

26

Ted thought he heard someone shout but the sound was lost, like hope. Another series of concussions, more demonic screams, more violent turbulence, a staccato battering ram attacking his flesh. The air around him seemed to burn. He felt as if he couldn't possibly survive and curled up into a ball, trying to think of home but only thinking of the ways in which he might die. He accepted death. There was nothing but death left for him...

Somewhere to his front, way beyond the rim of his helmet which had become the tolerable extent of his world, a huge grey vulture crashed into the ground, the force of its impact lifting him again, throwing him down again, discarded like a useless object. There was a silence so profound, so sudden that Ted wondered if he was now dead as expected. The silence was like a thick, sticky ooze that filled his head, yet all around him was a cauldron of horror, but even that seemed to fade, and, as he rolled onto his back, he caught glimpses of a greying sky through twisting snakes of blackness.

His nose was filled with a blend of pungent odours, different types of burning layered with different types of death and topped off with the smell of earth. Dinger's face appeared above his, streaked with mud, or blood, or both. He was talking, his words urgent but invisible.

Ted propped himself up on one elbow like a man waking from an operation. He emerged into a world a bit like the one he had known before but changed and quiet, as if in shock. He saw Snowball pulling Whitey to his feet, and a burning, crumpled ruin behind them. The shape was that of a Stuka and he could see the outline of its dead crew, trapped and beyond hope beneath the long, fractured canopy. He wondered if this was some sort of justice. Dinger stood, towering above him and shook his body like a dog trying to get dry before extending a hand.

He helped Ted to his feet and then spoke but no sound came. *Rather deaf than blind*, thought Ted.

He looked down, checking that his body was complete and began walking towards the hill once again, assuming that his men would follow him but powerless to do anything about it if they didn't. The air crackled with life and death but Ted heard none of it as if he had been shut off from the world he'd known.

Briefly, he checked over his shoulder and saw his three friends, noticed Dinger's look of near despair but said nothing in case his voice betrayed him. The ground was littered with shards of metal, lethal bomb splinters, masonry and the pathetic fragments of a person. He saw a young woman's leg, or maybe that of a girl, and remembered the terrible vision of death he'd witnessed just minutes (or was it seconds?) before. A brown lace-up shoe remained on her foot, still polished and clean in contrast to the shredded stocking on her leg. He was reminded of a snake shedding its skin. Bile rose in his throat and he spat, as if doing so would help his stomach hold on to the last meal he'd had. He couldn't even remember what it was, or when he'd eaten it.

To his right he saw a thick, green overcoat and looked away at once, not daring to find the rest of the girl's body within. A hand clasped him on the shoulder, making him jump. Ted stopped, turned slowly and spoke.

'What?', he said, hearing only a muted reflection of that single word somewhere inside his head. Snowball looked at him intently, searching his face for recognition or understanding. Ted read the words on the other man's lips.

'Are you okay?', he said but Ted just gave a helpless shrug and turned away again as if only hopelessness could ever suit his mood. He needed no direction, no instructions.

***

'He's down here, Corporal Dexter. Probably shouldn't say this but I'm not sure if he's really in charge anymore. You'll see what I mean when you get down there; drink taken and all that, if you know what I mean. He's still giving orders, but no one is following them and he doesn't seem to care too much.' The words came to Ted dully, as if through a tunnel filled with straw. He'd left Whitey, Snowball and Dinger above ground in a room that passed for the cookhouse and was now following the Company Sergeant Major into the basement. He frowned at the older man's words, puzzled at the strange behaviour he was hearing about.

'Why, sir?', he said. They paused outside the door.

'He just can't cope. Survived the Great War, unscathed, or so it seemed. Maybe this is one battle too many. He's a decent enough man but he's hit the bottle now. Says it's all hopeless.' The CSM raised his eyebrows. 'It's hard to disagree.' He put a hand on the door handle but paused. 'Just go through the motions, Ted. Salute, yes sir, no sir. Just go along with it. I expect one of the other officers will relieve him of his command soon. They're just trying to put off the evil moment.'

'So long as it's not Pomeroy', said Ted. In the gloom he saw the CSM pull an uncertain face. Ted wasn't permitted to express an opinion on the matter of an officer's character or proficiency, but he assumed that they were past the need for adhering to the niceties of military etiquette. When you were told that the OC was due to be relieved of his command, the whole basis of the regime in which you operated was coming undone. Aside from that,

Ted could only see the little girl meeting her terrible death and the imagined interminable despair of her parents. His mind was filled with nothing else. If only he could clear that image.

Ted marched in, halted and saluted, astonished at the eerie subterranean world he had entered. The OC was hunched over his desk, his head down, writing, the shadows cast by an array of flickering candles more distinct than his actual body. Ted stood, the CSM at his shoulder, both men waiting for some sort of response that was not forthcoming. Major Finlay's black fountain pen scratched over an indistinct army form spread on the wooden desk next to a whiskey glass half-filled with amber spirit. The only other sound was that of guttering candles and the occasional heartfelt sigh from the man himself. Ted realised that his hearing was coming back.

One of the candles died, releasing a thin smoke signal into the choking air.

'Corporal Dexter, sir', said the CSM eventually, circumventing normal procedure to suit their new situation. This was an army that was fast becoming alien to him. No longer did it offer the old certainties, the rights and wrongs, the blacks and whites. The OC looked up briefly, the merest smile on his face before returning to his work. Ted risked a questioning glance at the CSM who shook his head and then looked fixedly at some point to his front. The silence continued for another thirty seconds, as if the officer were making the point that he would deal with his NCO when he was good and ready and not before. Ted felt fatigue taking hold of his body, starting with his eyes, which began to sting. The lack of oxygen and abundance of waxy fumes didn't help. He felt as if he was on the set of a horror film. It just needed Bela Lugosi to walk in to complete the scene.

30

'Right. Where have you been Corporal Dexter?', asked the OC finally, laying his pen down very precisely at right angles to the sheet upon which he had been writing. This act signified, he thought, some sort of adherence to properness, an indication that things were normal, despite the disintegration of the world around them. It was his job to maintain standards, to set the correct example.

'At the canal, sir', replied Ted, looking ahead. He wondered if he was here for a debrief or a reprimand.

'Why where you there? At the canal?' The OC thrust his jaw out combatively as he spoke but his eyes were calm, dulled by drink.

'Captain Pomeroy put me there with three fusiliers...'

'Captain Pomeroy?'

'Sir.'

'Why?'

'To delay the Germans, he said, sir.'

'Three of you?'

'Four, sir. Me and three fusiliers.'

The OC sniffed, reached for his glass but then pulled his hand back in a belated act of abstinence.

'What good could four of you do?', he asked but before Ted had time to reply, he spoke again. 'And did you?'

'Did I what, sir? Delay the Germans?'

'Yes.'

'Em, not really sir. There were some Belg...'

'Doesn't matter', he said waving a dismissive hand at the soldier. 'Get your head down. I'll speak to Captain Pomeroy. Off you go.' His head was once again bowed to the papers in front of him. Ted felt the CSM nudge him and he saluted, about-turned and marched out, a series of acts that seemed to go entirely unnoticed by the officer.

'It's not going well?', asked the NCO, venturing an unaccustomed opinion.

'Not well at all, Ted.' The CSM glanced around to check that the two men were alone and then spoke to Ted conspiratorially. Ted felt himself to be an unlikely confidant for this man, a warrant officer. 'Word is we're all heading for the coast, eventually. The rate at which the French are surrenderin' is leaving our flanks exposed. We either pull back and evacuate or lose the whole BEF. Not a word, though.'

Ted nodded, open-mouthed and then said, 'not a word, sir.' He walked off but the sergeant major called him back.

'Who's TCP?', he asked quietly. He looked around him to check that no-one else was listening to their exchange. Ted smirked.

'That's Captain Pomeroy', explained Ted. 'Where have you heard that, sir?', he asked.

'Just the lads. They say it. Here's TCP or where's TCP? Stuff like that. So, TCP stands for That's Captain Pomeroy?', asked the CSM.

'Well the C doesn't actually stand for Captain, sir. It stands for cu..', said Ted before the CSM cut him off abruptly.

'Ah. I get it now. TCP is That .... Pomeroy.'

32

'Yes sir. Very disrespectful', said Ted, impassively. He wondered if the CSM avoided using the expletive for religious reasons. What sort of sergeant major didn't swear?

'And I hardly dare ask… but what do they call me?'

'They call you the sar'nt major, sir.'

'That's nice.'

'Yes sir. Respectful.' Ted smiled and wondered if the entire hierarchy of his company was slowly going mad. Starting from the top and working down it would take a while before he, a mere lance corporal, would be affected.

***

Ted found a patch of floor near Dinger and turned his bedding into something resembling a bed. His mood was circumspect. He had expected his war to be a repeat of the Great War, but hopefully a bit shorter. He had expected the British Army to win…

Chapter Three

The men were kicked awake in turn to find themselves looking down the barrel of a German gun. At the end of the room stood their sentry, Private Anson, radiating misery with a beaming German next to him, looking like the hapless British soldier was his prize from a peculiar raffle. Anson appeared bowed under the weight of his shame. The German kept the muzzle of his MP38 tucked firmly into the folds of Anson's greatcoat. The exhausted soldiers continued to rise in turn, each one making the same shocking discovery; they had been captured by a small German patrol as they slept. A pile of Lee Enfields and a couple of Bren guns lay in the furthest corner looking like factory rejects. Two Thompson sub machine guns were propped against the wall beneath the window, separate to the other weapons as if they might become prized loot.

'What the hell happened, Anson?', shouted Sergeant Parr, angrily. The invisible shrouds of sleep had fallen from him more quickly than the others. His voice and his stare were accusing. He knew how to intimidate. 'You'd better not tell me you fell asleep.' The sentry looked down at his boots and said nothing, his silence taken as guilt by the members of his platoon. One of them shouted out, 'You useless bastard, Anson', before being knocked to the floor by the butt of a Mauser rifle. He lay there, his hand to bloody face, dumb accusation in his eyes.

'Alle, von die Sie Ihre Münder schließen. Sie sind jetzt Gefangene von dem Dritten Reich.'

'What's that mean?', muttered Miglorine, from the corner of his mouth. He was trying to make sense of his shocking new circumstances by any means possible.

'Gawd knows, mate', said his oppo.

When each of them was on his feet and aware of the change in their situation, another German soldier spoke.

'Außenseite jetzt. Richten Sie aus und warten Sie auf den Transport.' The British soldiers looked at each other, perplexedly.

'Go out!', shouted an older German, clarifying the original order. The soldiers shuffled out, disbelief and anger slowly giving way to something like guilt or grief. The early morning air was cold and their breath swirled in miserable grey clouds before their faces.

'What now?', muttered Mig.

'Take us to Germany, I suppose.'

'Shit. I can't believe it.' He felt closer to despair than at any time he had ever known. Their captors casually paraded up and down the road in front of them, all wearing the same disdainful look *as well they might*, mused Miglorine. A few Germans had captured an entire British platoon without a bullet being fired, hardly a great day for the army. He thought of how the news of his capture would be received at home, saw his mother crumple to the ground, suffering her own personal defeat, blaming herself, as mothers do, for not keeping her son safe. From the corner of his mouth Miglorine's oppo spoke, 'Why don't we sneak around the corner and hide while no one is looking', he said.

Miglorine thought of his motorbike and nodded, hoping that some sort of basic plan was taking shape. He glanced over to his far right were a group of Germans stood in a little Teutonic huddle, smoking and chatting, betraying their human origins, and then glided around the corner of the barn, he hoped like a ghost.

The BSA M20 was sitting where he had left it and next to it was a chicken coop big enough to hide under.

Miglorine scrambled underneath the wooden structure and rolled himself into a ball, waiting for the other man to join him. He curled his legs tighter, making more room for the other soldier but it seemed as if he had suddenly got cold feet. He wanted to climb out and find him, suddenly realising that he was scared to undertake his escape – if that's what it was to be – on his own. The next series of events assaulted his senses in a frantic jumble of horror, as first he heard a shout in German and then a shot. For a fraction of a second there was only silence, so profound that it seemed to freeze the cold morning air and paralyse everyone at the barn, regardless of their nationality.

That fraction of a second was ended with the unmistakable sound of weapons being cocked and then machine gun fire. Miglorine heard men call out and saw his oppo collapse, falling into view from the corner of the barn. There were screams, some of which carried on briefly after the firing had finished and then he heard pistol fire and the sound of men being bayoneted. He didn't know how he recognised that sound but it was an unmistakable melange of grunts, tearing and stifled screams. He wanted to puke but clamped his mouth shut knowing that his survival hung by the slenderest of threads. His terror was complete. Miglorine of the Buffs felt his blood run cold as if he was already a corpse.

Assailed by the urge to run, he nevertheless fought to remain calm and stay in his hiding place, one which the Germans had not even considered searching yet. He didn't quite hold his breath but he kept it shallow despite the panic he felt.

Miglorine felt sure that the German troops would conduct a rapid search of the barn for any survivors or witnesses and, having done so, would take steps to silence them. But instead, they seemed to suddenly panic, as if assailed by guilt, and he saw them run off down the road to a truck. Unseen, he sat up and looked carefully at the scene, still hidden in the gloom. A German officer was confronting the men now, remonstrating with them. He shouted, almost hysterically and pushed one man in the chest, nearly knocking him to the ground. Nevertheless, he urged them into the back of the vehicle and after a few seconds it sped off.

Mig thought he should check for any survivors but knew that there were none – the Germans would have been thorough, as was their reputation – and so Miglorine collected his bike, grabbed the nearest Thompson through the window, slung it over his shoulder and took a deep breath. Despite the cold, the bike started with relative ease, its engine ripping apart the silence of early morning with a convulsive roar.

Moments later he manoeuvred the BSA past his fallen comrades, scarcely giving the indistinct pile of bodies a second glance, then raced off into the night, with no idea where he was headed but his mind filled with unspeakable horror. Tears pricked his eyes. He felt himself to be an unlikely survivor; neither the toughest nor the weakest man in the platoon, and certainly no more or less deserving of another helping of life than anyone else.

No one could dodge a bullet... but a survivor was a survivor whatever the reason.

Chapter Four

'It'll fly, John.'

'That's what I'm worried about.'

'There's not much anyone can say.'

'No.'

'It was all so simple before the war.'

'Safer anyway.'

'It can't go on for much longer.'

John gave a short bitter laugh. 'Presumably it stops for us when there is nothing left to fly, or no one left to do the flying. Those two events should occur simultaneously, I would say.'

There was silence between the two men as they walked back to the dispersal hut. They passed a French Dewoitine interceptor parked on the grass like an outsized toy. Its colours looked strange and garish, its roundels seeming to mock the colours of the RAF. The little planes had fared badly against the Luftwaffe's Messerschmitts like boys sent to do a man's job. The heroism of the pilots wasn't enough to bridge the shortfall in performance and armament, a phenomenon with which John was now sickeningly familiar.

'I can't see a way out of it for you, John', said the mechanic at last. They paused. John's face was creased in confusion and his stomach knotted as if some sort of premonition had taken hold of him.

'What do you mean?', he said tonelessly.

'Look, I know I'm not supposed to say this but I think about what it must be like for you and all those other poor buggers getting hacked out of the sky. To keep sending you up is such a bloody waste – it's criminal. Not a waste of planes – they are only fit for scrap – a waste of good men. But there is no escape…'

'Donny, Donny, just stop. It's not your fault, or anyone else's.' John looked heavenward. 'It's Hitler's fault', he said, plainly. 'It's just how it is. You're right – there is nothing that you can say or do.'

John wanted to placate his troubled friend. Plainly, the mechanic felt guilt at having a relatively safe job. Their numbers would remain virtually constant even as the pilots' numbers dwindled. They weren't equals in life and certainly not in death.

'Yeah, John but it's just shit. The whole thing…' Sergeant Donoghue stopped mid-sentence. He looked over at the pilot quizzically. John Guy raised his eyebrows in a question.

'What?'

'Heard something…'

John pulled a face, dismissive, but then he heard it too, a frantic buzz like some huge insect might make. Rapidly it became a disembodied howl, a surging wave of latent terror.

'Comin' in low', said Donoghue. 'And fast…'

The first Bf109 leapt the hedgerow at the end of the airfield like a gazelle, followed by two others acting as wingmen. At once they opened fire with their cannons and the air became hot with high explosive, filled with battering concussions. Guy and Donoghue hit the grass and flattened themselves into the fabric of the earth, hoping that whatever metal laced the air above their heads would not be impeded by their bodies. The German fighters roared over them, creating a pressure wave and subsequent vacuum that seemed to rip the atmosphere apart, like invisible tissue. In a moment they were gone and John looked up to see their tiny forms receding. He assumed that they were finished, that one strafing run was all they would risk, lest they fall prey to patrolling Hurricanes.

'We can get up, Donny', he said and the other man rose like a wraith, pulling himself away from the comforting earth with something like regret. Around them men emerged from cover, like a plague of cunning moles, unafraid of daylight, and others ran, urgently needed to fight fires or give medical attention. The base came to life again in an instant, busier than ever, the ground crews tending to whatever jobs had been created by their attackers: fires, medical assistance and the rest.

'Bastards', said the mechanic, brushing himself down. John assumed he was referring to the Germans and smiled, glad to be alive. The little French fighter plane still sat in its place, seemingly undamaged, but beyond that they could see other planes burning, Fairey Battles of their own squadron, flames licking the air, greedy for oxygen. Three fire tenders raced to the scene and behind them a little brown-painted ambulance sped along a path, its bell ringing frantically. There was little that either man could do. They began walking back to the squadron lines.

'There were no pilots for most of those planes, anyway', commented John.

'This could be your lucky day, John', said Sergeant Donoghue. 'They might have got your kite. It could be the miracle you needed.'

'I don't believe in miracles, Donny. Besides which I can see the bloody thing over there next to the hangar.' He pointed. The big single-engine bomber normally piloted by Sergeant Guy sat like a huge brown crow, intact, disappointingly ready to fly.

'Oh.'

'Precisely. 'Oh' is right, Donny. The only way that plane is going to get destroyed is with me in it', he said looking down at his boots. 'Unfortunately', he added. They listened to the crackling of burning aircraft, heard a shout go up – something to do with ammunition – heard another shout, a reprimand this time, and then the air was again filled with the noise of powerful aero engines. The Messerschmitts had returned, coming in low again, fire spitting from their wings, adding to the chaos they had left behind fifteen seconds earlier. John caught sight of an airman cut down as he sprinted for cover, saw another man turn the barrel of a Vickers guns towards the enemy aircraft and begin to fire. John dived to the ground again but Donoghue was too late, hit by a heavy bullet that tore his chest apart bloodily in a spray of flesh. His ruined body pitched forward, thrown to the ground.

A moment later the Messerschmitts were gone and just the noises of their one-sided battle remained. John turned his head, knew that his friend was dead, his body ruptured, mechanically savaged. His mind filled with the unfairness of it all. Poor old, Donny who had agonised about what he saw as his friend's near imminent and unavoidable death now lay dead himself, a victim of the bitterest irony imaginable. John's emotions seemed to spill into the ground, there to be soaked up by tender soil, for when he stood, he was ready for the next part of his day, divorced from the tragedy of Donoghue's demise. He wondered what was wrong with him and then glanced over to where his plane still stood undamaged. He remembered Donoghue's words to him – not his last words but close enough – *'It'll fly John.'*

'That's what I was afraid of', he said aloud, paraphrasing his own reply.

Chapter Five

Ted never saw the OC again and never heard of the man's fate. In effect he disappeared and was never discussed, as if he had been an embarrassing Victorian relative who had sullied the family's good name by impregnating the chamber maid. Later, when he had time to reflect upon these peculiar times, he supposed that he had been taken away to some retirement home for barmy officers; a sort off happy hunting ground with pipe smoke and chairs covered in cracked red leather. There he could spend his remaining idle days in a bath chair on a crisp English lawn, watching the peaceful world go by, reflecting on better days of half-imagined victories.

At zero five-thirty, Colour Sergeant Baker rudely kicked Ted and his men awake. Ted didn't like Baker. Baker didn't like Ted. Had they been of similar rank the situation might have suited Ted perfectly. However, Baker outranked Ted by some margin and rarely missed an opportunity to antagonise him. The army, Ted had realised, was largely but not by any means exclusively, populated by men who enjoyed power and opportunities to inflict minor pain and discomfort on their underlings.

In a less disciplined army Baker might have been shot by his own men, such was the degree to which he was unloved, for he seemed to revel in other men's disdain, almost striving to make repugnance a virtue. Ted was always reminded of some sort of grumpy woodland creature when he saw Baker's face. He had the red, bulbous nose of a drinker and the yard brush moustache of the professional soldier. He was perpetually dishevelled and quite the wrong shape for the uniform he wore. His belly protruded, his shoulders sloped and his battle dress touched at all the wrong places.

'Pomeroy wants you and your little gang of pixies to go on a recce', he said, nastily. He talked with a sneer in his voice. An image of Baker being harangued by his wife for some minor domestic indiscretion flitted through Ted's brain and he smiled involuntarily.

'Where?'

'What the fuck are you smiling at?'

'Nothing, Colour', said Ted, insincerely. 'Where does Captain Pomeroy want us to go?'

'That way', said Baker pointing.

'The cookhouse?'

'Outside, smartarse. East', he said. 'Towards the flamin' Germans.'

'A recce? But we already know where they are, Colour.'

'Listen lad. Just fuckin' go.' Baker rubbed his fat forehead and sighed wearily.

'He just wants us out of the way, Ted', interjected Snowball.

'Your little wintry friend is right, Corporal Dexter', said Baker. He looked over at Snowball with a mixture of disgust and gratitude.

'Fair enough. He just wants us to disappear…'

'Or die, Ted. Whichever's easiest', said Snowball.

***

'You see what I mean, though. Look where you have got us, Ted.'

'I do see what you mean, Snowball but don't feel that you've got to hang around. We're well clear of the company now. You can go wherever you want. They're going to be heading off for pastures new soon. No one is going to know, or care what happens to us.' Ted spoke with undisguised exasperation as if some of Baker's unpleasantness had rubbed off on him. He smiled without humour, utterly fed-up with the whole thing.

'I didn't mean that, Ted. But it's what I was saying before – that 'cos no one likes *you* we get all the shit jobs to do.' Despite his words, so plainly spoken, Snowball was reluctant to fall out over it.

'Whaddya mean, no one likes me!', said Ted, indignantly. He heard Dinger sniggering. 'And you can shut up too, Dinger, you wee bastard.'

'The officers and that, Ted. They don't like you, I mean', explained Snowball, earnestly. He slid his helmet from his head and ran a hand through his matted hair, his face creased with concern. He didn't want to rile Ted but he was convinced that he spoke the truth on the matter. Ted was a man he admired greatly but he had reservations about him too.

'Some of them do', said the NCO, defensively. 'Maybe. Pomeroy, for one.' He looked over at Whitey as if seeking reassurance, but the tall man said nothing and glanced away, unwilling to be drawn into the argument. Whitey had removed his tunic and shirt, revealing a body so thin as to allow light to pass through it.

'Bloody hell it'll be some bullet that catches you', said Ted, changing the subject.

'What?'

'You! You're so bloody thin, wee man. Shootin' you would be like shootin' at a broom handle.'

'Balls', said Fusilier White, a touch of colour suffusing his bony face.

'That's better', said Dinger. 'I can see you when you blush!' Ted laughed despite the strain he felt, a stifled guffaw and nothing more but enough to set the others off. For a moment their cares were forgotten and even Whitey tittered gamely.

'I'm glad I have some entertainment value', said the unfortunate White. 'Now, if you don't mind, I shall return to my duties', he added with theatrical dignity.

'Which are?', asked Snowball. Whitey just shrugged and closed his eyes against the sun.

They lay in the sunlight, each man alone with his thoughts of home and some better, safer life. Ted sat with his back against a tree trunk, nominally keeping watch, but in reality letting his mind wander through a circus of disconnected thoughts. Snowball lay next to the Bren, his finger idly tracing the outline of the gun's working parts. Out of sight, Ted could hear Dinger's heavy breathing, which eventually became a gentle snore. Whitey also seemed to be asleep, his eyes shut, his mouth slightly agape. Now and again he sighed, as if enjoying a dream in which his modest hopes became the real stuff of his life.

Ted smiled and then wondered how he had managed that small feat – that co-ordination of facial muscles – in such dispiriting circumstances. He realised that he wanted, indeed expected, very little from life. Those few things about which he might wistfully think were practically unobtainable. Simple pleasures, that was all: warmth, food, comfort and safety – not much to ask for, he thought, but unobtainable nonetheless. Maybe not the food, he corrected. He'd never gone hungry in the army but there was still time for that, and if they didn't get killed first there was every chance that they would become POWs. Exactly how much food did the Krauts spare for their prisoners? He shut that thought from his mind.

He was weary and dismayed but every now and again he felt a surge of optimism, the origin of which he could not trace. *What was good about their situation?* He struggled to think of an answer. The sun was shining; that was good and infinitely preferable to the wind and rain that seemed to plague their pre-war training in England, where manoeuvres had always seemed to take place in mud and foul weather, like re-enactments of the Great War.

No one was currently shooting at them or endangering their lives, which was also good. Even better was the fact that they were away from company lines and therefore more or less free to do what they liked, as they were doing now. Their orders were to carry out a recce patrol to establish the enemy's location, but they were in fact sitting on the edge of a copse in the corner of a field, resting. Ted had made no effort to find the Germans. *They'll find us*, he'd explained and this explanation had been gratefully accepted by the men under his command. It was obvious that the enemy were coming this way. They weren't likely to take a wrong turning and get lost. High above them he saw a squadron of bombers.

They were twin-engine aeroplanes, stubby wings, slender fuselages, Dorniers, perhaps? He wasn't sure. A few single seaters flew as escort, and he knew that these were the dreaded Messerschmitts.

From their direction of approach he knew they had to be Germans anyway and he further assumed that they could only maintain such perfect formation on the outward leg of their sortie before they had come to the attention of the British and French fighters who would surely disperse them. They posed no direct threat to him and he couldn't quite equate their presence to the damage and mayhem that they would eventually cause. Someone would die soon, blown to pieces by the high explosive delivered by these planes, but it wouldn't be him, nor would it be the defenders of Cassel.

Absentmindedly, he undid another tunic button and then sat upright to shrug the jacket off altogether. He rubbed a hand over his chin, thought about the wash kit in his webbing and the need for a shave. It would have to wait, they could be attacked at any minute, although it looked unlikely. In every direction he could see only signs of peace, especially now that the bombers had passed over. The war, he realised, came in fits and starts. It had probably always been that way.

He thought of his father in his trench in 1915, say. Not every waking hour was spent dodging bullets – it could not have been so or no one would have survived and the war would have ended in days, the armies spent, their ranks emptied. The carnage, when it came, was more terrible than could ever be imagined, he knew that, but mass slaughter was not on the cards every single day.

He lay back down again and sighed. The weight he usually carried on his shoulders – his responsibilities – had transferred itself to his stomach where it sat now, seeming to crush him. Ted could go to sleep lying here in the sun, but he knew that when he woke his problems and fears would remain and might seem all the more shocking and crippling by comparison with the pleasant world of dreams in which he might have temporarily taken refuge.

How peaceful the world seemed now. The sun's warmth further dispelled any thoughts of calamity and death. No one should die on a day like this, he mused.

For the next twenty minutes he let his mind wander of its own accord and it rewarded him with images of tranquillity and happiness of the sort that neither he, nor anyone else he knew, had ever really experienced, even in peace time. The beautiful glades and copses through which he moved in his thoughts were like nowhere on earth, or so he thought. That they were like nowhere in *Belfast* was closer to the truth. He smiled again, closed his eyes, felt a wave of fatigue course through his body and forced them open again; someone had to stay awake.

For a moment he thought about Captain Pomeroy and his relentless urge to push Ted out of the way. Why was that? What was his problem, or more to be point, why was Ted, specifically, a problem to him? He pursed his lips.

The aircraft was a distant dot that circled almost unseen and unheard. Its engine note came and went on the breeze as it flew a slow, lazy turn in the sky. Ted watched with a detached fascination, safe on the ground, letting the plane flit in and out of his half-remembered, half-invented recollections. It hung in the air for a tiny eternity, huge swathes of time compressed into moments. It seemed as if nothing was happening anywhere in the world and Ted allowed life to pass him by, enjoying the greatest but most fragile freedom of his life. He shut out the terrible possibilities, kept them at bay, the plane serving as an allegory of the distance between him and his problems.

He watched as two butterflies engaged in their own miniature dogfight just feet from where he sat and marvelled at the dexterity of these two sophisticated aviators with the simplest of lives. He marvelled too at how they could fill their world with such darting movement. Their aerial combat seemed unending, their energy boundless. Neither insect compromised nor conceded an inch of airspace, determined to win their duel with unflinching but pointless valour. At times they were a blur of white, and Ted thought he could hear their wings beating urgently as they fought to remain aloft. He envied them their short but carefree life. *So what if they survived just one season*, he thought. *It was what you did with your time that counted.*

A few hundred feet up the birds seemed to rule, and he craned his neck awkwardly against the skinny tree to see them engage in their own display of aerobatics. Ted sighed. The sigh mutated into a yawn and the desire to sleep overtook him.

'Is that plane one of ours?'

Ted looked over at Snowball. The soldier was propped up on one elbow like a young blade on a country picnic.

'Dunno. No one is shooting at it or doing anything about it', replied Ted, reluctant to be drawn back into the violent life that had recently been thrust upon him.

'What time are we going back, Ted?'

'When we find some Germans', answered the NCO, enigmatically. He was in no mood for another of Snowball's lectures, partly afraid that his friend was correct in his assessment of Ted's standing within the company and partly to maintain the idyll that existed either largely, or perhaps solely, within his head. Snowball nodded but said nothing more, until…

'It's a beautiful day.'

'Eh?'

'It's a beautiful day', he repeated.

'Yes.'

'What are you going to do after the war?'

'Dunno. Haven't thought about it much', lied Ted. There were times when he thought of nothing else. He imagined that the same must be true of all soldiers. The problem for him was that his ideas of peacetime, and the part that he might play in it, were such a jumble that he could never hope to put them into words. He glanced at Snowball, who gave him a knowing look. 'Well, it's different for me, isn't it?' he said. 'I was a soldier *before* the war.'

'So was I', said Snowball plainly.

'Aye but you joined *because* the war was coming. I joined because…'

'Because you just wanted to be a soldier. It doesn't make much sense when you put it like that', said Snowball, thoughtfully. 'Don't mean to be rude, Ted, by the way', he added.

'I suppose you're right. But it explains why I find it hard to answer your question about peacetime. This…', he held his hands out to encompass the war as it currently existed for him and Snowball, 'should be a dream come true for me. Soldiers must join up hoping to fight…'

'But that's not true, is it? This isn't a dream come true at all. You're as scared as the next man.'

'Worried. Not scared', corrected Ted, bristling just a little at the suggestion.

'Worried, scared… it's practically the same thing. One is just a more extreme version of the other.'

Ted laughed and looked at Snowball askance. He said, 'What did you do before the war, Snowball? Were you a professor of English at Queen's or something?'

'Fishmonger.'

'Fishmonger!', said Ted with a derisive snort. 'I can't picture you monging fish, somehow.'

'You'd be surprised. You don't have to be thick to be a fishmonger.'

'I never suggested… Is that plane getting closer?' Both men turned to watch the distant aeroplane becoming less distant. Its engine note became more distinct, more even in tone.

'Could be heading this way', suggested Snowball, non-commitally. He shielded his eyes with one hand and followed the progress of the distant aircraft.

'Could be one of ours', said Ted, although he didn't really believe that to be the case; the Germans seemed to be masters of the skies. They watched in silence as the aeroplane droned ever closer, its shape becoming clearer but no more recognisable. For a moment, Ted's brain seemed to lurch away from the present, and from all the certainties he had ever known, to some abstract world of imponderables and unpleasantness.

He pictured some men lying dead, sprawled out in grotesque postures only possible in death. He imagined himself approaching their horrifying, earthen deathbeds and then gazing down at faces he knew. Those faces were the embodiment of calm and quite at odds with the carnage of violent death apparent all around them. How such tranquillity could be found in the midst of terror was beyond comprehension. When he sighed there was tremor in his expelled breath.

'You look like you've seen a ghost, Ted', said Snowball. For a further moment Ted said nothing, wrenching himself away from the dreadful possibilities he had just visited.

'Erm, what? Let's get goin' Snowy.'

'Are you okay?'

'Fine but we'll get out of here, I think. Wake the sleeping uglies.'

'Fine, Ted, I'll wake these two', said Snowball, nervously. He looked on in alarm at the NCO, wondering why his good mood had disappeared so rapidly. The plane flew over as they darted about purposefully, getting ready for the move. Its shadow followed ominously like a phantom crow.

'What's up, Ted?', asked Dinger. He had sensed Ted's alarm the moment he was shaken awake.

'That plane is a Jerry spotter', said Ted.

'Has he seen us?'

'I think he has now. If he's got a radio, he might be calling up all sorts of problems for us. So, we'll put a bit of distance between us and this spot.' Ted looked at his men,

54

each of them dressed and in their webbing, ready for their return.

'Let's go.'

They ducked involuntarily as the German plane, a Henschel 126, swooped low again. Ted glanced upwards to see the observer grappling with his machine gun, bringing it to bear on his new moving target.

'Get down!' he shouted, just as the first bullets plucked at the earth around them. It was an inaccurate burst, no more than a snatch on the trigger. None of them was hit and they scrambled to their feet, running for cover to a patch of scrub. They charged through thicket, long tendrils of vegetation snatching at their clothing and threatening to pull them face-first into the rutted clay. The plane turned, its engine note stretched out from the Doppler effect, and then swept down upon them again. This time it was the aircraft's forward firing machine guns that were brought to bear, and bullets once again sliced through the air around them, nicking leaves and smashing branches before losing their momentum. Ted turned to see Dinger caught upright in a wall of brambles. His face was open with panic and he tried to fling himself to the ground but the vegetation supported his weight, aiding his crucifixion. The first bullet caught him in the back and he howled in agony and terror as it tumbled bloodily from his ribs, leaving his chest torn open. The second bullet hit his back at a lower point, was deflected from a bone and spent its remaining energy trapped within his torso, spinning out a deadly course through his vital organs. The screaming stopped abruptly and his head sank to his chest.

Ted heard Whitey sobbing and took hold of his tunic as the Henschel wheeled around again.

'Rest the Bren on Snowball's shoulder and start firing at that bastard!' he shouted. Whitey nodded, open-mouthed with terror, but already Snowball was next to him hefting the machine gun onto his shoulder and crouching, his head turned away from the barrel to protect his face from the muzzle blast. Whitey's composure had returned, his instinct to survive taking control. He cocked the gun.

'Wait until he's close enough', said Ted but the plane was travelling at two hundred miles per hour and the time came soon enough. Whitey squeezed the trigger, sending a burst of .303 past the propeller disc. Ted watched the brass casings tumble down Snowball's back in a hot, shiny cascade. The pilot veered over to port and released some tiny bombs at the same time. For a horrifying second Ted just stared as they drifted to earth.

'Holy...', said Ted but the bombs landed far over to their left, tearing up clumps of soil, throwing them high into the air. He found Snowball and Whitey crouching. 'Next time, keep firing and have another mag ready to put on.'

'This gets worse, Ted', said Snowball pointing. Ted looked into the distance, gaping as the first of four Stukas peeled away from its formation, falling to earth like a bird of prey after a field mouse. The others followed suit, each in turn, adding to the diabolical cacophony.

'Bombing Cassel', shouted Ted. 'Let's concentrate on our wee friend here. He's comin' back by the look of it. The Henschel swooped upon them in a shallow dive, machine guns flickering flame and another four bombs released, falling to the ground and heading right for them. Whitey was firing already, emptying a magazine in seconds, the Bren chugging away with great accuracy. Ted was astonished that he could hear the brass tinkling as it fell to the ground over the sound of battle. They were engulfed in a cauldron of fire, jagged shards of flame slicing the air in every direction, snatching the oxygen out of its natural home, consuming it. A series of sharp concussions lifted them from their feet, punching the air from their chests and then discarding them like leftovers from a giant's picnic.

Ted saw the world revolve and spin, its normal parameters stretched and distorted as he tumbled. A wall of ridged clay soil came up to meet him, breaking his fall as the edges of his vision contracted and then closed in.

Chapter Six

John cast a glance around the gloomy briefing room, wondering if there were fewer lights on to disguise the lack of bodies present. The shadows, decked out in the shape of folding chairs, could have been the phantom remains of the men lost on previous sorties. Gone was the elation of earlier missions, not that that it had lasted long in any case, diminishing at a rate greater than the loss of pilots. There was no nervous laughter or hushed chatter, and no ghoulish humour – the time for that was long past. .

On their first mission – it seemed like years ago now – they had lost no aircraft, and the men had returned to their base optimistic that their bomber really was good enough to fight a modern war, that the boasts about its performance were not hollow. The Fairey Battle had been a revelation just a few years before: as fast as a fighter, well-armed and capable of carrying one thousand pounds of bombs. It was sleek, modern and deadly.

The truth, however, became evident on the next sortie when they were required to attack German positions in Belgium in support of an offensive by the Belgian Army. They had dropped perhaps one bomb on its target and lost three aircraft. One of the Battles had simply exploded in mid-air for no reason that anyone could see. The others had been lost to opportunist Messerschmitts who had swooped upon them, hunting them down with derisory ease. John had watched in despair as they had swarmed over the lumbering bombers, scattering them and picking off individuals, first wounding and then killing them like easy prey.

Later, in his bunk, he wondered how any of them had actually made it back. It was almost as if the Luftwaffe had been delivering a warning – *this is what will happen if you stray into our territory again*. Perhaps it was a ridiculous notion, he mused, but it still fitted the facts. John felt like he had been allowed to escape and take the warning to those who might follow. However, those casual assassins up there waiting would not be so merciful the next time.

The next few missions were flown with heavy fighter escorts, and the rate of attrition slowed but the losses didn't stop. The aircrew certainly felt more confident taking their planes over enemy-held territory with a coterie of Hurricanes visible and ready to take on the deadly Messerschmitts of the Luftwaffe.

The surviving crews, of whom there were fewer and fewer, grumbled that it was no longer worth putting so many planes in the air for the sake of dropping what was such a tiny bomb load, and often missing in any case. Before long they were losing Hurricanes and Battles at such a rate that it was decided to suspend operations, but the demands for precision bombing still came in and the suspension never took effect. *This was the result*, he thought bitterly, looking around an empty room. The squadron's ghosts must pity them, he decided. Ghosts outnumbered the living by some huge margin.

They stood as the replacement squadron leader entered the hut. He hadn't flown a mission with them and didn't yet have an aircraft to fly. It didn't seem to matter much; within hours he was unlikely to have a squadron.

'Sit down chaps. Won't keep you long', he said. There was a barely disguised apologetic note in his voice. John guessed that he was twenty-five years old, his tunic pressed and free of decorations but a regular no doubt. The man looked at his six aircrew – two pilots, two gunners and two observers – smiled hesitantly, and gave his briefing, thankfully omitting the stirring words that normally presaged such an event.

59

'The target is the main road bridge over the Lemontaigne Canal. The Belgians are hoping that, if it can be put out of action, they stand a chance of holding the German assault in this region', he pointed to a map which was so brightly illuminated that its features were blanched, washed out, obliterated. 'Can you see this okay?', he asked peering out at his small, darkened audience. No one spoke and so he continued.

'Obviously, there is a limit to what can be achieved with two aircraft. I was hoping that my Battle would be delivered in time but it hasn't come yet.' John noted the apologetic tone again. *You can have mine*, he thought. They made a note of timings, code words and grid references.

Outside in the fading sun he said to his observer, 'Poor Squadron Leader *whatever his name is*. No aeroplane. I bet he was just dying to get shot to pieces like the rest of us.'

The other man, also a sergeant, gave a mirthless laugh. He said, 'how do you feel, John?'

'I don't know. One way or another, this has got to be *it*, so to speak. They can't really send us out again.'

'It does sound rather like a last-ditch type thing we're doing here.'

'My favourite bit is where they tell you to go and get some rest. How are you supposed to rest?'

***

The first rays of the sun spilt out over the lip at the end of the grass runway, heralding another summer's day alive with colourful possibilities, new life, freshness. John paced round his aircraft, checking the surfaces in a last visual inspection. He felt sick in some strange combination of hunger and dread. His mind was dead, as if in practice for the real thing. Sometimes he pictured himself making the low-level run over the bridge, the plane lifting as the bombs fell away, the surge of power, the turn, the weaving journey home, a stream of .303 from the gunner keeping the Luftwaffe wolves at bay, shells careering past, overtaking but ultimately tumbling to earth, spent and wasted. He saw the airfield and a squadron of Hurricanes pouncing on his pursuers vengefully, righting a wrong. He would land, have the meal he had passed up at breakfast, enjoy the sweet-bitter taste of beer slipping down his throat.

But other times he saw only his death and his hands curling up, consumed by fire as he fought to keep the stupid, useless old crate in the air for another few seconds of torment. Always he thought of his hands, remembered the anguished cries and tears of another pilot who'd landed his burning bomber on the field. His hands where blackened effigies as they took him away screaming, like some grotesque sculpture rendered in ebony that signified malevolence and pain. The hastily administered morphine had seemed slow to take effect.

The armourers had finished loading the bombs and stood back as if admiring their work. In reality there was nothing to admire; the bombs were tucked away out of sight so as not to upset the aerodynamics of the big aircraft.

'Ready to go, sar'nt', said the corporal in charge.

'Thanks, Tam. It's not so long ago we used to look at this plane and think it was the best bomber in the world.'

'Maybe it was at the time, John', said the corporal. He used the pilot's name when he was out of earshot of his crew of erks. Some of them had only been in the RAF for a few months. 'Things move on quickly. The fighter boys were still in biplanes when we got these.'

'Yeah', said John, sadly. He saw that the other pilot left in the squadron, a pilot officer recently posted in, had finished his checks and stood expectantly next to his plane. He waved at John.

'Ready, sergeant?' he called.

'Suppose so, sir', said John. His voice carried a cheerful lilt as if he still believed in the possibility of his own survival. Officers expected their men to be happy and enthusiastic and for John the habit of appearing so apparently died hard. 'Better go, Tam', he said to the armourer, his voice now a monotone.

'Good luck, sarge', said the corporal. He felt himself suddenly swamped by emotion. You could pretend that there was no 'us' and 'them' when it came to relationship between aircrew and groundcrew, but there was. Tam thought that he would never see John Guy again. He shut his mind to the awful possibilities of the pilot's death. He could never really comprehend what it must be like for them but he could come close. The truth was he simply didn't want to contemplate their probable fate, for he knew that they died horribly.

Moments later the remaining aircrafts' props slowly turned over, grindingly, wheezingly, and then the Rolls Royce Merlin engines erupted into a mechanical medley of sounds which soon settled into one harmonious roar. The observer checked his maps for the last time and the gunner checked his Vickers gun, ensuring that it was the functioning masterpiece of engineering required for the forthcoming adventure. It had long since stopped being an adventure, of course.

***

They hurtled through the clouds at two hundred knots, each man keeping a close eye on the skies, knowing that an encounter with the Luftwaffe might last only seconds, during which a hundred tiny decisions might be made and forgotten, superseded, corrected, wasted, amended. They feared the Bf 109 most of all. The German pilots were skilful and seemingly fearless, driven on by some sort of controlled recklessness and fervour. They courted death but always seemed to slide away from its final grasp, whereas the lumbering Battle merely trundled epically into every trap set for it, like some old, doomed warrior.

John thought of the one advantage that the incredible German advance had brought the RAF – they didn't have to fly far to reach their targets. The disadvantage, of course was that that they, the Germans, could be on top of them in no time, over-running the airfield or anything else that stood in their way. Once the airfield was in their hands – as seemed inevitable – they could themselves bomb any British target with ease.

'Target below. Almost overshot. Let's get down there. One pass only, drop the eggs and get out.'

'Roger', said John in the terse language of the radio. He watched as the lead aircraft banked and then he followed it down in a large spiral that would take them out over the bridge. The world revolved on a different axis for a moment and John kept an eye on his instruments, ready to pull out. The first bursts of flak exploded harmlessly as the surprised gunners fought to bring their guns to bear. The scene that rolled out before John's eyes told him the state of the battle at that precise time, with Belgian resistance obviously having collapsed and the Wehrmacht streaming across the target bridge like methodical worker ants caught in the disdainful glare of a hovering predator.

He saw men in grey uniforms scurrying for cover and trucks dispersing, horses bounding, barely under control.

The lead Battle leapt as it released its load of bombs and tried to gain height desperately before flying into a flak burst and exploding. John watched in horror as the plane separated into huge fragments which shot out to the limits of their aerodynamics before beginning to drift to the ground like giant confetti. A bullet-shaped flaming fragment fell in an elegant but remorselessly earthbound arc, having discarded large awkward sections that tumbled and weaved erratically through the agitated air. He flew through the aftermath of the other plane's destruction, perhaps even through the vaporised remains of the men to whom he had so recently spoken, unable to avoid them. He winced as debris bounced off his aircraft's wings with the sound of heavy rocks rolling down a metal roof. Behind him the observer tried to sight the bombs, and as they fell away, he felt the sickening lurch as the great machine lifted, as if suspended on a huge piece of elastic.

'Let's go', said John but the words came out as a strangled parody of speech. He was coated in sweat, a dank, damp fear that invaded his body, for he knew that things were set to get worse. Evil bursts of flak groped for the big aeroplane like drops of ink diffusing in water. Each black pom-pom was laced with deadly shards of hot, sharp metal spinning outwards at hundreds of miles per hour, a thousand random tin openers. He could feel their impacts but the great plane kept on flying, responding to the input of his hands and feet as he fought to make their escape. He heard nothing from his two crewmen until the rear machine gun began to open fire. As they pulled free from the scene below with a sickening lurch, he caught sight of his bombs reaching the ground. Only one had hit the bridge, hurling a truck sideways into the canal, contemptuously swept away by some obscure physical laws like a foolhardy fly swiped from a breadboard.

John wrenched the Battle around, saw the bridge was still standing and caught sight of the twin-engine Messerschmitt Bf 110 on his tail. His brain accepted a miasma of information in less than a calculable split second, his hands and feet working of their own volition to drag him towards another tiny victory for the empire, in whose service he had been trained and for whom he now fought.

'Got company, John', said the gunner, his words bursting through his headset.

'Seen. Keep the bastard at bay and we might just make it.' John took the ungainly bomber through a series of sweeping turns as if to make it hard for the gunner to find his mark. The Messerschmitt was also a big aeroplane but one equipped with a heavy armament and a fair turn of speed. John knew that even one hit might be enough to end their homeward journey prematurely.

He looked around desperately, hoping to catch sight of some Hurricanes to drive off his pursuer but it was just the two of them fighting it out, a cat playing with a mouse, knowing that it would eventually prevail if it just kept its prey in sight. John saw tracer whipping past the Battle and heard the rattle of the big machine gun in the rear cockpit. There was a pause and John realised that the gunner was changing magazines. Sure enough, the defensive fire started up again moments later.

He could picture the gunner deftly removing, stowing and replacing the big drum magazine, cocking the gun and then continuing to sweep the skies behind them with supersonic metal. It was a tiny pinprick against the barrage of heavy calibre machine guns and cannon of the German fighter. He didn't think they could shoot it down, but perhaps just prevent that fate occurring to them.

He wrenched on the control column to gain some height, cursing the slow responses of the bomber. It had the same engine as the Spitfire and Hurricane but there the resemblance ended. The Battle was easy to fly but as agile as an outhouse. He felt the sweat lining his uniform, felt his muscles ache and tire as if he couldn't go on. Moreover, he felt that the outcome of this struggle was already decided and that he was delaying his inevitable demise, but he kept going, kept them in the air, fighting. *How did you surrender anyway?* You fought to the death because there was simply no alternative.

The aeroplane shook and rattled as it took a hit, a single bullet punching through the fuselage with a dull thump. It flew with impaired agility now… and agility had never been its forte.

'Got us!', he shouted into his microphone but there was no reply. The plane still flew and responded to his control. They tore through the air at nearly two hundred and fifty miles per hour, the ground below a carpet of browns and greens flashing past and blending into one murky mustard-coloured blur. Their current proximity to the earth rendered an examination of detail impossible.

They flew over a tumultuous stream of pastureland, a seething, high-pressure river of pastel shades, a verdant jet squeezed out at unimaginable pressure. Only a glance at the clear skies above gave any indication of the tranquil calm that could be achieved even when flying.

John wondered if the rest of his crew was still alive; the firing had stopped now and no one responded to his voice. He felt the plane take another hit, a thump like a collision between two vehicles, then a shudder and a series of deep groans as the fuselage protested at its rough treatment. The engine seemed to miss but he might have imagined that. What he didn't imagine was the stream of smoke that came from it. His options were collapsing in their scope; a pyre of twigs consumed by flame. He thought again of those burnt, disfigured hands and hoped that they would never be his.

He knew that their fate was sealed and that they would die in this stupid plane in this stupid country. He cursed and felt tears of frustration and a sadness so intense it was almost an ache in his soul. He would be cheated of his chance of life, one that had been so filled with promise. Surely there were others who deserved to die more than him? Yet the big bomber still battered its way through the air. Suddenly, the airfield came into view, a foreshortened oblong of grass, a squat control tower and a few emergency vehicles waiting for the unlikely return of two aircraft. He tried to drop the undercarriage as he scrubbed off speed and listened for the dull 'thunk' that told him the wheels were down, but he listened in vain and realised that they remained retracted and utterly useless.

The Messerschmitt overshot, the pilot surprised at John's rapid deceleration. The German rear gunner fired a few token rounds their way, his first chance for action not to be missed and desultory ack-ack snaked up from the ground to try to bring the fighter down. This fight was over, however. All that remained was for John to land.

'No undercarriage boys', he said into a dead mic. He hoped that that was all that was dead. He saw a flash of flame from the engine cowling just below the exhaust and knew that he had one chance and if he messed up, they wouldn't get airborne again for another attempt. Oily, stinking flames licked the side of the fuselage and he winced as acrid fumes pushed into the cockpit for the first time. John choked and forced back the canopy, losing height, pulling up the nose to pancake safely on the grass.

He was glad that they had at least managed to leave their bombs behind for they were going to come down hard despite his best efforts. The ground was a blur of even green. He saw the fire tender pull away from its parking spot and an ambulance taking up position at the place where they thought he might come to a rest. They would have to be quick.

John stopped the engine and the prop slowly glided to a halt as if unconcerned at the chaos that would soon descend upon man and machine. The belly touched down with an empty thud, the prop buckled painfully and for a moment they slewed to the left and then the right, having bounced a few inches back into the air. The air was knocked from his lungs. For a second time they hit the grass and this time the big plane stayed rooted to *terra firma* as if on rails. John saw a spray of grass and soil erupting from beneath the wings, felt them slow, saw the fire start to go out for want of oxygen and then they stopped.

With a silence so intense it shocked, John sat back and heaved a sigh before unbuckling his safety harness. Ground crew began to scramble over the wings just moments later, earnest locusts, desperate to help even as they tore the plane to pieces to retrieve the crew trapped inside.

'We're home', called John, on the edge of hysteria. He didn't know how they had made it but somehow they had. There was still silence from the rear of the long cockpit. He heard the canopy section being wrenched open as hands reached in to pull him free and spotted his observer being lifted out with difficulty. The gunner was slumped as if trying to hide from his rescuers.

From a jumble of voices someone said, 'Are you okay sar'nt? Sergeant Guy are you okay?'

'What about the others?', he said but no one seemed to answer or he couldn't hear what was said above the urgent din. As he was carried from the wrecked plane and put on a stretcher, he thought he saw two bodies being laid out on the grass some distance from the ambulance. 'What about the others?' he said again but again there was no reply. John heard another voice, an educated one, before he lost consciousness. 'Get him on a stretcher and off to hospital', it said.

Chapter Seven

When the afternoon sun finally encroached upon Ted's eyelids, he found himself next to a hedge that ran the length of a bank of soil, down one side of a field. He studied the grass that poked out from between a few randomly laid stones and realised that he was looking at the remains of a wall. A few leaves from the hedge fluttered stiffly in a breeze and Ted continued to look on, unwilling to move, to think about his situation, or the fate of his friends. To stay still and let nature take its own ruminative course was the easiest option, with all initiative lying in the hands of a greater power, or more likely, with chance. He was alive – which was generally to be taken as a good thing as far as he could recall – but he felt that any further analysis of his situation was likely to dramatically reduce his sense of well-being.

The factors that impacted upon his current existence were very negative ones in the main. Chief amongst these was the war with Germany and the corresponding collapse of Allied resistance. He considered these to be an impediment to his continued good health and welfare.

Ted's thoughts milled around in his head, like old men out for a winter stroll to make sure that they were still alive until, with a sudden and rather shocking clarity, Ted foresaw a train of events in which the British were forced to skulk behind the English Channel and wait for the inevitable invasion and defeat. This apocalyptic vision came as clearly as a Pathé news show played out on the big screen, but he consoled himself that so long as he lay there none of this would happen; disaster would be delayed if not averted. There could be a temporary suspension of despair. He forced a smile.

None of which made any sense, of course, but he decided, for want of a better alternative, to stay where he was, at least until a plan came to him. It was the voices – German voices – on the other side of the hedge that persuaded him that this was not the time for such idiotic complacency. These Germans were not a distant enemy, an abstract entity dealing death from miles above like the Luftwaffe. They were here and now and could kill instantly. It was a truly shocking discovery. Ted could feel his heart thumping in his chest and he wondered why his enemies couldn't hear it. He was comforted by the fact that they obviously had no idea he was so close… but it was a small comfort and nothing more. He imagined that he could smell cologne or sausages, the things that Germans ought to smell of.

How long had he lain there like carrion? The ground war had caught up, or perhaps overtaken him. The transitory safety he had imagined just seconds before had been snatched away from him, cruelly reclaimed by another owner. He wasn't safe; far from it, in fact.

That they weren't looking for him or even expecting him to be there was good, of course, but he needed to increase the odds in his favour. He lay still and listened to the Germans talking, understanding literally one word in ten. The mood of the soldiers was easy enough to determine. These were men who were relaxed and confident, victors and not fugitives like him.

'*Geben Sie mir eine Zigarette Sie Bastard. Nicht einer von den Französischen derjenig.*' Some words need no translation, he realised, grimly.

'Wir werden in England bald sein.'

Ted felt alone, vulnerable, completely isolated from the company, the battalion, the whole BEF in fact. He might be a single British soldier afloat in a cruel sea of Germans. He twisted his head, suppressing a groan as battered muscles were made to work. He felt as if he had been repeatedly punched in the back. A pall of smoke rose from Cassel in the distance, and in the foreground there lay the mortal remains of his men. Sadness, tempered with nausea, pain, distress and weariness washed over him. Dinger was still caught in the brambles, his body slowly subsiding, a botched crucifixion; Christ without the salvation. Two other brown lifeless heaps he recognised as Snowball and Whitey. A fresh wave of sadness swamped all his other selfish thoughts and emotions. He wanted to talk to them, tell them that their deaths had some purpose. He wanted to bury them, or at least know that they would be buried, especially Dinger whom he'd known longest. Dinger deserved better than to be left hanging there like an obscene scarecrow.

There was nothing he could do for them.

Ted lay for another few seconds and then crawled closer to the hedge. Incongruously, he would be better hidden the closer he got to the hedge although that meant also getting closer to his enemy. For now, it only took one of them to stand up and he would be seen. In that event he could play dead but there was always the chance that one of them would send a bullet his way just to make sure... besides which he had no idea how long they intended to stay there. They didn't sound like men in a hurry, and soldiers, be they French, British or German, given the chance to take it easy, away from their officers, would do exactly that, spinning it out for as long as they could. Some things transcended nationality.

Ted lay at the edge of the bank, directly below the hedge's stunted foliage. He felt as if each breath he took was as loud as a trumpet call and that he must inadvertently attract the attention of the enemy soldiers. His worry only deepened when he realised that the nearest soldier was actually reclining against the very hedge that offered Ted concealment. He could see it bulge elastically as the man leaned against it. He heard him burp as he chomped noisily on a piece of bread. The soldier cried out to his companions.

'Das nächste Picknick wird auf dem Strand sein, bevor wir England überfallen.'

'Sie werden so Fett bis dahin sein, dass sie Sie hinterher verlassen werden', came the reply. It was followed by uproarious laughter. Only Ted felt like crying. Even if he had understood it he couldn't imagine himself laughing.

For what seemed like agonising hours he listened to their desultory banter, but in reality it was fifteen or twenty minutes before it began to die down and another fifteen or twenty before he heard the first gentle snores. He dared to look up and saw the nearest soldier's back against the hedge and the gentle swell of his breathing from within his uniform tunic. Ted peered through the hedge at the point where the roots became the first woody branches and where there were few leaves. He saw four other soldiers on the opposite bank lying in the sun, men clearly at peace in the midst of war. Strange how they could find relaxation and calm in such otherwise desperate circumstances, he thought. Their next orders could send them to their deaths and yet they were able to block such possibilities from their minds in order to enjoy a tiny fragment of peace. Life snatched from death, peace in war.

He looked at the unfamiliar belt equipment of the German: a cylindrical tin which he knew held a gas mask, a water bottle, a rolled-up cape, a grenade and round the front, just within his vision, ammunition pouches.

Now was the time to make his escape. Ted leaned back from the bank slowly and looked around at the route that offered him the best chance of making an unchallenged withdrawal. His options were few. To his right, the field followed an upward curve whilst the height of the hedge remained almost constant. After twenty yards or so he would be plainly visible to the Germans. Moving left offered him greater concealment but would mean walking in the wrong direction and further into enemy territory. Going back the way he came entailed a journey away from the British lines, whilst going straight ahead meant crossing the road. A dogleg to the left and then crossing the road later on, before continuing forwards might be his best option, but he was still unsure of his safest route.

Of course, he reasoned, the Germans were asleep now, but just then one of them spoke. No one replied but he knew now that there was at least one enemy soldier still awake for certain. Ted rubbed a hand over his face, containing the panic he felt, thinking urgently about an answer to his problem. An image – almost a vision – flitted through his mind: the grenade. With that he could kill the Germans, subtracting them from the equation, removing the conundrum wholesale. However, he balked at the idea of killing them – was he ready to be a killer? – and wondered if he could even reach the weapon.

Carefully, he leaned against the bank again. The German soldier had shifted slightly with a sleepy sigh and the grenade was now within reach. He scrutinised its design with the expert eyes of an infantryman; a long handle with a screw cap on one end and a cylinder, like a can of food, which he knew was packed with explosive, on the other. There was no obvious pin or other means to prime the bomb. Ted pulled a face. Without knowing how to use the grenade there was little point in taking it. The answer must lie in the screw cap, the only apparently moveable or detachable piece he could see.

As he reached through, his sleeve snagged on a treacherous little branch and the dry leaves shook like elfin percussion. Ted swallowed, closed his eyes for a second, released his sleeve and then tried again. His knuckles brushed the hem of the soldier's tunic but just moments later the tips of his fingers made contact with the grenade. He hoped that it would come smoothly from the German's belt... but it didn't, of course. At that moment the soldier broke wind, sat up slightly and unhooked his belt, plainly not asleep at all. Ted froze, his arm still reaching through the hedge like that of a drowning man clawing forlornly above the waves for the calloused hands of a rescuer. With horror he saw the German turn slightly and then realised that he was doing so to shrug off his webbing, which he then placed in an untidy pile under the hedge before sliding down the bank to lie in the sun-baked ditch.

Ted rolled his eyes in exasperation and released the breath he had been holding. His little explosive treasure was closer than ever. He carefully withdrew his arm yet again and waited for a count of thirty, before reaching into the hedge for one last time and taking hold of the screw cap with his fingertips. His mouth ran dry, his tongue sticking to his palette. He could practically smell his own fear. How long before he was discovered? He dislodged the grenade and pulled it through, making no sound.

He looked at the ungainly bomb as if it were a recently discovered artefact of dubious provenance and value. Ted wondered if he dared to use it. If he didn't manage to kill all the soldiers at once, or at least fearfully disable them, he would have to continue the fight with his rifle, a poor choice for close contact fighting unless he fitted his bayonet. Even then he wasn't sure if he had the stomach for close combat. It had almost been comical in training when they had been taught to charge at a straw dummy suspended from gallows, screaming their battle cry of *Faugh-a-Ballagh*. He couldn't remember how the ancient Irish words translated but he smiled at the recollection of them shouting 'fuck-a-bollock' as they stabbed their inert, inoffensive and strangely compliant enemies.

To kill a man from a great distance with a well-aimed bullet was one thing, but to kill a man when he was practically within arm's reach was quite another. The phrase 'arm's reach' suggested rescue, if anything, not the act of killing. He fought back his nerves but the sickly dread of taking life rose like bile in his throat, almost paralysing him. Ted knew that he was running out of options and that dwelling on his predicament was unlikely to make the situation better.

An image of the bomb clattering onto the road but not subsequently exploding filled his mind. In his thoughts he could see the Germans suddenly alert, perplexed, shocked but, crucially, unharmed and ready to fight back.

Ted tentatively twisted the screw cap but it didn't move until he applied greater pressure. He was now sure that the means to prime the bomb lay inside the handle. Each turn created a tiny squeak, which was either inaudible or quite deafening, and he wasn't sure which.

The distant sound of a motorbike, a guttural grumble, made him pause. His hand was being forced; whatever his plan was he had to carry it out now before the Germans stirred. Quickly, he unscrewed the cap, heedless of the noise, letting a tiny ceramic ball on the end of a piece of string fall into his hand. He frowned and silently mouthed the words, *'what the hell is this?'* He held the grenade in his left hand and the string in his right; there was only one thing that he could think of to do now. The motorbike crested the road maybe two hundred yards away. It was travelling at speed, putting distance between the rider and some devilish foe in pursuit. Ted grasped the ceramic ball, stood just as one of the Germans stirred, pulled and then hefted the grenade into the centre of the group. It was out of his hands now, both literally and metaphorically.

Ted's hasty plan had not included provision for the arrival of a motorbike.

'Mein Gott, eine Handgranate!' came a German voice. Ted glanced at the approaching motorcyclist just as he ducked behind the hedge, thought that it might be a British soldier, closed his eyes and rolled into a ball. He heard another German cry cut off by the explosion. The ground rocked, leaves were blown off the hedge and landed like roasted paper. He heard a scream, the squeal of brakes and an engine racing as the bike toppled over. There was a pause broken only by some muffled cursing, a scuffle and a shot fired. Ted had regained his feet and tied to vault the hedge but it was too tall and he fell backwards into the field, coming down hard on his angular metal water bottle. Despite his terror and anguish he found time to feel idiotic, like a stumbling hurdler. He heard another shot, then another.

'Shit!', he cried and rose to his feet again. From the other side of the hedge he heard a groan and a quick whiff of cordite assailed his nostrils.

'What the fu... oo are you?', said a soldier in British uniform.

'I'll explain in a minute when I get over this hedge', said Ted.

'I was coming down 'ere on me bike and I saw these Krauts and then they flippin' blew up!' said the soldier as Ted finally scrambled over the hedge with difficulty.

'I threw a grenade', he explained.

'You nearly bleedin' killed me', said the man. Ted smiled at his London accent. The man was indignant.

'I didn't know you were coming down the road.'

'I shot 'im', he said pointing at a German NCO whose body lay crumpled and bleeding in the road. 'I fink the others were dead. I've never killed anyone before.'

'Check that the rest of these Krauts are dead', said Ted, pointing to the scattered figures on the ground. He could now see that there had definitely been only five of them.

'I think *I'm* dead', said his new companion beneath his breath but he hobbled around the site of the massacre and checked the men with a swift kick to the ribs. One of the Germans lay there headless.

'I fink ee's dead, don't you?', asked the new man facetiously, pretending to scratch his own head in puzzlement.

'Could be.' Ted looked at the other soldier. He was of equal height to himself, thin and wiry-looking beneath his webbing, battledress and leather jerkin. His skin was swarthy, like a man used to working in the sun. One of the Germans gave a low groan and the man looked over at him without pity.

'Let's get out of here. What's your name?', asked Ted, eager to get through a short list of pleasantries very quickly.

'Private Tyrone Miglorine of the Buffs. People call me Mig.'

'I'm Ted', said Ted, holding out his hand. As they shook, he asked, 'Can you get us out of here on that bike.' Ted's rifle was pointed vaguely in the direction of the one survivor, a man whose life was clearly ebbing away, but he was looking at the despatch rider as he spoke. 'We are way behind German lines here', he added, hoping to make a strong case.

'Do you know which way to go, because I'm completely bloody lost!'

'Aye, but we might run into some Krauts on the way.'

'Okay let's go. Transport and someone who knows the way sounds like a good combination to me. I've not got much juice in the tank though.'

'Doesn't matter, let's hit the road' and he strode over to help the other man right the bike.

'What are you going to do with him?', said the rider pointing at the German. He wondered if they should shoot him. Was that the humane thing to do? Ted looked at the pale, terrified face of the stricken German soldier. Blood seeped out from a massive wound to his chest and the man was trying to hold himself together with what remained of his strength.

Ted's well of compassion was suddenly dry. He said, 'just leave him. He's going to die, anyway. Let's get out of here.' The BSA started again with some reluctance, perhaps protesting at the abuse it had suffered recently and with Ted on the back the two men set off.

Ted clung on tenaciously never having been on a motorbike before. He felt as if the next ragged gear change would definitely be the one that dislodged him and sent him backwards into the tarmac. The wind burned at his eyes as they sped off down the road and he wondered if he was going to have to tell his driver to slow down lest he tear into the middle of a party of Germans. But he needn't have worried because after about three miles the bike's engine began to cough and sputter. It finally cut out and they coasted down a long, straight tree-lined incline for about another three hundred yards like schoolboys playing on a stolen bike. When finally they stopped, the other soldier turned to Ted and said, 'Shit.'

The word was obviously a favourite of his and so far he had used it entirely appropriately to describe the situations in which he had found himself.

He kicked at the starter again but nothing much happened, apart from them both almost falling off their stationary mount.

'No petrol?', ventured Ted.

'No petrol', confirmed the Don R. They both dismounted like disappointed cavalrymen. As if to affirm the analogy, the despatch rider let the bike fall over, like a suddenly dying horse.

They stood beneath an archway of trees that lined and finally covered the road. To the left Ted saw a gravel path that led to a flat grassy area, and again he could picture the well-to-do French family sitting there next to their Citroen having a picnic. *Better times*, he thought wistfully, although his own family had had neither the time, nor the money, nor the inclination for such fripperies themselves. It was some sort of ideal that he perhaps yearned for now… now that his own life was going to hell in a handcart.

The Dexter family had never possessed a car either, so any picnics would have been in the local park, sitting on permanently wet grass beneath a mildewy tree. Bank managers and factory owners had cars; men who fitted out the cabins in ships built in Harland and Wolff didn't. He could imagine *Monsieur* swigging wine and getting quietly sloshed whilst *Madame* did her best to ensure that the children ate the rind of their Brie and did not run out into the road to be hit by the baker's van that traversed its boiling summer tarmac twice a day.

'Shall we go?', said Mig. Ted turned around, his reverie dissolving like a ghost taking fright. His new companion stood with his arms by his sides like a defeated boxer, looking at him with mild curiosity.

'Aye, come on. We're heading for the coast, right?'

'Are we?'

'That's where everyone else is going.'

'I didn't know that.'

***

The two men chatted as they made their way along the road, only taking care when they neared a bend or crested a rise, for fear of catching up with the advancing Germans. Mig told his new friend about the massacre and Ted listened in shocked silence, hardly able to believe that the Germans were capable of such things. He intended to escape if at all possible but had always considered surrender as a definite possibility – plan B in effect – until now, that was. He still believed that events such as this massacre did not represent the norm for captured soldiers, but it was alarming to have his contingency plan taken from him so rudely.

They walked for hours. Ted thought it unlikely that the Germans would have placed any sentries facing back into what had become their own lines. They would surely assume that they were in pursuit of the British and not, by any means, surrounded by them. Ted also presumed that they would spot or hear the Germans first and that as two lonely, isolated figures they would attract little attention so long as they kept their distance.

The sun warmed their backs but before long they were feeling its energy sap theirs. Mig removed his leather jerkin, tucking it into his webbing. His Thompson sub-machine gun rested on an ammo pouch and his helmet was tilted back on his head. Subconsciously, both men had fallen into step and the clump of their leather-soled boots on the tarmac beat a steady rhythm that kept them moving, like a tribal drum tapping into some deep buried instinct that kept the ancient hunter on the trail. The road seemed endless, nothing more than a grey swathe cut through a land of infinite meadow inhabited solely by cows and butterflies.

That two such disparate creatures could live so harmoniously might have been a source of great wonder, had it not simply been part of a transient myth that drifted through Ted's mind. Of its own volition it had created, developed and rejected this version of events, as if giving Ted a clever picture to think about as he wound his way through this alien, dangerous land. The air smelled floral fresh, at odds with the general stink that wafted up from his battledress tunic and from the terrifying version of hell that rolled through this bucolic semi-wilderness in violent spasms.

Ted longed for a bath, some beer and steak and potatoes, not necessarily in that order and not necessarily in isolation either. He'd never previously drunk beer whilst in the bath but he didn't rule it out. He smiled at the thought, recognising it as harmless whimsy. Eating steak and potatoes in the bath might prove more difficult but he knew that he would welcome the opportunity to find out for himself.

Without pausing, he took a swig from his water bottle. The water had a strange powdery taste to it that he had never been able to eradicate no matter how many times he rinsed the offending container out.

He took a hard tack biscuit from its wrapper and crunched on it. It was just filler that stopped his stomach from rumbling, and nothing more than that.

He offered a broken rectangle of biscuit to Mig but the other man shook his head with a look that said, *I'm not that hungry.*

'Are we definitely going the right way?', said Mig, at last. Ted had sensed that the question was coming as they plodded along, seemingly without purpose.

'Roughly. We're headed roughly the right direction and we've got no choice but to follow this road. I've got a map', he said, tapping his tunic beneath which the folded map lay.

'And when we get to the coast, then what?'

'Get on a boat and go home.'

'A boat?'

'Aye. You know what a boat is, don't ya? Remember when you came to France, you got on a big metal thing that moved…'

'I know *what* a boat is, thank you. I just didn't think that I was going to be getting on one again so soon.'

'How long were you lost for?'

'A couple of days.'

'Really!', said Ted incredulously. 'And you didn't see any British soldiers?'

'Yeah, I did, but none of them knew where my unit was so I just kept looking. They all gave me food and petrol an' that…'

'But no one told you?'

'Told me what?'

Ted shook his head. They had stopped now; carelessly staging their discussion in plain view of whatever enemy forces might be around. Ted tilted his helmet back and wiped sweat from his brow with a cuff.

'The BEF is being evacuated from the channel ports. They are going to get us all off from Boulogne and Calais, take us home. The French are surrendering in their tens of thousands. The only reason I'm here is I got separated from my company.'

'Just you?', asked Mig.

'No, there were four of us…'

'That's still not many…'

'Well, anyway that's the script. That's why we're heading to the coast.'

'Shit', said Mig.

Chapter Eight

The barn could have been the French National Museum of Faeces (Le Musée National Français de Matières fécales) such was the extent, range and variety of exhibits. Admittedly, had that been the building's intended use, they had been very haphazardly stored, with one animal caring very little for the deposits of its predecessors, but nevertheless it represented something fairly unique even by the standards of French barns.

Neither man cared very much about the overpowering odour, such was the depth of their exhaustion as they slumped against the wall onto hastily constructed paliasses of straw. Mig had drawn his leather jerkin around him like a short blanket and was asleep, it seemed, within seconds, his mind filled with pleasant dreams that could never match the reality of his waking hours. Ted found sleep harder to come by and not just because of the cold. He felt alone despite the presence of the other man.

This odyssey across northern France was not to his liking and with extreme tiredness came attenuation of hope and confidence. His task was a difficult one, if not impossible, and at the very heart of his near despair was the feeling that the rest of the British Army had got to the coast much quicker than him and was already on its way home to Britain. The alternative possibilities were no better: they had got to the coast but there was insufficient transport, or they were not at the coast and the transport idled at ports being bombed by the Germans.

He had tried to take a last look at the map before he settled to sleep but it was already too dark to see the maze of lines and colours. The truth was that he had lost his bearings, although he was still sure that they were heading in approximately the right direction. Should he go for Boulogne or Calais? Was there any point in doing either? Were the Germans taking prisoners or using a more terminal approach to the problem of dealing with captured soldiers? Mig's recent experiences had placed that idea firmly in his head.

He shuddered at the thought of surrender and recalled the Londoner's description of his fortunate escape.

In the gloom, he could pick out the rafters above his head. He knew there was a hole in the ceiling and in the roof above, but such was the intensity of the blackness that enveloped them he couldn't pick out the night sky... nor did he really want to; he wanted to sleep. Ted tried to clear his mind of comforting memories, realising that they were of no use to him. He needed to think clearly and to be realistic about what his immediate future held, but no matter how hard he tried thoughts of better times ran through his mind, seeming to jostle with one another, vying for his attention. An image of his mum and dad's house in Belfast loomed large.

It was the same as the house to the left and the one to the right, the one behind and the one across the road. It was the same as the one behind the one behind, in fact everywhere you looked there were houses just the same. And yet that house was unique. That house was where *his* mum and dad lived, where the fire always burned, where there was a hot meal on the table every night and enough hot water to have a bath every week if you wanted one. He pictured his dad sitting in *his* chair, a tatty wingback affair with a gaudy Victorian pattern, reading the Belfast Telegraph, paying special attention to the obituaries, which seemed to fascinate him for some reason.

Maybe he just loved the fact that he had outlived someone and it didn't matter whom. The newspaper appeared just too large and the young Ted had often wondered why his dad bothered with his evening wrestling match; man pitted against paper. Every now and again his dad's hand would drop down to the floor to pat the dog's head. The dog would look up from his slumber and sniff the proffered hand, which would then be withdrawn.

'Ted, take Seamus for a walk, willya, son', his dad would say, eventually. Ted had never understood how the dog had ended up with a Catholic name.

His mum, on the other hand, seemed to spend her day in the kitchen as if she couldn't survive without the hundred tasks she set herself to perform. She washed, cleaned and ironed continuously, a slave to her own high standards, to Protestant perfection; no one set foot out of the door without a clean shirt.

Ted saw less of his brother, a policeman stationed in County Armagh, near the border with the Irish Free State. It had been Ted's intention to join the RUC too when he was old enough but they'd told him that he was just too short. Not much, but enough seemingly. Personally, he would have sworn that he was the requisite five feet eight but they said otherwise, and even having a brother already in the RUC made no difference.

It was that rejection that prompted him to join the army instead, and until a few weeks ago he'd had no regrets. Whilst his brother might have had to deal with the occasional bullet from a piqued 'Free-Stater', as he called them, he was unlikely to have to take on the Wehrmacht, unless of course things went very badly wrong indeed.

He didn't want to think about that possibility, the Germans in Northern Ireland. Instead, he tried to think about food – usually a mistake when you don't have much – but he finally dozed off, sure that in the morning they would find some sustenance. This was a farm after all…

***

The sun was still low in the sky and the air was cold when he awoke. Mig's bedspace was empty but his leather jerkin lay there, which Ted took to be an indication that he was coming back. Ted stretched where he lay, yawned, rubbed his eyes and yawned again. His stomach rumbled in painful protest. He patted his rifle like an old friend, taking comfort from its presence, and then he stood to examine their location in daylight. Against a tableau of blue skies, streaked with lackadaisical clouds, he could pick out a byre and a farmhouse.

A two-wheeled cart rested against the wall of the byre, looking very much like something that had fallen into disuse. The building itself had once been white but the paint was peeling off with years of exposure to wind and rain. Repairs had been started on the roof, a fact witnessed by the piles of brick-red tiles stacked neatly alongside.

Unsurprisingly, the farmhouse itself appeared to be in rather better condition, but somehow just as deserted as the rest. It wasn't too hard to picture it at the centre of a bustling enterprise with tractors and trucks to-ing and fro-ing, geese and hens waddling about without purpose and a dog caked in manure, tied up, alternately basking in the sun or barking at visitors.

However, something was missing. Noise and smoke from the chimney, perhaps? Even on a hot day they would have a stove burning to cook and bake, and clearly wherever the owners had gone their livestock had gone too. Ted peered onto the road and then cocked an ear in that direction but there was no sound: not the rumble-clank-squeal of tanks, the smoky clatter of trucks or the gentle clip-clop of horses. There were no voices singing, nor the regular clump-stomp of men marching in time. For a moment he seemed to exist in a peaceful world, and he closed his eyes slowly, as if doing so would help to capture and retain this carefree place for a time when he might need it.

Ted breathed deeply, almost a sigh, in recognition of the fact that he was creating a lie. His hands ran through the puddles of condensation on the windowsill and he opened his eyes. For a second he thought he saw a figure at the side window of the farmhouse and almost gasped in something akin to terror, until he remembered the little Londoner who called himself Mig.

He followed a weed-strewn path to the farm, entered cautiously like an intruder and found Mig cooking eggs on a tiny gas stove.

'Morning', said their cook, cheerily. 'I was going to do you breakfast in bed! I found some bread – not too fresh – and meat – but it stank. These eggs are okay though.' He seemed cheered after his night's sleep and the prospect of food.

'So, a big plate of fried eggs for breakfast?'

'Yeah. Not bad, eh? Bit of energy for the journey.'

Ted nodded and laughed. Mig's enthusiasm was infectious and although not a great fan of eggs he had to admit that they did smell good.

'I've boiled some water but I've run out of tea bags and powdered milk', said Mig.

'I've got some somewhere. And some fags.' Ted patted his pockets and then produced the goods, like a low-rent magician. He smiled with a sort of restrained satisfaction. A cup of tea wasn't much to get excited about.

'Tea, fags and eggs', said Mig counting the ingredients for their feast off on his fingers. 'Not exactly the Ritz but it'll do.'

They sat at a table that had four legs of matching length and on chairs that didn't. Mig winced as he supped his tea, burning his mouth slightly. He constantly forgot that milk powder did not cool the boiling water as fresh milk did. He devoured the eggs as if he hadn't eaten for some days and Ted did the same, casting aside the table manners that his mum had nagged into him.

Don't put your elbows on the table. Don't speak with your mouth full. Keep your mouth closed when you chew.

And so, it went on and on, over and over, until he learnt. Every now and then his dad would chip in with something like, *come on lad, you're a Protestant, y'know,* but there was a twinkle in his eye as he said it, as if he didn't take his own remonstrations too seriously. Ted found himself smiling at the memory.

'What are you smilin' at?', asked Mig looking up from his tea. He'd been blowing on it with great gusto, eager to take a proper drink.

'I was just thinking of home', he said.

'Mmmm. Best not to. You'll only get fed up. Don't think about it until you're in Blighty and you get told you're on leave. In fact, don't think about it until you are actually on leave... back in... wherever you're from', said Mig, risking a sip of tea. He rested his cigarette on the edge of the table. 'Where *are* you from?', he added, as if he should show some interest in his new friend.

'Belfast', replied Ted.

'Ireland.'

'Northern Ireland.'

'What mob are you in?', he asked Ted.

'You might be a spy', joked Ted.

'Yeah I am. I'm disguised as a private in the Buffs.'

'Well, you had me fooled. I'm in the Royal Irish Fusiliers.'

'Do you lot wear those big green hats with the feather stickin' out?'

'The big green hat is a caubeen and the feather is a hackle.'

'So that's your lot that wear that?'

'No', lied Ted. He intended to tell Mig the truth almost at once but he'd moved onto a new topic before he got the chance.

'Did you enjoy your breakfast?'

'Aye, very nice it was. The eggs were good. Did you find any other grub?'

'Not searched everywhere yet but there's bound to be other stuff. There's a bottle of wine', he added, pointing to the sideboard, where there was indeed a bottle of wine.

'Don't drink wine', said Ted, emphatically. 'Don't like it.'

'Nor me', agreed the Londoner. 'Have you ever had it?'

'No.'

'I 'aven't either.' They both laughed. 'More of a beer man', said Mig. Ted nodded his agreement. Soldiers drank beer, not wine. Wine, he supposed, was for officers and homosexuals.

'Are you a regular?', he asked and Mig shook his head.

'Territorial. Joined up in 1938. I drove a van before the war, delivering ladies undergarments to shops and market stalls.' Ted laughed. He could picture the man doing exactly that.

'Undergarments?'

'Knickers.'

Ted laughed.

'It's true. Great job, it was. Drivin' round London, stopping off at the ladies' shops, 'avin a brew and a chat and then off to the next shop. Same thing there. Like I said, a great job.' He sipped his tea, wistfully, ensconced in comforting memories. 'You could have as many pairs of tights, stockings and women's knickers as you wanted.'

'And you actually wanted these, did you?' enquired Ted, doubtfully.

'Yeah, of course', said Mig. He was astonished at Ted's question. 'Not for me, personally. They're a great way to get the birds.' He drew on his cigarette, lost in that faraway time, and then sipped his tea. He was appraising the life he'd had almost as if it was about to end. 'Still that's all gone now', he added sadly.

'The war?', asked Ted.

'Marriage.'

Chapter Nine

The interior of the ambulance was painted in a pale green gloss that brought to mind a wooden rocking horse John had once seen as a child. He remembered the toy well and how he had wanted to climb on its back, but somehow this was the sort of toy that no one seemed to play with. His mother's friend, Mrs Dunkerley, was wealthy and had children roughly John's age, but they never wanted to play, or at least not with him. In fact, sometimes they did not even bother to come downstairs when they visited, as if they were imprisoned in a tower or under a spell that prevented them from doing anything that might be considered fun.

The horse, now that he thought about it, symbolised what was wrong with the family as a whole: well-heeled neglect. Mr Dunkerley was never at home, might not have existed; the children were always called that, 'the children', as if their mother wasn't sure of their names; and the toys were for show. The horse looked brand new, the only attention paid to it being from the cleaner's duster. They had everything except contentment. How Mrs Guy and Mrs Dunkerley had ever become friends was a mystery, unless the fact that they were so clearly mismatched was the secret of their mutual attraction.

They lurched noisily through a solitary pothole and then through a series of them.

'Bloody French roads', complained the medic. John looked over and nodded but didn't speak. He felt light-headed and just slightly ill, as if he could be sick on demand but not involuntarily. He drew his hands from under the blanket to look at them, to reassure himself that they weren't burnt. He dreaded that more than anything else.

'You okay, sar'nt?', enquired the medic.

'Fine corporal. Bit sick, that's all. Don't think I really need to be in this ambulance.'

'Better to get you checked out, sar'nt. You'll soon be flying again', he said cheerily. He intercepted John's dark look. 'Which is the last thing you want to hear.'

John didn't bother to argue.

'You'll be going home soon, anyway, sar'nt. We all will.'

'Home? England?'

'So, I hear. Evacuation. The Frenchies are surrendering left, right and centre. Pulling the BEF back to the coast and getting them home.'

John pulled a face and wondered if what he was hearing was just part of the jumbled confusion upon which his life was currently based. He felt disconnected from reality, although he seemed to be able to pick out what was real from what was not, as if he was making a journey through a patchy mist that drifted before his eyes, carried on a soporific breeze. The facts, if that's what they were, were plain enough and likely to be true; it all made sense according to his view of the war.

He knew that things were going badly, and when that happened a retreat – or in this case, an evacuation – was a likely outcome if it was possible. But somehow, he felt like these things were happening to someone else and that he personally would never be taken from the war after such a short struggle. He didn't feel part of the whole. He was an outsider, rattling along in this old (it was actually almost new) ambulance. *He* was an irrelevance. Sleep or unconsciousness took him, dragging him into a heavy-eyed, comfortable world.

The medic cast a glance in his direction and noted his slumber.

'Best thing for you mate.' He had seen the squadron decimated. Sergeant Guy was just about the only pilot left and, as far as he knew, they no longer had any aeroplanes, or none that were fit to fly. They'd joked about it in a macabre way; as soon as they ran out of planes they could go home, although no one had foreseen that they would reach that point quite so soon.

'Soon be there, Albert', called the driver. The medic could only just hear him above the racket of the engine and transmission. He braced his feet against the wheel arch as they ran through another series of potholes. If the Germans could move their army along roads such as these they deserved to win, he thought grimly. As soon as they had dropped their patient off at hospital, he was going to urge a return to the airfield to ensure that they were not left behind when the inevitable happened.

He looked at the pilot again and wondered if they should all just head for the coast without delay. After all, he reasoned, the first seeds of chaos had already been sown and he seriously doubted if anyone would miss them. By the time they got home to Blighty the circumstances behind their diversion would be forgotten in all likelihood; they would just be glad that someone had escaped, if that escape were really possible, of course. Even if that weren't the case, they could make up an excuse.

He thought about shouting this suggestion through to Jimmy, the driver. He opened his mouth to speak then shut it again. It wasn't a bad idea, though. *Live to fight another day.*

'Oh shit!', came a shout from the front.

'What?', shouted Albert.

'Oh shit!' repeated the driver as he applied the brakes. The ambulance trundled to a halt, the engine was switched off and silence followed.

***

The feldwebel had been ordered to take half of the platoon on what the young leutnant hoped would be a flanking manoeuvre to capture an entire company of demoralised British soldiers. He fervently hoped they were demoralised anyway because, despite the pounding they had received from the artillery, it was clear that they still outnumbered his men at least two to one. But if he could capture an entire company of the enemy it would do his career no harm at all. He had given his sergeant the hard job; getting two half-tracks across the fields and the road unseen to affect the great surprise that was needed for his plan to work.

He knew that he could do it. The sergeant was a veteran of Poland and as tough as they came, a resourceful man and most importantly someone to blame if the plan didn't work. You were never taught the importance of scapegoats during officer training but it was obvious, when you thought about it.

And he had thought about it often.

War was a treacherous game and sometimes a little subterfuge – nothing too obvious – was needed for one to emerge with the credit one deserved.

The feldwebel was well aware of all this and distrusted his platoon commander implicitly. However, the half-tracks coped well with the fields and their hard-packed, corrugated surfaces, and they seemed to avoid detection despite the dust they kicked up. The roar of their engines was rather hard to conceal too. His men knew what they had to do and would fight intelligently and with the appropriate amount of courage. They weren't reckless and he didn't want them to be, for reckless men got you killed too easily.

So far, the plan was working. Ahead, he could pick out the tall hedge that he knew must line the road he needed to cross. He signalled to his driver to slow and stop. The second vehicle followed suit. With a sigh he prised himself from his seat and gestured one of his men to follow him. They set off across the field to reconnoitre, keeping a wary eye out for British soldiers.

He could see no gate leading to the road and realised that they would be required to drive over and through the tall hedge to continue their journey. It wasn't impossible to do, merely difficult, but he needed to know what lay on the other side. The two soldiers peered cautiously through the thicket and bindweed to find a steep drop down to the road. The feldwebel tried to imagine the vehicles surmounting the hedge, hopefully crushing it and then rolling forwards onto the tarmac. He stood back and squinted. Having done this, he would then decide whether to keep to the road or proceed through the next field as ordered. Things never looked quite the same in reality as they did on a map. The leutnant would have to accept his decision, whatever it was, based on the situation as he found it and not on what the young officer would like it to be.

He had his doubts about the whole enterprise. His old sergeant major had once told him that the greatest service a young officer could offer to his platoon sergeant was to take a bullet that might otherwise hit someone useful. The officer's plan was crap, he thought, taking no account of the terrain. He could picture the half-tracks rolling forwards and onto the road without much difficulty, but equally he could visualise them turning turtle, or getting stuck as they surmounted the hedge. These hedgerows were stronger than anyone thought. He scratched his chin as if that might help. He turned to the private, an intelligent lad from Kassel who had been a draughtsman before the war.

'*Können wir über dies erhalten?*', he asked. Can we get over this? The soldier looked around him doubtfully before he answered.

'*Wir sollten ein Tor suchen.*' The sergeant already knew they needed a gate, just as he knew that there wasn't one.

'*Es gibt einen nicht*', he said, crossly. There isn't one. He was thoroughly fed up with the whole enterprise: they would have to drive through the hedge. He beckoned the leading vehicle to trundle forwards and this it did, bellowing smoke from its exhaust. He signalled to the driver that he should speed up and the great mechanical beast shot forwards under acceleration. Both he and the private stood back as the half-track charged the hedge like a huge snorting bull. He hardly dared to look as that shark nose plunged deeply into the woody vegetation with a noise like a thousand tiny fireworks exploding as myriad branches snapped, dryly.

For a second the green wall took on a distended shape, like a pregnant woman's belly, and then the half-track burst through the other side, its wheels in the air as the tracks pushed it inexorably forwards. For a moment it appeared as if the whole wagon was trapped, suspended in nothingness and without any support, but gravity wrested control once again and it toppled forward onto the tarmac with a thump.

He heard shouts from inside and wondered if he should order the troops out of the next vehicle to spare them this rocky journey. A helmeted head poked over the side like someone climbing out of a deep well and the feldwebel shouted at them to get down.

Was he going to risk the second vehicle in a similar fashion, he asked himself? It had worked once and so the answer was 'yes' and he beckoned the driver to follow suit.

If it had worked once, why not twice?

The half-track rumbled forwards more cautiously this time because the main obstacle in their path had already been breached. It was this caution which proved to be their undoing for, with the sergeant watching in horror, the wagon slowly began to twist sideways as its tracks climbed over the slight apex which edged the field and which was normally obscured by the hedge.

'Mein Gott!', he spluttered and hardly dared to look as the half-track began its inexorable slide onto the road. He saw two men jump from the back in panic just before it toppled lengthways into the ditch and crashed down with a sickening thump. The engine roared and the tracks spun ineffectually before the shaken driver had the presence of mind to switch off. He looked over at the private.

'Mein Gott, der wir sind in schwierigkeiten jetzt', he said unhappily. The private nodded; they *were* in trouble, or rather the NCO was. It wasn't his problem; he was only a private. They scrambled down onto the road to join the rescue party that had formed. Possible British bullets were forgotten as they began pulling their friends from the

stricken vehicle. No one was really hurt, nothing more than bumps and bruises, but their ability to carry out the allocated mission was severely compromised. The sergeant stood back, like an artist surveying his latest work, and swore. The half-track lay in the ditch like a squat dinosaur, and was about as much use to him.

He swore again, then regained some of his composure, detailed two sentries, each with a light machine gun, and set about the recovery. A wire hawser was attached to the side of the stricken vehicle whilst its roadworthy counterpart was manoeuvred into position. The second vehicle would then reverse slowly taking the strain and then hopefully righting its ditch-bound companion. All being well, the latter would still be fit to drive. There was no reason that the sergeant could see why this simple operation wouldn't work. His confidence began to return. His men looked on, then backed off lest the wire should snap, its loose end flailing around like a demonic and deadly whip.

He cupped his chin between his forefinger and thumb, contemplating the recovery that was just beginning.

'*Dies sollte arbeiten*', he said guardedly and to no one but himself. This should work. Then, above the roar of the engine, he heard one of his sentries call out.

'*Aussehen Feldwebel einige Brite.*' He followed the man's pointing finger up the road to the spot where a British ambulance had lumbered into view. The British had indeed arrived as the sentry had said.

***

'Whadya mean, oh shit?', asked the medic. He stood and peered through the tiny oblong window that overlooked the cab roof.

'Oh shit', he said. A group of bewildered looking German soldiers stood in the road gazing at them, mouths comically agape as if the ambulance and its little crew had just descended from heaven. Their near paralysis did not last long however and Albert saw the nearest German soldier, prone, snuggle his cheek into the butt of his machine gun, preparatory to firing.

The older man, clearly their NCO, cocked a sub machine gun and gestured to his troops to advance with caution. Albert looked down at John Guy and then back out through the window to see Jimmy clambering down from the cab and putting his hands in the air. Albert's throat ran dry and he decided to run. He tapped the heavy revolver on his hip for reassurance, a fleeting image of some sort of cinematic cowboy showdown flashing through his mind and disappearing again. Jimmy shouted to him.

'Come out, Albert. Hands up and all that. They know you're in there.'

Well they do now, he thought bitterly. For a moment he hesitated. *Where would he run to? Could he outrun a spray of bullets from a German machine gun? Had Jimmy actually saved his life?*

'Albert. It's okay. They're friendly. Well, not friendly exactly', blathered the driver. 'Friendly's not quite the right word but...'

'Right Jimmy', he shouted, shaking his head. 'I'm bloody coming.' He looked again at John Guy, peaceful and unaware of the drama. A quick glance out of the window showed him that the Germans hadn't come any closer. Perhaps he could still do something to help; his last act in fighting the war.

This would be his last throw of the dice, his last contribution to the war effort. Quickly, he loosened the leather restraints on the stretcher and unclipped his pistol belt. He placed the heavy revolver on the pilot's chest. So long as Jimmy said nothing more, then this man might have a chance of escape when he came around. As a last measure he reached for a woven blanket and draped it over the unconscious pilot.

'Good luck', he whispered and clasped John by the shoulder. He opened the door, stepped down to the road and cautiously stood to one side of the ambulance, his hands raised. 'Take me to your leader', he muttered defiantly, but he felt like crying.

Chapter Ten

Ted placed one foot in front of the other like a dogged robot. It was simple enough. He didn't even have to think about it, but for some of the time at least he thought about nothing else. He let his mind take him elsewhere, to his childhood, to the future he wanted, or to the future he might get, but always he came back to the dull rhythm of his own footfalls on grass, or tarmac, or mud. At times it seemed so pointless, and at others it seemed like the most important thing in the world.

His ears became attuned to the terrain so that he felt as if he could determine what lay below the surface of the ground beneath his feet. That much of it, particularly the vast fields they traversed, sounded like shallow graves did nothing to lighten his mood. Briefly, he wondered about the battles of the Great War, and this thought came into sharp focus along with his own father's dry, succinct recollections of that terrible conflict. That had been the war which would make any future war unthinkable, a virtual impossibility. They would never repeat those mistakes, they thought.

It was a bitter irony of course that the Great War had made a rematch inevitable. Did his father and his father's generation feel cheated of the one benefit they could possibly have accrued from their participation in the 'War to End All Wars?' One thing was for sure: his father certainly didn't feel as if he'd returned to a 'land fit for heroes', as the political rhetoric of the time had presumed.

Ted heard Private Miglorine whistling gently to himself a few feet behind and wondered what thoughts ran through his mind as he trudged along, but soon Ted was back in his childhood, an odd mix of events real and imagined, of opportunities taken and others left ignored. He imagined himself climbing Black Mountain and looking down on the great city of his birth, with its river and docks and factories arrayed like a vast board game.

In reality, he had never actually climbed the mountain. It was just there. He could climb it any time – if he ever got home again – and therefore probably never would, unless he made a special effort to do so. If he ever got home again, he would never leave, not for any reason. If, if, if. There were too many comforts and too many certainties associated with his old, dirty city to ever think about giving them up again. The problem was him being a soldier and this being a war. It was a bad time to start making plans.

Ted wondered if Mig had similar thoughts or was he one of those easy-going souls for whom life was a straightforward unfolding of entirely expected events. He had never been that type of man himself – not even close. He could marvel at soldiers he knew whose spirit was indomitable, who showed courage and resourcefulness, but never felt as if he was like them, or could justify standing next to them, either actually or metaphorically. There was a word for these stout-hearted men but he didn't know it. Were they *stoics*, he wondered?

'Are you okay?', he asked Miglorine, turning and pausing for a second. They both cast a glance at the enemy aircraft high above them, flying in perfect formation and untroubled by the RAF.

'Fine. Just ploddin' along, you know.'

'If you want to take a break or anything, just say.'

'Alright mate. I'll let you know.' Mig smiled and Ted nodded.

Ted's thoughts drifted again as they strode onward, as if he were fading in and out of consciousness. He wasn't bothered by the Germans and didn't really expect to see any of them again other than the Luftwaffe, whose attentions were firmly fixed on bigger targets than two lost men in the French countryside. He slipped from near despair at times to unjustified hope, thinking that they would prevail over their dismal circumstances, making it back home to fight again. He had no desire to fight again however, none at all, and the very thought of combat, either now or in the future, made him feel sick. Perhaps he had used up his small reserves of martial valour. Was that only natural and could he somehow replenish his stocks? He sighed.

Now and again a cow would wander along the field next to them or set a course to intercept the two men like bovine well-wishers. Ted stopped and allowed his hand to run over the nose of one of these great creatures.

'Don't get many cows in Belfast', he said.

'Don't trust 'em', said Mig. 'They'll be just as pally with the Krauts when they come this way, believe me.'

'Would you trust a British cow?', joked Ted.

'Some of 'em', said Mig.

'Do you know how to milk a cow?'

'I'm from London', explained Mig. 'Why? Are you thirsty?'

'Just a thought. Milk's good for you.'

'If it's been pasteurised.'

'Oh aye, right enough. Best leave it, then.' The cow tried to lick his hand but he pulled it away just in time.

As they set off, the cow blinked its big eyes as if disappointed at their poor opinion of its loyalty. He was a loyal French cow perhaps.

The road followed an undulating course over, or round, a series of hills, grazed by cattle for centuries. To begin with the men crested each hill cautiously just in case a party of Germans lay in wait on the other side, although Ted considered such an eventuality very unlikely. By the time they had been walking for two or three hours, such caution had been abandoned, the effort required to crouch and crawl too much for them.

Their feet ached and their spirits sagged along with their shoulders, as if each step drained them of the hope that forced them onwards in a destructive, self-defeating cycle from which there was no escape. In this way they almost walked into the arms of the Wehrmacht, becoming prisoners, taken without a fight. It was Mig who saw them first and pushed Ted into the roadside ditch, landing on top of him a moment later.

'Bloody hell!', he spluttered, the breath knocked from his lungs with shock. Mig crawled into a dip next to the Ulsterman and together they watched as the ambulance door opened and the Royal Air Force medic corporal stepped onto the road, hands raised. Slightly further down the road, another erk was walking, his arms in the air also, towards a group of surprised-looking Germans. Both wore blue battledress and had white armbands with a red cross visible.

Clearly, until seconds before, the Germans' attention had been focussed on the recovery of the peculiar looking truck lying in the ditch.

'Shall we get out of here?', hissed Mig but Ted shook his head distractedly, watching the odd little scene play out before him with a mixture of awe and pity. What must those airmen be thinking now, he wondered and hoped that he wouldn't be experiencing similar emotions any time soon. He lowered his head slowly behind the ragged grass, suddenly feeling as if they were exposed and obvious, like tall, black horses in a field of stocky, white sheep.

He saw shapes dance before his eyes and released the breath he'd been holding. As he did so, he spotted movement in the back of the ambulance and felt himself almost leaning in to get a better look. A figure in the shadows sat up and peered from side to side, looking like someone unexpectedly risen from the dead.

'Shit!', said Mig through clenched teeth. The German soldiers' concentration was firmly fixed on the two airmen, a number of rifles pointed in their direction, fingers hovering over the triggers, or planted on the trigger guard. Ted felt infected by others' tension and held his breath, again, waiting and watching, scarcely able to comprehend the nature of the drama he was witnessing. A German rifleman detached himself from the group as the two airmen walked slowly into captivity. Ted could almost feel their despair and terror as their few certainties were handed over to the enemy.

Haltingly at first, and with a backwards glance over his shoulder at the sergeant, the soldier began to pace up the road towards the abandoned vehicle. Ted was reminded of a wilful but cautious child set upon some forbidden exploration. At once he was decisive, then unsure, his initiative crippled by isolation of purpose; no-one had told him to check the ambulance; no orders had been given to that effect. He was ten yards from the vehicle when he halted and drew his rifle into his shoulder, but still at the low port. At the same moment, the figure in the ambulance seemed to topple backwards onto the stretcher with what Ted thought must be an audible thump.

Ted looked from the ambulance back to the soldier, trying to divine what reaction might follow. The German tipped his helmet back slightly as if to let the air get to his forehead and then glanced guiltily over his shoulder again. It occurred to Ted for the first time that this one man might have reached what should have been an obvious conclusion; had there not been another man in the back of the ambulance, a patient, of course, then the medic would have ridden up front next to the driver. His logic, intuition, whatever it was, was perfect and yet he had his doubts.

He looked again at the abandoned vehicle, then seemed to cast a glance up the road to the exact spot where Ted and Mig lay concealed. Ted felt as if their eyes met and then a shout from the main party of Germans distracted this lone explorer. He paused, undecided, then reluctantly returned to the group just as the stricken half-track was pulled upright with a tremendous crash. The vehicle rocked on its suspension for a moment as a couple of the soldiers applauded and cheered ironically. Even the sergeant allowed himself a wry smile.

The Germans chatted idly as their prisoners were bundled on board. Less than a minute later they had driven off and a further minute saw them out of sight and earshot, the ambulance forgotten.

Chapter Eleven

In his dream he was back in childhood again. Mrs Dunkerley had just produced a packet of expensive biscuits, the sort they sometimes had at Christmas. He felt his mouth produce a rush of saliva in anticipation of a treat he might well not receive. His mother, for reasons that made no sense to him, would always refuse the proffered biscuits as if she knew they had been poisoned. It was something to do with pride, whatever that was, but he just wished that she could set this pride thing to one side a bit more often.

It all seemed to depend on whether or not Mrs Dunkerley had said something that annoyed his mother. If she had – no biscuits. If, however, they had been getting along, and his mother hadn't felt as if her friend was out to score points, then biscuits were a real possibility. It was a stupid game, but he could recognise all the moves, explain the reactions and counterstrokes. He knew when his mother was bristling with silent indignation at some slight or other and he knew when she felt that inexplicable closeness to her odd friend. Perhaps Mrs Dunkerley needed his mother more than she needed Mrs Dunkerley.

The plate had just been set on the occasional table, left there like bait, while their host went to fetch the teapot. He knew from his mother's scornful mutterings that Mrs Dunkerley was very proud of her table – her *occasional* table. *If it's only occasionally a table, what is it the rest of the time?*, John's father had once joked. They had all had a titter at that, even

111

John who had no idea what it meant. His mother's friend had returned in this dream, glancing in the direction of the plate, swiftly counting the biscuit array and finding that none were missing. John was ravenous with diabolical biscuit cravings but knew that his mother would sooner have broken his arm than let him take one without the proper decorum being shown. The biscuits were venerated, a sign of prosperity and solid British decency.

'Do have a biscuit, John', said the bountiful Mrs Dunkerley upon her return. He looked from the biscuits to his mother and then to his host. It wasn't as simple as just *taking* a biscuit.

'Are you okay mate?', said Mrs Dunkerley. He looked at her again. He wondered why her voice had changed and why the biscuits had gone.

'Can you hear me, sergeant?', she said, her voice changed yet again. With shocking suddenness, the whole room had gone now, taking Mrs Dunkerley and his mother with it. John frowned, half in sleep and half in wakefulness. The white-painted ceiling with its elaborate cornices was gone, replaced by something much more utilitarian and painted a pastel green. Two men wearing helmets stared down at him as if they were examining some peculiar biological specimen they had just stumbled upon. John said nothing as his mind raced to catch up with his new situation. For a moment he no longer wanted the stupid biscuit, only his mother and the security and humour of her presence. Everyone wants their mother in times of distress, or so he'd been told, and he was prepared to believe that.

'Ee's comin round, Ted', said one of the men. He meant him, John Guy. The other man, Ted, looked in and then spoke in a broad Ulster accent.

'You okay, sergeant?', he said, an earnest, honest look on his face. He seemed like someone he could trust; an Ulster Scot, a reliable breed, as far as he knew. He responded with a stupid question, the answer to which was supremely unimportant.

'Who are you?', he said. If he'd been asked to write a script for a play about his experiences in France in 1940, he would not have included that line. It just sounded too corny, too much of a cliché. The soldier looked doubtful, perhaps confirming the irrelevance of the question.

'I'm Ted', he answered. Did the man need more clarification, he wondered? 'Lance Corporal Dexter, Royal Irish Fusiliers. This other boyo is Tyrone Miglorine of the Buffs. We've just found you here. You were nearly taken by the Germans, you know.'

John nodded and then sat up, noticing for the first time the weight of the pistol belt on his chest.

'There was a medic', he said. 'And a driver.'

'The Krauts got 'em', said the other man, Miglorine. 'Nearly got you as well. We watched it happen. They've only gone a few minutes ago.'

'We need to get you out of here, Sergeant. Can you walk?'

'Yeah, I can walk. I'm not sure why I'm in this ambulance', he said, swinging his legs over the side of the stretcher. For a moment his head seemed to swim and images of various lurid tides swelled and crashed in his brain. A spray of sweat grew on his forehead and bile rose in his throat as if propelled there by the lunatic contractions of his stomach. He heard one of the men say, 'he's goin' to faint' and an arm reached out to stop him falling backwards but the moment passed like the sun coming from behind a cloud.

'You didn't look so good there for a minute', said the Ulsterman.

'I crashed my plane. Must have banged my head or something but I'll be okay. Can I have a drink or something?' Ted placed his water bottle into the pilot's hands and the man drank, taking little sips as his mother had advised in childhood. Ted looked on at the sergeant, saw the colour return to his cheeks, a flow of pink displacing the jaundice yellow of his skin.

'We're heading for the coast. If you want to join up with us you can do', said Ted. Beside him Mig nodded.

'Might be easier than doin' it on yer own', added the Londoner.

'The coast? I probably need to get back to my squadron.'

'Your squadron has probably flown back to Blighty by now', suggested Ted.

'I doubt that somehow', said John without explaining further. 'Is everyone going back? Back to England?'

'There's an evacuation. The whole BEF is withdrawing to the coast.'

'Have the Germans won?', asked John. His mind felt muddled, as if someone had stuffed it with cotton.

'Not won, exactly', said Ted, glancing at Mig. 'But they seem to be *winning*. Either way we're all going back home and leavin' the French to it.'

'My God! So, whereabouts are we headed?'

'That's the thing, sarge. We don't know exactly but it's got to be Boulogne, Calais or Dunkerque. We've been heading in roughly the right direction and hoping to pick up a few clues on the way but there are Germans about and bits of fighting here and there. I don't think anyone's too clear on what's goin' on.'

'Ted's got a map', said Mig, hopefully.

'That's something', said the pilot. His senses seemed to be returning in a flood. A map was something that he could use; a prop to give him a sense of purpose, to justify them taking him along. 'Let's have a look at this map and then we'll get going', he said. 'If you still don't mind me tagging along?'

The map was passed to him and Ted pointed out what he thought was their position. He watched as the airman scanned the surrounding countryside transferring obvious landmarks into his mind and then checking them against the folded paper. Neither soldier spoke whilst he did this, content to fall back on someone else's expertise to extricate them from their joint dilemma.

Finally, John spoke. 'This is the road we are on', he said jabbing a finger decisively on the oft-folded map. 'The coast is about twenty-five miles from here, depending on which direction you head. As you said we have three ports to choose from but either way we will be travelling through this little village here, which is called Braaten. Sounds more German than French. I reckon it's five miles and we could be there before dark, maybe get some food and somewhere to sleep.'

He looked at the two soldiers expectantly, suddenly aware that they might have had plans of their own and that he had come in at the eleventh hour and taken over. He out ranked them of course but probably needed them

115

more than they needed him; on the ground a soldier's expertise was so much more useful than that of a pilot. He might only be a burden unless he made sure that his presence was actually of some benefit to them.

'Sounds fine, sarge', said Ted, with an apathetic shrug. If someone else wanted to lead them then so be it.

The pilot sensed the NCO's change in mood. He was eager to have these men's company and assistance. He said, 'I'm, John by the way. John Guy.' He held out his hand. 'Some people call me Johnny but I really don't mind what I'm called.' He smiled and then shrugged as if to say, *take me or leave me*.

Ted cast a final glance at the ambulance, rejecting its implicit offer of transportation on the grounds that it was too conspicuous and they were likely to catch up with the troops they had so recently evaded. Had it been a *German* vehicle, behind German lines, that might have been different.

They walked for almost two hours in single file, Ted in front and Mig bringing up the rear, stopping to listen, or observe every now and again. John was happy to tag along as a passenger. He'd heard about the Americans developing a thing called autopilot, where a plane flew itself, and compared his current situation to that. Someone else was in control and that was fine by him. If they needed his help it was available. In a short time, he grew to trust these two men whom he barely knew. They represented the best that the army had to offer, and perhaps he was fortunate to have stumbled upon, or more aptly to have *been* stumbled upon, by men of character and fortitude. Or so it seemed.

Alternatively of course, he might be deluding himself. They might be the two worst wretches ever to don the

King's uniform, a fact which he had yet to discover. Maybe they hadn't yet shown their true nature, but he thought he had the measure of his new companions and he was glad to be heading west towards freedom with them rather than east towards captivity by himself.

The pistol belt felt heavy and awkward around his waist, an unaccustomed burden. But he was glad of it. It gave him the chance to fight back should they encounter the enemy on this peculiar odyssey. The ground crunched under their feet and before long they had unintentionally fallen into step. He allowed himself a little smile, all thoughts of recent disasters and triumphs edged out of his mind.

Occasionally, he would glance at the surrounding countryside of undulating hills, fields and copses, home to a million tiny plants and animals whose short lives would be played out unaffected by the calamity befalling man. That these two things could happen simultaneously was a source of amazement to him. This bucolic idyll was waiting to be consumed by war for the second time in a quarter of a century; his own childhood games and his father's terrible nightmares made real, whilst elsewhere in the world life carried on and people prospered, lived and died as they had always done. Even with the skies temporarily clear of enemy aeroplanes and no German soldiers in sight, the threat of war felt like a strong hand grasping his shoulder.

A butterfly, a blur of blues, flickered fitfully before his eyes like a silent taunt and he swiped it away, unwilling to suffer the gregarious simplicity of its life.

'This place should be over the hill', said Ted pausing. The men crouched instinctively, closing in to confer. 'If we're going to spend the night there it might be best if I go in and have a look around first, just to find a spot to kip in and some food.' Mig and John nodded. 'So, if you two find somewhere just on the other side of the hill to conceal yourselves, somewhere where you can see me and then I can signal you when it's okay to come down. Okay?'

'Yip', said Mig.

Braaten was a long, stretched-out village bordering the main road that would lead them to the coast. Roughly halfway down its length stood an outsized church; the only remarkable building in a setting of squat cottages, it towered above the trees, reaching for unattainable heavenly glory. Did it offer them usable salvation or only the esoteric sort espoused by the clergy? They watched Ted's receding figure as he made his way to the town like David making his first nervous approach to Goliath, the idea of actually slaying the giant not fully formed in his head. He looked somehow vulnerable but defiant nevertheless.

'Will he be okay?', asked John.

'He'll be careful. He knows what to do. Besides it doesn't look as if the place is crawling with Krauts.'

'It's not as if we can warn him if we see any.'

'No. He'll just have to take his chances.'

Ted resisted the temptation to glance over his shoulder, imagining that if *he* were being watched, doing so would alert his enemies to the presence of John and Ted. The village (or was it a town?) grew in size as he drew near. He was reminded of a seaside town, built to follow the line of the coast, except that this place had no beach, or dancehall, or ice cream parlour...

It had the church, of course, a horrible, brooding monstrosity built in dark stone that seemed to drain hope from his frail body. For some reason, which he couldn't explain, the presence of God's house made him worry about the next section of his mission. He felt as if it was watching him like some sort of baleful sentinel, filled with malice. His foreboding was palpable like a lead-filled waistcoat pressing him earthward. No doubt it was a Catholic church too and those, for some peculiar Protestant reason lost in the tangles of Irish history, were the worst of all. He was glad he didn't have to explain his concerns to his new English friends; it would sound ridiculous.

His mind took yet another trip back to childhood and his Dad's gentle taunts about Fenians and his mum's half-hearted reprimands at the use of such language. The exact problem with Catholicism was never quite made clear, as if no one actually knew what it was themselves, only that it was there and had to be recognised as such. This church, the one at the end of the road could be a Protestant church of course. They had Protestants in France, he was sure.

It dominated everything. Ted supposed that it offered their best chance for a place to sleep; where better than the house of God, after all? He was a merciful God, or so he'd been told in church by the Presbyterian minister who harangued them for their earthly weaknesses and in gentler fashion at Sunday school. God was merciful but vengeful too. How could he be both?

Upon reaching the T-junction, Ted paused, kneeling and scanning, looking left to the houses that led to the distant coast and right to the houses that led away from it. He bit his lip as if doing so would help him make a decision, then swiped some dirt from his knee as he straightened.

The church it was.

The houses all seemed unoccupied, apart from one where smoke spiralled from the chimney in a thin trail. Their gardens were large but unkempt; the householders apparently unenthusiastic gardeners, united in a desire to create their own scrubland estates enclosed by dilapidated fences. Each was a study in ruin and set to get worse, as the town's population had mostly left and with them the prospect of even the most half-hearted attempts at garden maintenance.

Ted propped his tired body against a telegraph pole that leaned to one side as if it had been hit by a truck. To the left, the wires were correspondingly taut and to the right they were slack. The only things that thrived were the weeds and Ted wondered idly if the forthcoming and inevitable German occupation might be exactly what this town needed. They would bring order to the chaos. *Every cloud*, he thought. He closed his eyes for a second and realised that he was subconsciously creating a delay. *What exactly was the problem*, he asked himself?

His trepidation was profound, almost a physical barrier that paralysed him when he most needed to act decisively. There was more at stake than just his safety.

'Come on, Ted', he muttered. He sprinted across the road in a half crouch and then hid self-consciously behind a sturdy pillar at the corner of the church wall. He felt and smelt the moss and lichen that lined the stone, hoped to find something soothing in its texture, but failed to dislodge the feeling that his every action was being observed by a spirit suffused with perverse, gleeful rancour. Ted frowned and tried to dislodge the gross unease that stifled his initiative. Something was draining his strength, nullifying his fortitude and making him less than the man he needed to be. *Was it the church*, he asked himself?

For the first time he noticed a car at the main gate to the churchyard, the inverted chevrons on its grill visible in the gloom and one door open as if in preparation for a quick, godless getaway. Keeping close to the wall, he approached the tall gates that represented the only break in the defences designed to keep the heathen at bay. Ted peered around the corner, almost expecting to see a party of Germans sitting in wait for him but there were none, just a statue of Jesus, his arms welcome-wide and a beatific smile on his face.

He was an enigma rendered in plaster or marble, his face like that of a washed-out Mona Lisa, inscrutable and laden with meaning, that either wasn't really there, or simply could not be fathomed. For a second, Ted tried to make sense of his world and to reconcile it with the one that Jesus might have liked, marvelling at how little progress had actually been made in achieving the goals of the man who claimed to be humanity's saviour.

As a boy, Ted had gone to church, dragged there by his mother each Sunday. Jesus, God and the rest were just abstract figures who existed simply because he hadn't bothered to object to the idea. Without the evidence of his own eyes he believed, but only because that's what everyone else seemed to do. Only his father remained tight-lipped on the subject, attending church irregularly and seemingly prepared to take his chances with the threat of damnation. Once he had been chastised by his wife for his lack of devotion and had responded curtly with the words, *'If you'd seen what I've seen.'*

He did not elaborate but everyone knew that he was referring to his experiences in the Great War, and from then on he went to church when it pleased him, which was rarely.

Those who had fought in the trenches seldom spoke of it, and so it was with Ted's father. Even when Ted had told him of his decision to join up himself, he knew better than to ask his dad what to expect. For his part, his father kept his counsel, expressing neither enthusiasm for the idea, nor disappointment. *I knew you would son'*, was all he said.

Next to the car was a suitcase, battered and discoloured, a remnant from another generation's travels. It was creased and dog-eared like an old book, made from some sort of shiny brown material that was supposed to look like leather and might even be leather. Ted couldn't tell if it was expensive or cheap, only that it was well worn and its owner was nowhere to be seen. He paused, his initiative returning in tiny waves, and then looked at Jesus, still disquieted by the son of God's unearthly silence.

Did this Roman Catholic Jesus despise him? He turned to look behind him, catching sight of the hill and remembering the two men he had left behind and who depended on *him* for *their* salvation. Their destiny was entwined with his and he hoped that the faith they showed was not misplaced; who was he to assume that he could be anyone's saviour? Maybe that is why Jesus frowned at him.

'Sort yourself out, Ted', he said in muttered reprimand. He walked through the gate, forcing himself to do something decisive, wresting control of his faculties back from the inertia that had gripped him. His boots crunched on a gravel moat with the noise of a scratch-rattle timpani, and he skipped across onto the grass from which numerous headstones and sarcophagi rose. He knew with certain knowledge that to tread on a grave was unlucky, although for whom this bad luck might occur or how it might manifest itself was a continuing mystery.

Presumably being dead, like those in the grave, was considered enough bad luck for anyone. Years ago – ten or fifteen – he and a boy called Tommy Boyle had walked through a graveyard on their way home from school and Ted had accidentally stood on a corner of grass below which someone's relative was buried. Was this, being abandoned in a country and about to meet a terrible fate, his bad luck stemming from that incident? If it was, then he could only say it had been a long time coming but he wasn't about to repeat the same mistake now, especially with Jesus watching.

He eased round the last resting place of *la famille Perdotte*, marvelling at the sheer number of people crammed into one grave. He hoped to reach the church's side door but paused next to a headstone, beneath which was buried just one man, Marcel Ankoplar. A voice stopped him in his tracks and again he was transported back to a childhood of minor infractions. He was always caught and always entirely without a cover story.

'Monsieur?'

'Oh, God, you surprised me', said Ted. The priest looked perplexed. He held his hands out, palms uppermost; a gesture of supplication.

'Peux-je vous aider?', he said. There was no obvious fear showing in the man's young face. His looks were bland, a man who could go unnoticed where it not for the uniform of his profession. Clearly it was he who owned the car and was intending to desert his parish, or was it the case he was merely trying to catch up with a parish that had deserted him?

'My friends – *mes amis* – need to stay here for a night. *Un nuit*. Also, some food', said Ted miming someone eating with terrible table manners. His awkward patois had some effect, however.

'Amenez vos amis, je vais chercher des couvertures. Il n'y a pas d'Allemands sur.'

'Okay', said Ted, hoping that he understood the man's reply, something about blankets and a lack of Germans. 'I'll go and get them.' He ran to the foot of the hill, leaving the perplexed clergyman to organise some sort of reception, and waved his arms high in the air so that John and Mig could see him. He watched as the two distant figures stood. Ted waited while they trotted down the road, allowing a breath of warm wind to pass over his upturned face.

They joined him a few minutes later.

'The church', he said, turning and pointing. 'The priest will put us up for the night and feed us.'

'Wafers and communion wine?', asked John. Ted just shrugged.

'So, no Krauts about?', asked Mig. They were at the gates now and Ted ushered them inside as if he were an innkeeper welcoming much-travelled guests.

'Not according to the priest. He doesn't speak English but he seems okay, I suppose. Might not be hanging around either; that was his car at the gate.' The men entered the church like true sinners, aware that they deserved nothing more than damnation, and stood in an unholy clump as if waiting for some fate that was easier to bear as a group. Their footsteps had echoed loudly in the large hollow space they now occupied, and the silence that followed their entrance was profound, an irreconcilable mix of nervous anticipation, relief and fear.

'Messieurs', said the priest as he returned laden with grey blankets. Ted approached and took the burden but at once the priest scurried off again.

'Our beds for the night', said Mig as he lifted two blankets from the top of the pile. 'Where does he want us to sleep?'

'Up there looks best to me', said John, pointing. 'Near the pulpit. At least there's some carpet on the floor. They edged forward just as the priest emerged again from a previously hidden door near the choir stalls. In his hands they saw, wine, cheese and two sticks of bread. Ted was shocked at the hunger that suddenly gripped him. The priest smiled and shrugged apologetically.

'This is good. *Tres bien*', said Ted. *'Merci.'*

Chapter Twelve

Multi-coloured shards of morning light streamed through the stained-glass windows, suffusing the dust with shades of blues and greens that were undetectable on their complex but miniscule surfaces.

The door to the church was set at right angles to the rows of pews that defined the aisle. It was at the end of a short, broad corridor or hallway, at which the priest would stand at the end of his service to bid *'adieu'* to his flock as they returned to their flawed lives after a brief communion with God. It was only this architectural accident that gave the three men time to take cover when the German commander decided to have a look inside. He was a Protestant from Bad Salzuflen and, although a churchgoer, would not normally have stepped inside a Roman Catholic church for any reason. However, his curiosity was pricked by the strange building that dominated whatever crumbling hamlet this happened to be.

He had forbidden his men to enter, not trusting them to keep their hands off the valuables they might find inside, and had left them devouring their breakfast in that animalistic way they liked to affect. Killing Frenchmen was not enough for them it seemed, they had to eat like savages also. *An orgy of digestive gratification*, as one of his fellow officers had described it. Unfathomably, his was the only platoon that did this. It was as if all of Germany's cannibals and freaks had been put under his command, and had it not been for his lieutenant's badges of rank, he feared they might have eaten him too. They terrified him.

They had sped through France on a whirlwind tour of destruction and mayhem, seeking out places of interest and beauty and levelling them... well not quite. Still, he hadn't had a chance to stop and see what made this country tick, to experience whatever passed for normality in a peaceful setting, or even to discover why the French were their enemies. He personally had no gripe with the French, knew little or nothing about them, in fact. He sighed as he passed into the church, forgetting his hunger and glad to be away from the enthusiastic offers of overcooked, preserved meat of questionable lineage that were constantly thrust at him.

'Eat some of this, Herr Leutnant!'

And he would force himself to look at some remnant of marbled sausage comprising offal and fat, looking like a cross between a police baton and some large animal's sex organ. The smell alone made him retch but he'd eaten such things often enough, lacking an alternative. Even the coffee they made, these lunatic soldiers of his, had too much of everything in it. Too much coffee, too much sugar. Somehow, he'd got used to it.

At once he noticed a smell that he thought of as perfumed dust, reminiscent of his visits to an aunt's house in Detmold. Smells and sights and sounds flooded back to him. Vegetables boiling in a big pan, a fire crackling in the grate and overstuffed chairs in the living room: all of these things momentarily vied for his attention and then were gone, leaving only the present. A statue of the Virgin Mary looked at him inscrutably, not apparently caring that he was the invader. His footsteps seemed to reverberate in the church building which was essentially just a great hall with an ornate roof, deep windows and wooden fittings.

He felt the need to be respectful, although he was sure he was alone. Or was God in attendance? Was *He* really watching him as he crept around *His* house where he, a German, had no right to be? What did God think of a Protestant entering a Roman Catholic church? Did he care? Did he exist? The lieutenant had begun to have his doubts. The more *poilu* you saw dead, the more tank soldiers you saw burned into the structure of their tank, the more pitiful wailing of injured men, soon to die… it would make the Pope think twice.

Here, in this place of God, perhaps he could restore his faith, or at least take a rest from his doubts. Suddenly, he wanted to lie down and sleep. He wanted to wake up in a different place, a different world if needs be, one where he was safe and no one died, or at least not in the horrifying ways he'd witnessed so far. Asking God if he had deserted him did no good, when the question perhaps ought to be, 'had *he* deserted God?' He knew there were no answers, not even in this place, and then he wondered if he deserved a god of any sort.

He could smell candle wax before he saw the tell-tale drips that looked like long, white icicles clinging to the wooden side piece of the pew. The rest of the church was spotless, or so it seemed to his cursory examination, and the incongruity of that tiny mess failed to lodge in his busy mind. Slowly he strolled to the front of the church, his boots clacking on the wooden floor. He intended to absorb some goodness or fill his lungs with hopeful air. For a second, he considered never coming out again.

What would they do about that?

Shoot him.

He gave a derisory snort, aimed at the people that had sent him here to fight a war in which he had no interest, and then loneliness swept over him and he wanted to cry. For how long did he have to do this absurd job for which he was so profoundly unsuited?

'*Monsieur?*'

The officer jumped and put a hand to his chest as if to still his pounding heart. He hadn't noticed the priest. How long had he been standing there watching the outward signs of a dozen different emotions drifting across the stage that was his face?

'*Bonjour*', he stammered.

'*Bonjour*', said the priest. He looked at the German officer, as if searching his soul for vestigial goodness and then cast a sidewards glance, intercepted only by Ted, at the three men cowering on the floor next to him. The brief look was laden with meaning but sadly, Ted didn't know what that meaning was. He'd only just got them there in time, each one wrenched from the sleep of the good. The priest could betray them now, if his loyalty had suddenly switched to the new rulers of France. Ted tried to think it through but that and every other thought was caught up and lost in a hurricane of words and images being blasted indiscriminately around his brain. He felt panic about this situation over which he had no control.

'*Je suis désolé*', said the officer, apologetically. The priest said nothing. '*J'admirais juste vous etes l'élglise.*'

'*Partir de la guerre?*', asked the priest, archly. Privately, he doubted if the German was really an admirer of churches as he claimed. He shot a sly look at Ted, the latter wishing he understood the precise nature of the exchange he was secretly hearing. He was impressed that the German spoke French and wondered if they all did. A peculiar image presented itself; the German Army sitting in vast classrooms learning to speak the language of the countries they were about to invade. *Would they be learning English soon?*

'*Oui. Partir de la guerre*', confirmed the German officer with a weary sigh. He quickly realised that he had no right to expect sympathy from the French priest. In response the French man raised his chin slightly, as if having summoned the courage for a minor act of defiance.

'*Mais c'est vous qui amené la guerre ici, bien sûr.*' But it is you who brought the war here, of course.

'*Je partirai*', said the German, with an air of embarrassed humility. He now felt as if his country had somehow desecrated God's house, rather than merely invaded France. That was worse.

Ted thought he heard the man click his heels but he certainly heard the sound of receding jackboots. Next to him, he saw John Guy blow air out of his cheeks in evident relief and moments later Mig did the same. None of the men moved an inch until long after they heard the church door open and then shut. Even breathing seemed like an extravagance. The priest stood stock-still like one of his plaster statues; a champion defending his cause.

'I don't think they will be outside for long. You can wait for them to leave, or I can take you out from the back door.'

'You speak English?', said John with amazement.

'It is not our custom to speak the language of visitors to our country but you are preferable to the Boche.' As he was speaking the men had gathered up their belongings and were inching towards the back door.

'You are taking your chances', observed the priest. 'I don't know where you are going but you will need to make your way directly out the door and straight across the field until you come to a gate. There is another field and then a road. The road is going to the coast.' With a click the door was open and sunlight streamed in, picking out an armada of dust. 'They can't see you but be very careful once you get to the road.'

'What are you going to do?', asked Mig.

'I'll do what men of God always do: pray and hope for the best. A waste of time, I know but it's expected, is it not?'

'I suppose', said Ted doubtfully as he left. 'Thank you.' The priest smiled wanly and closed the door behind them. Ted heard the lock being applied and then followed his comrades across the field. From the front of the church, he heard an engine starting up, heard a roar as it caught and turned to see a plume of black exhaust smoke shoot into the air.

They stayed close to the thorny hedges that bordered the field, avoiding cow dung, molehills and the attentions of the Wehrmacht. Somewhere far behind them, they heard an artillery barrage start, shaking the still morning air, and closer they heard an exchange of gunfire. The distinctive chug of a Bren gun duelled with the zip of a German MG34, the notorious but incorrectly named 'Spandau.' The war was following them, or had it surrounded them? Either way, it seemed that they could hardly avoid it for much longer.

At the road they stopped and crouched next to the gate. John looked at Ted's map, sucking on his teeth as he did so. When he spoke, there was a sigh in his voice.

'We follow the road that way', he said pointing to their left. 'But we come to a junction and there we can either head for Calais or Dunkerque, or we can set off cross-country for Boulogne. They paused, just picking up the sound of aircraft. Three and then four black specks came into view, bursting through a bank of cloud, disappearing into another, then bursting out again. John shaded his eyes against the sun.

'What are they?', asked Ted.

'Stukas', he said. 'I think they're Stukas, anyway.' They watched for another few moments. 'Yes, they're Stukas and they're heading for Dunkerque by the look of it.'

'So maybe we *shouldn't* head for Dunkerque', said Mig, raising his eyebrows.

'Or maybe we should. Maybe that's precisely where we ought to be going. If the Germans are bothering to bomb it then there must be something there that they want to destroy', said the pilot, an expert on the subject.

'Like the British Army?', suggested Ted. John nodded. The German dive-bombers had drawn level with the soldiers from their position over to the east. They droned onwards for another thirty seconds, the men following their progress helplessly and then, without warning, they seemed to fall out of the sky.

'Pity the poor bugger who's going to cop for that lot', said Mig, using an oft-heard refrain. The aircraft almost seemed to have been designed around a specification intended to depict evil as much as for aerodynamic and functional reasons. It was a theme enhanced by the devilish scream they emitted in the dive. The men winced collectively as if they were the intended target but forced themselves to watch, nevertheless. Bombs fell away like discarded refuse but then exploded on the ground, both the analogy and those in their path, dead.

'Shouldn't someone be shootin' 'em down?', said Ted and then offered a brief apology to the pilot. John shrugged. It was a good question. *Where was the RAF?*

He turned back to the map again as the German planes, having pulled out of their dives, sped back to their base.

'Dunkerque, Calais or Boulogne?', he said stabbing a finger at each one on the map as he spoke.

'Dunkerque', said Mig.

'I think Calais', said Ted. His companions looked at him quizzically.

'I was going to say Dunkerque as well', said John. It was clear that the pilot had little doubt that this was the most desirable destination. 'Why Calais, Ted?', he asked.

'It's a one-in-three chance. Calais is in the middle. We don't know which one is correct but if we head for Calais and that *isn't* the right place then at least we are equally close to the other two. If we head for Dunkerque, say, and it's Boulogne, we're miles away.' Mig nodded and looked over at the pilot who had yet to speak.

'That's a good point', he said at last.

'Calais', said Mig.

'Calais', agreed John and they stood while Ted opened the gate. If the BEF was being evacuated from Calais then they should be able to join them in a day or two. Ted smiled hopefully. Perhaps things were looking up. Maybe they would be safely at home in a day or two, eating properly and catching up on their sleep.

Chapter Thirteen

The sky was overcast and gloomy. Even the birds didn't sing, seeming to sense the war that was coming their way. They trudged down the road, not speaking, each man caught up in his own thoughts, or with his mind a blank. After an hour they stopped as a squadron of Junkers bombers surged overhead. An escort of twin-engine Messerschmitts flew above and behind them as protection.

'That's the type that shot me down', said John. He now understood the world of a foot soldier much better than they understood his world, and both of his new companions briefly wondered what it felt like to be hunted down and so nearly destroyed. Yet the battles that took place in the skies could never be more than an abstract for them, quite unreal. *This*, thought Ted, *this is real.*

'It must be frightening', said Ted.

'Yeah, I suppose it is. The plane catching fire is the thing we all dread the most'. He thought again about those burnt hands and grimaced inwardly.

Mig's stomach rumbled, angry at not being fed.

'Wish I had some fags left', he said, wistfully. The men began walking again, more slowly, as if out for a ruminative stroll.

'From the noise your gut's making it sounds as if you need food', replied Ted, smiling.

'Ah, but if I had a fag, I'd forget all about being hungry', replied Mig, with a certain skewed logic. John laughed and shook his head.

'Have some water', he said.

'I could just go to sleep', said Ted.

'You've only been up a few hours', said John. The conversation began to jump from subject to subject, each man seemingly not listening to his companion's words before taking his own thoughts in an entirely different direction. John sniffed at the air, imagining that he could smell the sea.

Mig had an announcement to make. 'In the following order', he said, 'I would like these things.' None of them broke stride as they waited for what sounded like a royal proclamation. 'A cigarette, a cup of tea and a bar of chocolate', he said, simply. He counted his heart's desires off on his fingers as he spoke, his Thompson snuggled under his arm.

'That's not much', said John, impressed at his fellow Londoner's asceticism.

'That's just the start, Johnny. That's what I want right now, you see. For lunch, I want some of that French bread and a big lump of cheese.' Ted pulled a face; that had no personal appeal. 'For tea I want spuds and a nice big piece of steak – well done – and peas. Then I want some apple pie and custard. Then I want to go to the pub and drink exactly the right amount of beer, go home and cuddle up next to me wife.' He nodded to indicate that he had completed his list and smiled, successfully blotting out any thoughts of the unquestionable absence of every single thing he had just mentioned.

'Just the right amount of beer? How much is that?', queried Ted.

'Depends on how you feel, doesn't it? Not too much. I know the right amount when I have had it.'

'I didn't know you were married', said John.

'Yeah. Got hitched just before we came out 'ere. She's beautiful my wife. Like a little sparra', he said with a dreamy smile on his face.

'You mean she eats worms?'

Mig looked for something to throw at Ted and then they laughed, their troubles temporarily forgotten. The men stopped at the foot of a hill.

'This way, I suppose', said Ted. 'Looks quicker to go over it than round it.'

'The road we want should be on the other side', said John, looking at the map. 'That's if we've come the right way.'

As they crested the hill, the three men fell silent. The road was where John had said it would be but they had not expected the column of French heavy tanks that had just rolled into view. They dropped from sight and then crawled a short distance to get into cover. There were plenty of stunted bushes, most of them a hollow tangle of branches with an outer coating of broad waxy leaves, offering ideal concealment. Ted crawled forward to a point where he could watch the tanks as they got into position.

'Don't fancy gettin' caught up in that lot', he said over his shoulder. John looked confused. Mig explained, 'You can't see much from a closed-down tank. They could drive over the top of us, or open fire without knowing we were there, or without knowing we were on their side.' John nodded. Moments later the tanks' engines seemed to roar in unison and the ground began to tremble beneath them. Ted watched as they span on their tracks through ninety degrees and began their crushing ascent on the hillside.

'They're comin' this way', he said. 'Thought they might.'

'What do we do?', said John, his mind still not quite adjusted to his new status of foot soldier.

'Curl up in a ball, old son', said Mig. 'It won't help', he continued, qualifying his advice, 'but it's what I do.' He watched as Mig did exactly that, transforming himself into a khaki hedgehog. He looked for a minute as if he was trying to draw his whole body into his tin helmet. A moment later he uncoiled himself and spoke.

'I once knew someone so small that they could get inside their own suitcase and pull it shut', he said, before curling up once more. John raised his eyebrows and wondered how exactly that titbit of information helped them in their current predicament. He looked over at Ted. Ted smiled and shrugged.

***

The hard earth seemed to be a perfect transmitter of vibrations and John's image of these squat steel robots intensified, taking on a new, more terrifying form of reality. Their sound too spoke of an unstoppable, uncaring charge carried out in slow time. They were an inexorable tide that would run them over, grind them to dust, like some apocalyptic vision of industrial warfare being realised. He looked at Ted, trying to gauge the inscrutable Ulsterman's feelings, pre-empt his actions. He thought that Mig might have unwittingly sacrificed himself to misfortune; that his means of surviving this terrible onslaught was weak and foolish and moreover, doomed to fail. To die so meekly at the hands, or rather under the tracks, of their allies seemed the greatest, most unspeakable act of self-treachery.

He wanted to run, to take his chances and make his own way to safety... And then he realised something that made him stay put and examine the state of his mind. Mig and Ted had no intention of dying, at least not in this way. They were survivors like him and they might have the skills and quick reactions to get them all out of France alive.

'They're spreading out and comin' this way', said Ted. There was no fear evident in his voice. 'We'll sit tight let them get past and then make our way to the coast.' The sound of massed tank engines was about to drown out his voice and the ground shook as if it was being subjected to a long, drawn out minor earthquake. 'They should keep the Krauts occupied for a while if nothing else.' John watched as Ted sat down again, his back to the low wall from which the bush seemed to grow. He removed his tin helmet, as if he had realised for the first time that it wouldn't save him from being crushed by a tank, and then patted his pockets, hoping to find some cigarettes. Ted saw the pilot looking at him and smiled. John nodded, amazed at the soldier's coolness.

The French tanks ground out their course at ten miles per hour, slowed by the incline and more vulnerable as a result. Dark petrol fumes swirled in the air, making a cloying gaseous patois with dust and grit, all carried on a slight breeze. They heard branches snap violently even over the engines' roar. Some of the tanks audibly changed down a gear, engines even louder as their progress slowed again. They knew that at least one of these leviathans was close to their hiding place, and then shockingly a track caught hold of the outer covering of leaves and ripped the supporting branch away like some demonic harvesting machine scornfully exposing a crop ready to be taken. A storm of leaf litter sprayed the men.

John saw the tracks and the wheels roll by, the branch still caught up in the tracks, waving around like a duster. A second later he was looking at the engine covers and exhaust, knowing that the danger had passed. The noise of the great vehicle receded faster than his images of the carnage it might have caused. They sat exposed, like three children who had been hiding under a blanket that had just been whipped away by an adult.

'Time to go, I think', said Ted as Mig uncurled himself, hesitantly. Mig looked over, first at Ted then at John, seemingly unsure of where he was or who they were. He seemed to be in a daze but then snapped himself out of it. He crawled out from the bush and then stood.

'Come on, let's go', repeated Ted, brusquely. He watched as John brushed himself down, a series of gestures that seemed designed to restore his confidence and bearing as much as to actually clean his uniform. He looked ready to continue, more certain of himself than the shaken man they had found lying in the abandoned ambulance so recently. The pilot smiled, the fact and the act of being alive the drug he needed.

'Come on Mig', said Ted. 'Let's get on that boat and get ourselves home.' Mig still stood watching as the tanks smashed through another hedge and disappeared into a wood. His shoulders were hunched and his hands thrust deep into his pockets like a man caught in a freezing rain shower with nowhere to go.

'Mig?', said John. The soldier just stood there. He spoke.

'Are we actually going to get home?', he asked, miserably.

'Of course', said Ted. He gave a little laugh that he hoped would sound reassuring and not betray his own doubts. 'We're not far from the coast. You'll not be eatin' that steak if you don't keep goin.' Mig nodded, but still he faced the other way as if wanting to follow the tanks to whatever fate awaited them. John and Ted began walking slowly, allowing the little Londoner time to compose himself and follow on, which he did in due course. After half a mile they came to a junction. It had once held a road sign but this had been removed. John pointed to the map.

'We're here', he said. 'Do you agree?' Ted nodded. Mig looked over at the map, shrugged and nodded. If Ted agreed then he agreed too because he'd not really looked at the map previously. 'Well, Calais is that way. Down the road for about half a mile, then turn right. Ten or twelve miles to go.'

Ted pointed to a hill.

'We could do with using that high ground so that we can have a look into Calais and see what is going on. From there we should be able to see the sea and, if there are any ships, then that might be the place to go.'

'Okay. Good idea. That okay with you, Mig?' Mig nodded and smiled, scarcely concealing his despondency.

***

A French tank lay abandoned by the side of the road, its garish camouflage of mottled yellows, browns and greens at odds with the verdant banks of the road and the meadow beyond. For all the world it was a child's toy of giant proportions, discarded from the pram and left to discolour, then break.

'We could hitch a ride in that', said John. 'It looks fine, doesn't it? It's not been knocked out, I mean.'

140

'Give it a go. We'll be okay so long as we don't run into any Germans.' Mig looked at the others as he spoke. 'I'll see if I can start it.'

'Neither of you are tank drivers, are you?', said John. The soldiers shook their heads. Mig fiddled about with various controls inside the driver's compartment but there was no sound that indicated an engine about to burst into life.

'It's been abandoned for a reason, of course', said Ted.

'I was hoping it was a case of French cowardice and that they'd left a perfectly good vehicle behind. I trained to be a mechanic before I became a pilot but we didn't work on a lot of French tanks funnily enough.' He opened the engine covers and tried to peer inside. From his lowly viewpoint he could see no obvious problems. 'It could have run out of petrol, of course', he shouted round to the front. He heard Mig operating the tank's switchgear and then another sound which at first he didn't recognise. For a moment he also thought he smelt petrol but assumed that his mind was filling in blanks, adding extra information to complete a picture he didn't need.

'I think it's a dead duck', said Ted to whomever would listen. He turned to survey the road behind him, unsure what had caused him to do so. 'Maybe we've spent too long here', he said, ominously.

'I was thinking the same thing', said John. In the distance they heard machine gun fire and then the boom of cannon. 'Sounds like the French and Germans have found each other.'

'Something's going on', said Mig suddenly. He was clambering from the driver's compartment like a rodent darting out of a hole in the ground.

'Aye, a tank battle', said Ted.

'Something else, Ted. There's something in the grass behind us. Something moving this way.'

'Like a leopard?', said the Ulsterman, facetiously.

'Like a bleedin' German, Ted, I'm not joking.' He jumped from the hull of the tank to the ground, scooped up his kit and urged the men to move with just a look. The first bullet hit the tank's turret at that very moment with a noise like a well thrown stone hitting an iron gutter.

'What in the name...', began John before joining the other two men on the ground. 'Someone's shooting at...' For the second time he didn't bother to finish his sentence, quickly recognising the need for verbal economy and for husbanding his reserves of courage. The two soldiers, trained to react and thus to stay alive, had been in the dirt, their noses pressed into the loose surface soil whilst the second bullet was in flight. It smacked the steel flank of the turret, instantly flattened and then dropped on to the hull like a tossed penny. They followed Ted's lead and crawled behind the tank, putting twenty-six tons of steel between them and the next few bullets.

'It seems like one German shooting at us but what he's doing out here by himself is anyone's guess', said Ted.

'The rest of 'em – the Germans – are miles away', said Mig. He pointed in the direction of the tank engagement they could hear. It sounded as if the French were putting up a fight – so often it was rumoured that they didn't.

'Well, I don't know what the hell is going on so let's just get out of here', said John. He looked down the road as he spoke, realising that they were going to be very short of cover. The road surface had a pronounced camber and was itself raised up above the level of the surrounding countryside by means of a broad earthen bank. Grass struggled for life in the sandy soil, yellowed and stunted. A series of fences transected the barren fields, seeming to grow out from the verge at right angles, like a hopeless spider's web. Nevertheless, each one would have to be surmounted, exposing the men as they did so.

'You two. Take to the ditch and keep crawling. When you get to those fences try to get through rather than over them.'

'And you?', asked John, concerned.

'I'll keep a look out for our friend and try to get him.'

'Get him?'

'Shoot him', clarified Ted, impatiently.

'We'll wait for you at the crossroads', said Mig, as he slithered out of sight. Ted looked behind him. The crossroads were about half a mile away, marked out by a forlorn signpost. He wasn't sure if the others would make it. He wasn't sure that he would either, but this perhaps gave them a chance. The decision had been easy in one respect because, as the only man armed with a rifle and considering the distances involved, it was only he who could really engage the sniper. Ted found himself a vantage point from beneath the abandoned Somua tank. From here he could observe without *being* observed. He was in the shadows, well behind the bogies – the small wheels over which the vehicle's tracks ran – and he had a clear view of the field.

He guessed that the rifleman must be four hundred yards away at least, although the presence of dead ground between them made it difficult to be more precise. Stunted clumps of grass offered the only obvious cover but if this man knew his game, he would avoid these in favour of something harder to single out.

Just how good was his opponent? Was he a trained sniper? He'd have to be an exceptional shot to stand much chance of hitting Ted from the distance involved. He could move in closer but that would mean risking exposure, something that he might do if he thought that his prey had begun to withdraw. For now, he waited and Ted did likewise... waiting for a mistake.

He watched as a fox drew itself cautiously from the long grass at the side of the road. Ted's mind seemed unable to rest and he idly wondered how this animal could remain elusive when the colour of its fur was so at odds with its surroundings. He thought of himself in a ginger battledress...

A movement!

The field was bisected by a raised line of grassy soil seemingly too straight for nature but not easy to spot with a casual glance. It appeared as if a giant had lifted the topsoil like a huge tablecloth, folded it once then laid it out again without smoothing the resulting wrinkle.

The 'wrinkle' might be deep enough for a man to hide behind, and at one end there was a hay cart, partly loaded but with piles of hay lying next to it as if someone was going to load it imminently, or more likely had been disturbed in the act of doing so. This was on the far left of Ted's vision, perhaps within his field of fire. In a sense it offered only isolated cover of the sort that a trained sniper would always avoid, but the ridge on the surface was also a potential escape route should one prove necessary. Ted fixed his gaze on the cart, looking for movement or the glint of sun on steel or glass.

Perhaps a minute passed in this way and his mind began to wander again. He wondered how long it would be before it played tricks on him. He recalled a soldier from another platoon swearing that he had shot a German during the night when he was on sentry duty. That was the Christmas of 1939. The shot had woken the whole company, probably the entire battalion. A few people had even heard him shout his challenge to the 'intruder' before releasing his shot. In the morning he had been questioned by the OC and Sergeant major but insisted that he had shot at and hit a German soldier. When asked if had wounded the man and that he might have crawled away, he insisted that he had killed him.

No dead German was ever found. At this point in the war the German Army weren't actually in the habit of sending recce parties out, but the soldier remained convinced that he had shot his man.

Ted twisted slowly, looking behind to judge the distance his two friends had covered so far. He could see very little. He cocked his rifle and then slowly drew it into his shoulder. He'd get one shot, just as his opponent would. He wondered if he was good enough to hit the man. Four hundred yards? It wasn't an impossible distance but even for a regular British infantryman, well trained in musketry and armed with a Lee Enfield – the rifle whose rate of fire had caused the Germans to over-estimate the number of machine guns operated by the BEF during the Great War – a little bit of luck would be required. A slight breeze blew from right to left – he would aim slightly to the right of his target when he got the chance.

He nuzzled the rifle into his cheek and placed his thumb on the safety catch, ready. His sights were adjusted to the required distance and he had the weapon pointing naturally towards his target, the blade of the foresight almost aligned. He waited. He waited until his elbows got sore and, as he waited, he wondered when the German was going to make his move, for it made no sense to stay put if there seemed to be no target for him. Surely, he must have suspected that his prey had given him the slip, thought Ted. Unless, of course, *he* had Ted in *his* sights but just couldn't quite get the clear shot he needed. The thought unnerved him.

He felt his nose begin to run and smelt the dirt in which he lay, a dry, dusty choking smell, laced with petrol. He noticed that the underside of the tank was very clean as if it had only driven a short distance from its barracks to be here. It came as a surprise to him that the noise of battle had receded. One side was victorious, and if it was the Germans, he might be expecting them to put in an appearance soon, whatever opposition barring their way now gone. He could take his shot, climb out from under the tank and dive in the ditch, all in the time it took the other man to take stock, but only if he had actually appraised the situation correctly. If the man wasn't in amongst the hay…

Movement!

Definitely. The German had sat up, slowly, imperceptibly almost and was now scanning the ground to his front with field glasses. As Ted thumbed off the safety catch, he took in the netting that obscured the binocular lenses. He breathed deeply, noting the foliage skilfully applied to his shoulders and his helmet. Holding his breath, he could just make out the darkened skin and he took the first pressure on the trigger, the foresight and rear sight in perfect alignment and he knew that he had his shot.

Aiming slightly to the right, into the breeze, the second pressure, the recoil punching his shoulder, the

German gone in an instant, knocked down like a fairground target, dead.

Chapter Fourteen

'You got him?'

'I got him. Let's get going', said Ted hastily, his tone curt.

'You shot him?', said Mig.

'No, I threw buns at him until he died', snapped Ted.

'Alright mate, alright', said Mig, feigning hurt. In truth he was taken aback at the other man's outburst. Ted said nothing more but set off without seeming to care whether his comrades followed or not. John glanced over at the other soldier pityingly, as if his emotions were reinstating themselves after a long absence.

'Don't worry about it, Mig. He's just killed someone. Not everyone finds it easy. Even if they've done it before.' His tone was conciliatory. Mig nodded. 'We'll catch him up', said the pilot.

High above them, two squadrons of Luftwaffe bombers made for targets on the coast. Their altitude robbed them of apparent velocity and yet their progress was inexorable. Ted glanced at the sky without interest but otherwise marched on, head down, as if he were walking into a blizzard. He tried not to think about the man he had killed but images of his face exploding flitted across his mind uninvited. Even at the great distance involved he had seen a spray of blood and matter, before the inevitable bodily collapse as the dead man's nervous system abandoned its efforts to keep him functioning.

When previously he had killed, as he knew he had, the truth of his act had been obscured by the chaos of death all around. His personal contribution was lost in a melee of similar actions in which men sometimes took the credit for each other's kills. Often an equal number of men died on each side; it seemed perversely fair.

The crump, crump of flak assailed their ears as British gunners fired into the bomber formations. They seemed to get the altitude right almost at once, although it could have been an illusion, and puffs of black appeared in the midst of the bombers, catching one which fell slowly back to earth with a stream of smoke from one engine.

John watched with some satisfaction until a picture of the terror in the cockpit crowded his brain; men fighting for their lives in an aircraft no longer under their control, nothing more than a tumbling coffin. At least the pilots had something to do, attempting to regain control of the great machine, of making their landing survivable. The rest of the crew could only sit there and hope, unable to bail out of the flailing fuselage. At times like these they stopped being the enemy and instead became fellow flyers.

'Think it landed in the sea', said John, finally, having watched the big aircraft suffer its agonising death throes until the end. No one else spoke. Ted continued his forced march, trying to put distance between them and the advancing Germans. Occasionally, Mig jogged a few steps to catch up. John was glad that his rugby training kept him fit. Each man was lost, alone in his own thoughts or thinking nothing, if such a thing were really possible.

They shared a common purpose but no bonhomie, no deliberate unity of action or resolve. Each had his private doubts, his private worries and fears. In the afternoon it began to rain; large, warm drops of water that darkened their uniforms by increments, each new pattern spreading and merging into its neighbour. Ted's battledress tunic gave off a musty odour as if it had just been unpacked after months in a case.

The road deteriorated in quality, its surface riven by fissures and potholes. From above it might have looked like a grey ribbon of map depicting some imaginary land of lakes and rivers; the work of a fantastical cartographer. Patches of concrete had been carelessly applied but nothing could be done to counteract the grandiose undulations that ran its entire length, as if the land on which it sat had contracted.

They stopped to stare at the body of a French soldier who lay in the roadside ditch like a crop sack fallen from a farmer's cart. A single hole in his temple indicated the path of a bullet, and there was no obvious exit wound. A Lebel revolver clutched in his right hand and an officer's side cap sitting next his body like a discarded letter told their own story. His eyes were shut, refusing to witness the events that had brought him to this last desperate act. He was at peace, serene almost, and if you didn't look at his self-inflicted head wound it was easy to imagine him sitting up and continuing with his life. Ted moved off again. John and Mig watched dispassionately as a single fly darted across the dead officer's face.

'I can't wait to get away from here', said Mig. John nodded.

'Nearly in Calais, mate. We'll keep going.'

***

A pall of smoke lifted from the town as if the inhabitants were warning them off, and overhead another wave of bombers set about the defenders, a sight which had become normal for them now. John glanced over at the puny anti-tank gun, its tiny barrel just protruding from a wall of sandbags. Five miserable looking, uniformly unshaven French soldiers sat nearby, looking very much as if they would bolt at the first sight of a panzer.

They represented an army in disarray, defeated in spirit but still fighting on the paper of a general's map. Their collective demeanour shocked the airman and he knew then that France was lost. He concealed his anger; anger that he had fought for a country that had given up on itself, anger that almost all of his friends had died terrible deaths in the air above these wretched men's heads. One of the gunners looked over at him with dead eyes.

John looked away to hide his disgust; sadly, they might need their help.

The sergeant with whom Ted talked at least still looked like a soldier, his uniform neat, worn with some pride. He couldn't have failed to notice the abject state of his men and yet was probably powerless to do anything now. Perhaps he was just grateful that they were there at all. One word of reprimand and they just might desert. The NCO clearly had an axe to grind with the British soldier to whom he spoke, for he had rediscovered the ability to speak English. John wondered how much Ted would take before he floored the Frenchman.

'Your bloody army is leaving us here to fight', said the sergeant. 'We fight so that they can escape', he said angrily, pointing at his own chest. He then pointed the same finger at Ted's chest.

'Stop pointing your fucking finger at me or I'll break it off', replied Ted. His voice was calm, belying the anger

151

he felt. John allowed himself a smile, never before having heard the quiet Ulsterman use the soldiery's favourite word. The Frenchman didn't exactly tower over Ted but he offered a more pugnacious physical presence, and yet somehow John had no doubt which one he'd want next to him in a fight.

'It is okay for us to die so that you can escape.'

'I'm just asking for directions.' He then added unhelpfully, 'I'm sorry that your soldiers run away but it's not my fault.' The sergeant took a step forwards, his face suffused with blood. Ted stood his ground and eyed the man levelly. An officer appeared from the entrance of a command post, his uniform almost immaculate but his eyes red-rimmed with fatigue and despair.

'Qu'arrive-t-il, le sergent?'

'Cet homme veut des directions to Dunkerque.'

'Bien, lui donner les directions alors.' Good then give him the directions. The officer looked at his senior NCO with a trace of disgust before retiring to the command post again.

The sergeant looked at Ted once more. 'Follow that road', he said pointing. 'You will find yet more French soldiers defending the town so that you can escape and go and hide in England.' His face was fixed with contempt born from the knowledge that his army had not performed well and would continue to fail when tested. Nevertheless, it galled him to give support to men who were, in his view, no more than deserters themselves. If he had been expecting gratitude from the British soldier, he was disappointed. Ted turned his back on the sergeant and spoke to his comrades.

'We're in the wrong place', said Ted, with disgust.

John felt his chest tighten with anxiety. Mig looked at the sky and controlled his breathing.

'You were both right', he added. 'We should be in Dunkerque.'

***

'Doesn't matter, we'll be there soon enough', said Mig, cheerily. They had set off once again. The rain continued to fall from a grey sky streaked with black.

Ted looked back at the French NCO as if about to speak. He looked into the man's eyes, noticed the raindrops settling like a glassy necklace around the rim of his Adrian helmet, and continued to walk in the direction of Dunkerque.

Chapter Fifteen

'After the war? Knickers. Women will always want knickers', he said. There was a pause. 'Mind you', he continued, 'some of the women I know don't wear them for long.' Mig looked over at the pilot and smiled. John laughed despite the driving rain. Just ahead of them Ted set the pace, the responsibility for taking them to the wrong town feeling like a weighty burden on his shoulders. Neither Mig nor John had even looked as if they were about to say something along the lines of *I told you so*. He wondered if he would have been so forgiving in the same circumstances.

A sudden gust of wind threw raindrops into his eyes and he wiped them away like the tears of frustration that a lesser man might have produced. It was done now. It had been his error and it fell to him to put it right, to get these men home. He felt that he owed it to them. He had to reward their faith, their support and their companionship. So often in the past those who put their faith in him had been let down, and he thought of Whitey, Snowball and Dinger, all of whom were dead while he lived on. Life was no fairer than death, and harder to manage sometimes.

He wasn't in the mood for inane conversations, but he understood their purpose well enough – to distract. He had allowed himself to become serious, morose perhaps, and he recognised this in himself, wondering if it was a fault. Had he ever been anything other than the man he was now, he wondered? He'd always been cheeky, he supposed, contemptuous of authority, but had he ever been light-hearted, easy-going or approachable? In short, had he ever displayed the traits he valued in others? There was something that made him think he had once been that other type of person, perhaps quite recently. Yet he could not readily draw upon any examples that might indicate that this had been the case.

He saw it in others: people who could tell jokes, people whose stories enthralled and appalled, even when their audience suspected that they might not be true. He knew people who were liked simply because they smiled readily and often. He knew people who charmed, all facets of a personality that was not like his.

Was this empty robot something he had become by chance? Had he always been this way? Or was it a latent self that had been hidden away, needing the terror of war to set it free? He dredged his conscious to find something good about himself. And all the time he placed one foot in front of the other, lessening the distance to home, or at least the next personal disaster that awaited him. A mind reader might have detected more than a trace of self-pity, but Ted's face was set, inscrutable and hidden.

Ted thought about John, the pilot. His strength of character was more apparent now, his personality an easily defined thing. Did he wish he was more like *this* man? He showed much greater resolve and courage than when they had first met. Of course, hadn't been well at the time, his mind hurt by the crash somehow, dazed and disconnected. Even as he came around, the fog in his head dispersing, he'd seemed aloof and withdrawn as if operating on a different, superior level to the two soldiers. No doubt he was a complex, intelligent man but now he seemed to enjoy the relaxed banter of his fellow Londoner, as if they both shared the same history of tiny happenings.

Where John Guy was complex, Tyrone Miglorine was affable, displaying an odd mix of vulnerability and determination. Ted wished that he could be like either of these two men without really knowing why. Their lives weren't so great, in fact no better than his right now. Behind him he heard Mig talking about the weather and allowed himself a grim smile at the Londoner's meteorological ponderings.

'If it weren't for the rain, the cold and the wind it would be quite pleasant out', he said. He heard John laugh but his reply was lost in the storm.

Ted fancied that he could smell the sea, and his mind retreated to a family holiday in Portrush as a kid. Now he smelt the sooty air produced by the train as it lumbered off towards the seaside resort in the north of his tiny country. The anticipation and the journey itself were perhaps more intoxicating than the time spent in the town, and more than once it had rained heavily, and yet these trips – the best holiday they could manage – meant more to him than any other childhood memory. He vowed to re-enact them when he had children of his own.

Ahead and to their right he saw a vehicle park. Quite at odds with the lush fields around it, it stood as mute testimony to the power of the British motor industry. It was a square, bordered by hedge and filled with rectangles, each one a truck. Morrises, Bedfords and AECs… Ted imagined that they had all come off the boat and been stored here before anyone had a chance to use them, some sort of stockpile of vehicular reinforcements. The men stopped for a moment to take in the sight.

'There's some money's worth there', said Mig. 'You could start your own hauliers with that lot.' The wind changed direction and they caught a whiff of petrol. 'Stinks, though.'

'It's a wonder the Germans haven't bombed this lot', said John, ever the airman. 'They're not exactly well hidden.'

'Come on. We might be able to hitch a ride', said Ted. Even as he said the words, he doubted that this would be possible. His simultaneous hope and despair collided and he momentarily felt as if he was doomed in some way. It wasn't just the fact that the army needed a signature for everything, permission, documentation – none of which they had – it was something else, something indefinite but present nonetheless. There was an eerie stillness to the packed field that made him think of a haunted place, an aura of abandonment.

It was a field forlorn and strewn with the cast-offs of a broken army, a poetic thought that he kept to himself for the meantime. As they drew closer, they heard the slow rhythm of a man at work with a sledgehammer. The sound he made boomed out like the din from a satanic foundry heard dully through the insulating ground above. Ted pictured a tireless slave in perpetual labour, glistening with sweat despite the chill of his own personal hell.

The entrance to the field was muddied with unaccustomed vehicle traffic, its gates lying open, gate posts askew. They peered into a grassy corridor lined with army trucks of various kinds along with a few towering Quad tenders, little Vickers tanks, which looked quaint and harmless and Universal Carriers, tiny turretless tanks armed most commonly with a Bren gun. Each had its engine compartment opened and when they looked inside, as they were bound to do with their schoolboy curiosity ignited, they found that enormous damage had been done by the lone wielder of the sledgehammer: engine casings cracked, wiring looms pulled out of place and severed, radiators smashed in and windows broken. The tyres had not been slashed.

'Perhaps, that takes too long or is too easy to fix', said Mig, gloomily. They quickly recognised the fact that they were unlikely to be 'hitching a ride' on any of these vehicles. They strolled through the field, curious, unbidden visitors, looking at a hundred thousand pounds worth of transport that had been reduced to almost worthless junk in a few hours. Eventually they caught up with the wrecker himself, a compact man, with a large hammer.

'Tattersall, RASC', he said by way of introduction. 'I don't think I can help you. The ones near the gate are smashed up and the ones I haven't got to yet are stuck where they are because of them. That one works', he said pointing at a small Morris truck. It looked brand new apart from mud on its tyres. 'But you can't get it out of the field, unless you can make it fly.'

'Shit', said Mig. Ted nodded, silently.

'Someone has decided that these can't be brought back so I have to make sure the Krauts can't use them. 'I've been doing this for two days', he said matter-of-factly. 'Would you like a brew and something to eat?'

'We would', said John but he looked over at Ted as if seeking approval. He still deferred to the Ulsterman, since it had always seemed like his job to get them to the coast and he trusted him to do that.

'Aye, some food if you have it too?', said the Ulsterman, hopefully. His stomach rumbled its assent.

'Got loads. Come on. I'll be glad of the company.' He led them to the back of a truck that had become his home. His bedding was stowed neatly and his rifle lay on top of his webbing. He clambered into the back athletically, despite his lack of stature. 'Welcome to my humble abode', he said spreading his arms in a welcoming gesture. Mig had only really ever met other Londoners before but he placed Tattersall from somewhere 'up north', a strange place about which he knew nothing. Ted though, had heard accents similar to Tattersall's, knew they came from England and understood roughly two thirds of what was said in them.

Only John was familiar with all the country's accents; he'd heard the lot in the RAF, whose regular units tended not to have any discreet geographical recruitment area. His own squadron had been populated by Welsh, Northern Irish, Scots, Geordies, Scousers, Londoners… a little bit of everything.

'A Yorkshireman?', he ventured.

'Aye, sergeant, that's right.' Tattersall played around with his stove until it burst into life beneath a miniature fireball that made them all sit back in surprise. 'Bloody lethal, this thing', he said. 'If the Germans don't get me, this will', he added contemptuously. Dangerous or not, it made swift work of heating the water in his tiny kettle, a civilian model given to him by his mother in Huddersfield just before coming to France. She worried about him dehydrating if he didn't have six cups of tea a day. He produced china mugs, tea bags, sugar and a tin of evaporated milk from a wooden locker under the bench seat on which he was perched. 'Now. I've got some of that French bread – a bit stale but not mouldy or owt, some meat paste, some cans of 'am and these 'ere biscuits which fell off the back of a Froggie general. And apples.'

'Anything', said Ted, his mouth watering. He had forgotten how hungry he was but now it felt as if his stomach was doing somersaults, excited by the prospect of food.

'I've also got these buns, which a nice lady gave me.'
Tattersall, a sort of food magpie, was proud of his edible
haul and the means by which he had obtained it. He
produced a patterned tin and prised the lid off with
difficulty. The buns looked like oblong fairy cakes. Each
of the men helped themselves. 'Just tuck in lads', said
Tattersall, happy to share. 'I've got loads', he added.
'Chocolate, tinned fruit. You name it. I'll never eat it all.'
He watched as his three temporary companions ate like
starving prisoners. Occasionally he sipped his tea. He
wanted to talk – just for the company and in case he went
mad from talking to himself – but he knew that he had to
wait, while his new companions gorged themselves.

'You can take some of it with you, you know. Mind,
you've not got far to go…' John looked at him when he
said this, the information lodging in his mind and a note
made to pursue this conversation when he had finished his
refuelling. 'By, you are 'ungry lads, aren't you?'

It was Mig who spoke first but only to comment on
the food. He said, 'this is great, mate.'

Tattersall smiled benevolently.

'Well, 'opefully it will put to rest the notion that
Yorkshiremen are tight. Not that I paid for this lot, mind.'

'Got any fags, mate', said Mig.

'Yeah, fags, of course', said the Yorkshireman. 'Fags,
wine, chocolates…' His voice tailed off as he reached into
another wooden box to retrieve three packets of cigarettes
and three small bars of Swiss chocolate. He had a surplus
of everything; enough to make a wartime shopkeeper
weep. He passed these to the men who took them
gratefully.

'You could open a shop', said Ted.

'Aye. Maybe.' A shadow of regret passed over his face. 'Customers are likely to be Germans though.'

'You said we didn't have far to go', said John. He sat back, his stomach full, and drew luxuriously on his cigarette. Smoking was a habit he had intended to break but it hardly seemed to matter now, with the German Army at his back. He could give up at his leisure if he made it home. Alternatively, a POW camp with its attendant privations would be a great place to wean himself off tobacco, he mused.

'Twelve mile, I reckon. Just keep walkin' and you can't miss it. There's a defensive perimeter around Dunkerque to keep the Germans out, and hundreds of boats out at sea. Thousands of men waiting on the sand for their turn to get on a boat. Loads of French among 'em but mainly the BEF.' His audience was rapt.

Ted noticed steam rising from his trouser legs as they dried in the heat given out by Tattersall's burner. It mixed with the cigarette smoke to form an odd, unbreathable gas and yet he felt no desire to move from the comfort of the truck.

'You've been there!', said Mig, incredulously.

'Oh, aye lad, that's where I came from. My lot were one of the first units to get here when they said we was evacuating. We 'ad trucks, see? Didn't take us long to get from where we were to 'ere. They're all back in Blighty now, I think. The lads, I mean.'

'Just you left?', asked Ted.

'Me, the CO and a few men just to help out with the evacuation. Volunteers. I got sent off here to bust up the trucks. I'd already walked from here to Dunkerque and then got sent back.'

'I don't think I'd have done that. Volunteering, I mean', said Mig. Ted nodded, impressed but he was beginning to think that it was time to move on. He pictured the German infantry just a few miles behind them perhaps, closing in stealthily while they ate and chatted as if they hadn't a care in the world.

'Well, someone 'ad to. Maybe I'll get a medal', he said with a twinkle in his eye. They sat in companionable silence for a few minutes, each man alone with his own thoughts. The rain drove against the canvas sides of the truck and Ted drew his collar up around his neck to ward off a cold that was more imagined than felt.

'You can stay 'ere, if you want', said Tattersall, breaking the spell of silence.

'We need to move on, I think', said Ted, realising that the others were free to do what they wanted. He couldn't force them to do anything and they weren't his responsibility. The alternatives to following him were fairly grim but it was their choice. He stood and clambered down from the truck.

'*Any* of these wagons still work?', enquired John, hopefully as he followed Ted.

'Well, that's the silly thing', said Tattersall. 'This one still goes. I thought I might use it to make my getaway – just to get to the beach – but, like I said, it's hemmed in now by the others. As soon as I'm finished 'ere, I'm on Shanks's pony.'

'Oh well. You're not staying on for much longer, are you?'

'Don't think so. I've already disabled all the trucks. I've just got to smash them all up a bit so that they are beyond repair. When I've done that I'll 'ed off.'

'You can come with us', offered John. 'You've done enough.' He looked at the little Yorkshireman levelly, offering him an escape.

'Ta, sarge, but I'll just finish off.'

'You'll still get your medal', added Mig. The RASC man laughed.

'I'll finish off. I'll be okay.'

Tattersall handed them some tinned fruit for the journey and they wished him good luck. As they turned on their heels toward the coast, the metallic clank of the sledgehammer resumed. He'd be done soon enough.

Chapter Sixteen

Another bomber stream flew over their heads, the din intimidating earthbound voyeurs and making speech virtually impossible. They watched as stick after stick of bombs fell onto the town they'd been sent to destroy.

'There'll be nothing left by the time we get there', said Ted.

'What sort are those?', asked Mig, nodding towards the enemy aircraft.

'Heinkels. Medium bombers', replied John.

'Is that similar to what you flew?'

'No, not really.'

'Is a Heinkel better than what you flew?'

'Anything's better than what I flew', replied the pilot, shuddering inwardly at the memory. He hoped that if he ever made it back to Britain he would not be made to fly a Fairey Battle again. Surely no-one could be expected to do that after their experiences in France where the big plane had proved to be a death trap.

They had left the road to follow a low stone wall that separated two fields, both of which shared a crop with bright, yellow flowers that none of them could identify.

'It's cos we're all city boys', observed Ted.

'Where're you from, Ted?', asked Mig.

'Sunny Belfast', replied the Ulsterman.

'*Sunny* Belfast?', queried John.

'It's irony, or so my teacher told me at school.' He asked the pilot where he was from and was surprised to learn that, like Miglorine, he was also from London.

'I've heard of it', he said, deliberately sounding doubtful.

'I lived in Kent for a while', said Mig.

'Is that near Africa?', asked the Ulsterman, dumbly. John looked at him askance and asked, 'do you know what a stereotype is?'

'Yes', replied Ted, poker-faced. They were walking more quickly now, buoyed by the fact that they were getting closer and closer to hoped-for safety. The bombers had finished their work and made a laborious turn out to sea before heading inland once more. Once the area was clear, a flight of Stukas plummeted to earth from on high like avenging angels.

'Pity the poor bastards under that lot', said Ted.

'It'll be us soon', said John. He glanced over the wall at the neighbouring field and was shocked to see a crash-landed Hurricane fighter. Its propeller was crumpled, but other than its apparent lack of undercarriage, the aircraft seemed in good condition, salvageable perhaps. Not that anyone would bother, he mused. The cockpit canopy was pulled to the rear and he could see the lifeless figure of the pilot sitting at the controls as if waiting to take off on his next sortie. An enormous burden of sadness descended on him, this followed by relief that it wasn't him in the stricken plane. At no point did he break his stride and he realised that the other two men, eyes fixed ahead, hadn't even seen the aircraft.

John guessed that the Hurricane would stay there for some time until the new rulers of France had a chance to deal with it. For now, it was a temporary memorial to the war *he* had fought, and so far, survived.

John envied the other men their firearms; Ted his rifle and Mig his sub-machine gun. He recognised it as a stupid waste of emotion, pointless, unworthy even. It wasn't just because each of them was capable of engaging the enemy so much more effectively than him with his revolver – although that should have been the main consideration. Rather he envied them their 'shoulder weapons', as they been known when he did his training all those years ago, because they gave you something to do with your hands.

He looked at Ted striding out in front so purposefully with his rifle in the low port and he knew that he felt comfortable that way. There was little doubting the man's expertise with the Lee Enfield rifle either. Behind him, he knew that Mig carried his Thompson in a similar fashion. It was a shorter-range weapon of course, but eminently suitable for keeping an enemy's head down.

Whatever – both of them had no need to put their hands in their pockets as he felt inclined to do. Had that simple but slovenly act not been forbidden in His Majesty's Armed Forces, he would happily have put his hands in his pockets now, if for no other reason, than to get them out of the way! He decided that he would relent if he became a prisoner of war and then laughed grimly at his own ridiculous resolution. He pictured himself behind a wire fence, hands in pockets… Such notions made the time pass if nothing else, and this was time he hoped was being spent in getting closer to home.

He looked again at Ted and felt a peculiar pride in the strength and resolve of the British soldier, as typified here. Or perhaps he was better than most, or just acting from self-preservation. But he kept going and had brought them so far already without giving in to any doubts of his own, and, thought John, he must have doubts.

A strong, gusty breeze laced with spray blew in off the sea, making them wet and cold. If the weather got worse, he hoped that it might encourage the Luftwaffe to stay on the ground. They, the three of them, weren't the target yet, but they would be once they got to Dunkerque. He wondered if this was what lay in store for Britain's towns once the Germans made up their minds to invade. For now, they just had to follow the wind-battered pall of smoke to know that they were heading towards the port.

'Looks like we can either head for the coast and follow it until we get there, or stay inland', said Ted. They had come to a dilapidated iron gate that looked as if it had been neither shut nor opened for years. The post to which it was attached had partially collapsed and thicket grew through and around the gate's bars, holding them firmly like a policeman restraining a violent drunk. Just beyond the gate was an overgrown path that split into three weed-strewn directions. To the left it appeared to lead towards the sea; they could hear and smell, rather than see, the English Channel. To the right it led in a slight dogleg to the road they had abandoned earlier to make their progress less easily observed. Straight ahead it led to a farm. It seemed as if the farmer had tried to blockade his property by putting a grey, modern-looking tractor across his gates.

'That's not going to keep anyone out', said Mig nodding at the vehicle.

'No', replied John. 'Just desperate to try something. These are terrible times for the French.'

'What time is it John?', asked Ted. The pilot wiped the rain from his watch glass.

'Nineteen hundred.'

'Why don't we stay here for the night?', suggested Ted. 'Get our stuff dried out, some food, some sleep and set off early.' Mig looked at John and then Ted. He imagined that the alternative might involve standing on a freezing beach, soaked to the skin, hungry and forlorn.

'Fine by me', he said. 'If that's what you think.'

'You have doubts, John?', queried Ted.

'I just don't want to miss the boat.'

He was right of course, for the German Army powered by Benzedrine tablets was constantly pushing forwards. None of the men knew that they had consolidated positions around the port and that the Luftwaffe had been charged with destroying the British Army on the beaches.

John relented.

'But I am bloody knackered. What's another day?'

The farm had a prosperous air about it, the house quite separate from the other farm buildings. It was white-painted and had a red tile roof, reminiscent of some houses in the south of England. They squeezed through a tiny gap between the tractor and the gatepost and made for the front door, which opened immediately. The men paused warily as a woman in her late thirties stood defensively between them and the house. She looked intent on blocking their path.

'I speak not much English', she said clearly. Ted shrugged and gave her a smile which he hoped might win her over. The woman looked apprehensive.

'Can we stay here?', he asked. *'Restez ici?'*, he added. He felt as if he had just stepped out of his own body and was looking at a stranger who spoke French. Precisely where these tiny snatches of a foreign language came from, he could not say.

'Yes', said the woman, drawing a hand through her auburn hair. 'You come in.'

Each of them muttered his thanks as they entered the house, feeling clumsy and dirty in the presence of this attractive female.

'Food? Yes?', she said. They nodded. Mig said, 'yes please', like a schoolboy talking bashfully to his best friend's mum.

They stood in her living room now. The grate was filled with logs but unlit. A thick wooden timber, cracked with age and painted black served as a mantelpiece and was lined with brass ornaments and a china plate which carried the inscription, 'Southend-on-Sea.' The woman ordered them to sit and they did so, although Mig lingered for a moment to examine the ornaments.

'I've been to Southend, you know', he said in the voice of a seasoned explorer. The woman nodded without feigning interest in this revelation and Mig blushed before taking his seat.

The woman sighed wearily and then spoke again, 'you want baths and wash clothes?'

'A bath maybe', said Ted, doubtfully. Could she really produce enough hot water for them to each have a separate bath? His mind raced back to the tin bath they had at home and the difficulty they'd had in filling it with enough hot water. He thought of his current filthy state and doubted if anyone would want his bath water after he'd finished with it. Then he looked at his two companions and decided that he didn't want their bath water after *they* had finished with it, either.

'Not washing our clothes', he said using his hands to wave the idea off. 'Too long to dry them', he explained. The woman shrugged and set off for the kitchen. Pans and plates rattled and then they heard her going upstairs, water being run into a bath.

'A meal in thirty minutes. Bath with water', she pointed at Ted as she said the latter. He took it to mean that she was filling the bath.

The bathroom, only the second such room he had ever seen in his life, was stocked with oils and lotions on a shelf, had a real bath which stood on short, elaborately decorated legs and taps from which spewed hot water which foamed and broiled under pressure. Suddenly he felt even dirtier than before and as he began to remove his clothes, he wished that they could be washed or, even better, burned and replaced with a clean shirt and a new smart civilian suit of the sort that no one he knew owned. This was wealth, he decided and as he caught sight of his naked torso in a full-length mirror, he was able to make the contrast with near poverty.

His body was a sickly white colour like a dirty sheet. His forearms were deep brown from toiling under the French sun with his sleeves rolled up. Put together it looked as if his arms were still alive after the rest of his body had died. He felt painful boils on his back and one in his armpit, the result, he thought, of not washing. He winced as he explored a bruise in his side just below his ribs but could not remember that injury even occurring.

He was used to his own stink by now to the extent that he didn't actually notice it anymore but when he removed his boots a new odour of even greater pungency assailed his nostrils.

'Phew! Bloody hell!' he said, peeling off a sock that was only fit for destruction. He did the same with his other boot and his other sock, his face registering disgust. He had just dropped his trousers when the woman came into the room. If she was shocked at the smell, the state of his underwear or the sight of his pale, marked skin then she hid it well. She smiled as she handed over a pile of fresh white towels. Either she was amused at his appearance, or the frosty reception she kept for unexpected visitors was beginning to thaw a little.

She pointed at a bottle on the shelf.

'Shampoo', she said, miming the actions of someone washing their hair. Ted nodded and she left him to his bath.

'Sham-what?', he muttered to himself as he climbed into the bath.

Ted let the warmth seep into his body, his eyes so heavy that he could easily have drifted off. Only his sense of duty and his hunger kept him alert. And he didn't want to drown.

He felt at least some of the dirt lift from his body and float to the water's surface like oil and debris from a sunken ship.

When he had finished, he pulled the plug and looked at his uniform with distaste. He towelled himself dry and was about to start dressing when the woman returned with underwear and socks. He hurriedly drew the towel round his waist but she appeared to be completely unabashed.

'The underpants of my husband', she said, archly. She smiled at him and he noticed how much it suited her.

'Thanks', he said.

'I have some army shirts - his.' Ted gave a shrug that in any language meant, *well, if I'm going to wear his underpants there's not much harm in having his shirt as well.*

She returned a moment later which a fresh, beautifully made officer's shirt. Ted cast a glance at the stinking rag on the floor and then at the laundered thing held before him.

'Beauty and the Beast', he said, taking the shirt.

'Pardon?'

'Nothing. Just a silly comment.' The shirt was just slightly too large but so much better made and more comfortable against his skin than the rag he had discarded. It had a slightly perfumed smell when he held the cuff to his nose. 'Might get followed home by a sailor in this' he said. She shrugged and he recalled the fact that no one ever laughed at his jokes even when they understood them. He turned momentarily and gasped when he saw the rind of dirt left around the bath.

'Oh my God!', he exclaimed. She peered in after him.

'Easy cleaning', she said and left the room. Moments later she returned with a sponge and another bottle. 'See this clean its!'

'Sorry about the mess.'

'Okay. You very dirty man', she said without guile, causing Ted to snigger.

'Quoi?'

'Nothin'. Just a funny thing you said.' She shrugged and carried on wiping the bath. He thought he saw a knowing smile play on her lips. Ted shaved as she ran a bath for the next man, huge dollops of grainy shaving soap plopping into the sink as he slashed at his face with his safety razor.

'Your husband's a soldier?', he said through a diminishing beard of lather.

'An artillery officer.' She said something else, which Ted took to be the region in which his unit was deployed but he really did not understand.

'We'll be off in the morning. *Depart matin.*' He pronounced 'depart' in the English way, or rather the Belfast way but she nodded. 'What's your name?'

'Geneviève Boutin.'

'You might have to do this for the Germans soon, Geneviève.' He spread his hands wide, indicating, he hoped, the house, the bath, the hospitality.

'Never for the Germans', she said with her eyes downcast.

When he came downstairs Mig rose from his seat and sometime later the process was repeated with John making the short walk upstairs to the bathroom from which he would emerge refreshed, clean and hopeful. No one spoke during their meal except to say how much they enjoyed the food.

'I hope you have some left for yourself', said John. Geneviève shrugged. 'You have plenty of food?'

173

'We own a farm…'

'Of course. Thank you for taking us in.'

'We'll come back and see you after the war, Geneviève', said Mig. He stumbled over the unfamiliar name but she seemed to understand him better than the others and smiled.

'You can bring a plate with your town on it!', she said, laughing.

'London', said Mig.

'What if the Germans come? *Les Allemends?*', said John.

'I don't want a plate from them.'

'No, I mean…'

'A joke. You still have time, I think', she answered. Ted thought that he detected a flash of fear in her eyes. 'The war is not over. My husband fights the Italians in south.'

'The Italians?', said Ted. He hadn't even known they were in the war.

'Oui', replied Geneviève. She seemed matter of fact about it. Mig looked down at his plate, pushing half a potato around on the end of his fork.

'I'm an Italian', he said finally. He thought no one had heard, for only silence followed but when he raised his eyes they were all looking at him. Ted gave a shrug. He could shoot him later.

'Better have a wee sleep before we set off again', said Ted.

***

Like men who had been sleeping though an agrarian dream, they were awakened by the sound of a cockerel. John sat bolt upright and wondered where he was. There was something about a plane crash and he thought he'd seen those burnt hands again… but he saw them too often to be sure.

'I think that's the deepest sleep I've ever had', said Mig. He patted the huge bed, appreciatively. 'There'd be about five of us in this bed back in London.' He looked down to the other end where Ted's head stuck out from beneath the sheet. 'Sleep okay?'

'Like a baby', confirmed the Ulsterman.

'John, did you sleep okay?', asked Mig. The pilot had the room's single bed to himself.

'I think so', he answered, running a hand though his hair. It sat up like the stuffing from a burst mattress.

'You're missing your Brylcreem, Sergeant Guy', said Mig, mischievously. The pilot put a hand to his head and pressed down on the thatch like someone testing the softness of a bed.

'My God', he said.

'Oh, to be a sergeant', said Ted. 'A bed to yourself, an' all. Must be great.'

'Yeah. Rank certainly has its privileges.' Their easy banter belied the danger they were in but perhaps it also suggested that they were getting used to each other, becoming friends, rather than three men thrown together in desperate circumstances. He liked and trusted Ted and Mig. He wondered what he would have done had he regained consciousness in that ambulance and found himself alone. He pictured himself walking, lonely, dazed… and into captivity. He could see the broad Germanic faces of his captors and their rifles and bayonets as they pushed him and manhandled him into a truck, in which a handful of other prisoners already sat.

He could see their pale, fear-filled faces looming out of the black, a hand reaching out, seemingly unattached to a body, hauling him aboard. There would be too little food – soup and stale bread – a long train journey to the heart of his enemy's country, and years of grinding, soul-destroying fatigue and cold. They had spared him that – so far. Now they just had to make that final part of the journey to safety. He owed it to them to get there, to get home.

It wasn't a compulsion to fly a bomber over Germany that would drive him on, rather it was his duty to these men. Maybe he would eventually feel an urge to kill Germans, but right now he just wanted to avoid them. If he got back to Britain they'd put him in a bomber again for sure, and that, he supposed, was the price of liberty. He'd earned his freedom with those seven bombing sorties. Seven times he had escaped death or mutilation, attacking an enemy who couldn't be stopped with seventy or seven hundred bombing sorties against them. But maybe his reward for that was life. Nothing more than that, just life.

To keep his liberty, however, he might accumulate a debt that had to be paid by climbing into the pilot's seat of a bomber again and risking his life. He could almost smell the oil, the wood, the fabric. Without realising he rubbed his thumb and forefinger together, imagining the texture of oil, of hot metal.

He closed his eyes against the vibration of the great engines that pulled the aeroplane into the dangerous skies. He straightened his back and raised his hands to his ears to block out the sounds of engines and tried to think of peace. John tried to think of a quiet place, maybe a meadow with birdsong and the soothing smell of flowers, but nothing could blot out the image of that bomber. A co-pilot took his seat next to him and spoke, but John heard nothing. The navigator checked his charts and the front gunner worked his guns and spun his turret this way and that. He felt his stomach contract as if in some long spasm…

'Y'okay?', asked Ted. John had fallen asleep but now he shook himself back to the present. He needed to concentrate on the journey back home.

'Miles away', he said with a sigh, but the involuntary tension in his stomach muscles remained, telling him that the visions he had would never go completely but wait in abeyance, ready to ambush him again. Perhaps when they became reality he'd be free of them. How dispiriting that the reality was so much worse than his worst imaginings.

'You mean you wish you were miles away. We all do', said Mig. 'Smells like there's some breakfast on the table.'

The table was laid but their hostess was nowhere to be seen. A white tablecloth and gleaming cutlery reminded them of peacetime, of normality.

'Shall we sit?', said John. Ted looked doubtful. 'I don't think we need to be invited chaps. The table is obviously set for us. They helped themselves to bread, butter and cheese. Moments later Geneviève returned with a plate of cured bacon, a jug of milk and a pot of tea. She left the room again and came back a moment later.

'I make food for you to bring', she said and held up packages wrapped in paper and tied with string. The men thanked her and she nodded and smiled.

'Breakfast on the table, sandwiches for lunch; it's like being at 'ome', said Mig. 'My wife's very good to me.'

'Did you get married because of the war?', asked John. 'You seem very young.' He took a sip of tea and winced involuntarily as the searing water burnt his tongue.

'I got married young because my Dad's bald.'

John looked at him as if waiting for the punchline to a joke.

'Ee said to me, *find someone before your hair falls out*. I just laughed and 'ee gave me a look and said, *or you'll end up with someone like your mother.*'

John snorted a laugh and said, 'he was joking, of course?'

'I don't think so', said Mig, earnestly.

Geneviève watched the men, a mixture of concern and affection written across her beautiful face. As if remembering some long-forgotten truth, she put a finger to her lips and tapped, clearly thinking. Then she moved to a carved wooden box, parked on a tiny shelf in a dark alcove, a place for emergency treasures. The lid came off with a noise like a suction cup being pulled from a wall. When she removed her hand from the box she clutched three packets of cigarettes and these she thrust at John, the man sitting closest to her.

'Gauloises', she said apologetically. The men thanked her discordantly through mouthfuls of food.

***

When they opened the door to leave, they noticed that the weather had improved. Ted thought of the men described by Tattersall, crouching on the beach, lining up, hoping to get on a ship. He thought of the frustration of being the man *after* the last man to board and the knowledge that you would stand in the freezing water for another hour or two or three. Men had lain asleep in the wind and rain, their clothes sodden, the sand hard against their emaciated frames. By contrast *they* had slept in a warm bed and eaten like kings. Of course, some of those freezing souls were now home. John and Mig looked over at him as he spoke absent-mindedly.

'But we're still in bloody France', he said.

Chapter Seventeen

One of Mig's teachers, Mrs Milford, had once told him that his mind was very active. He'd thought about that simple statement often and wondered, not about its meaning – that was fairly clear – but about its relevance. Was an active mind a good thing or a bad thing, or did it depend upon the circumstances, the advantages that life threw at you or the opportunities it snatched away? He wasn't even sure if the teacher had meant it as a compliment exactly. Was she subtly calling him a liar, perhaps, as he tried to wriggle his way out of some compromising situation or other in which he had been found? He really couldn't remember.

However, he did know that in some of the jobs he'd taken after school he'd have been better off with a *dull* mind. He'd worked in a factory producing bottles of lemonade, for instance. It had been a dusty, dark place, gloomy all year round but cold during the winter like some sort of Victorian workshop. There he had realised that a person whose existence was devoid of intelligent thought could prosper. Perhaps 'prosper' wasn't exactly the right word. They could *exist* with a modicum of contentment – that was it. *Exist*.

If a plant could have been trained to perform simple manual tasks then it would have made the perfect employee for the lemonade factory. Unfortunately for Mig, putting bottles of lemonade into a wooden crate was just slightly beyond the capabilities of earth's flora and it had fallen on him to perform this task.

After the first hour of a shift, he would begin to put the bottles into the crate in different patterns, spelling out letters, making a stunted star or a face before filling in the spaces with the remainder of the bottles, wiping away his art forever. There was only so much you could do with a crate designed to hold twenty-four bottles and he had abandoned that entertainment in favour of mental arithmetic. He set himself tasks.

How many bottles could he put into crates in an hour? If he filled a crate in ten seconds (he suspected it was slightly longer), then he could do six crates per minute, except that he also spent time lifting the next crate into place, so knock two seconds off for that and maybe it was five crates per minute. Five crates per minute would equate to three hundred crates per hour. But that wasn't quite right either because having filled a stack of five crates he had to wait until his mate had taken them away on a trolley. He then had to put the other trolley in place, set the next crate on and begin again.

By the time he had done the next five crates, his mate would have finished loading the last lot onto the lorry and returned with the empty trolley. He knocked some time off for that. He decided that it was two hundred and eighty crates per hour and although he knew that to get his answer he had to times this by twenty-four – the number of bottles per crate – he found that he just couldn't summon enough concentration to take the sum any further.

Some years later, during his time in the lingerie industry, he had again used mental arithmetic to calculate the speed of the little Citroen van they had given him, the speedometer of which was in kilometres per hour. Thirty miles per hour was just less than fifty kilometres per hour, and all his other calculations were simply permutations of that single conversion.

For now, he was guessing the length of his stride, trying to remember how many yards there were in a mile and how long it might take them to cover the eight miles that John reckoned they had left. He looked down at his boots, each one looming into view with a monotonous but unbreakable rhythm. Mig remembered that there might be Germans around, recce patrols, or fighting patrols, sent to test the resolve of the defenders. They also needed to be wary of stumbling across the British lines without giving the men in trenches the chance to establish their identities. It didn't matter who shot you dead – friends or foes – you were still dead. He raised his head and began to scan the area, but it was difficult to remain alert for long. They were so close and although they might not be the first to get on the beach, they might well avoid the queues by arriving later. The sun, peeking out from behind a moving screen of cloud, cheered him like the first pint of beer in the pub after a hard day's work, although according to his father he'd never actually done a hard day's work. He smiled at the memory. He'd see the old man soon enough. They were so close. So close.

Ted hardly dared to think about what lay ahead. He'd had the same thoughts as Mig; arriving as the queues were dying down, being shepherded onto a ship or a boat, anchor raised and off to Blighty. Simple. He imagined the bow cutting through the surf as they sped through the channel, Spitfires and Hurricanes overhead, keeping the Luftwaffe at bay, destroyers to front, rear and either side, watching for submarines. What happened then? He had no idea. Would they receive a hero's welcome? He doubted it. Heroes won battles. No one would see the heroic aspect of men who *ran* from battle. This was the British Army, after all. They were the Tommies, the BEF just like their fathers twenty-five years before.

Their fathers had fought like lions (and been led by donkeys, so it was said). If men who stood and fought were lions, then to what animal would they – the new BEF – be compared? Who would dare to say that they were the equal of the fearless 'contemptibles' of the previous generation? How could they ever hope to emulate those men or be their equals when they were ordered to cut and run? *But did he want to stand and fight?* he asked himself, as if prising open his own soul to look for signs of cowardice.

Most men weren't cowards, of course. Nor were they heroes. Most soldiers, for instance, were just men; scared for some of the time, blasé or distracted for most of it, living out their unnatural existences as best they could with occasional acts of reckless, and often accidental, bravery to tell their grandchildren about. He knew this not because of the heroes he had met – he was yet to meet one – but because of the cowards he'd met. Manifestations of cowardice came to him often, like spirits taunting him. He knew that heroism and cowardice were opposing sides of the same coin and that sometimes an act as fickle as the flipping of a coin might mark you down forever. There was no shame like the shame of cowardice.

The soldiers he had known were the living evidence that gave flesh to his theories of the ordinariness of man. By contrast he knew of three bona fide cowards, the latest being Captain Pomeroy – TCP – a man who acted with dash and élan at all times except when dash and élan were required. He was a coward without ever having to prove it. Cliché it might be, but it was the man's eyes that gave him away. Always the eyes he thought, nodding his head slightly as he walked. At the canal he had seen Pomeroy's eyes betray his weakness by increments, as the perceived time limit for his own escape had approached.

It was all very clear to Ted for some reason, as if he had an extra sense granted at birth. He could see the man's face – his large pointed nose underlined by a clipped moustache, his broad shoulders a physical contradiction to his character – as if he was standing there blocking their path. His presence was at variance with his nature, for he was a coward in a hero's body. Above all, he wondered why Pomeroy was always so eager to get him out of the way. The officer seemed driven by a compulsion that transcended mere antipathy. It was almost as if he thought that Ted was a witness to some criminal act he had perpetrated and that only his removal would prevent his exposure to the authorities. For that reason – and only for that reason – Ted realised that he wanted to meet up with Captain Pomeroy again. He had nearly cost him his life, after all. Nor was it too big a stretch to blame him for the deaths of Whitey, Dinger and Snowball.

They had all sensed an enemy nearby, but Ted and his men had embraced their fate with a grudging acceptance seemingly not conducive to Pomeroy, their supposed leader. He alone had an escape route.

Before that he'd seen it – cowardice – in Flanagan, and again his face swam before his eyes like a dislocated ghost. Then Ted remembered yet another soldier, also an NCO. The man's pre-war swagger and self-assurance had melted away the first time they were ordered forward to engage the Germans, desperation and terror written across his whole face.

His men had fought without him and prevailed, driving back a peculiarly cautious German attack. Not one man had ever spoken of his cowardice but his weakness was there for all to see, like permanent scars. He was called Ernie Orange, a name that should have made him a great Ulsterman when in reality he was nothing of the sort.

And at school there had been Sammy McClelland. Everyone liked Sammy, even Ted and yet he alone seemed to recognise the weakness that lay just under his skin. Again, it was his eyes, the way he flinched and the way they filled up with pathetic dampness at the slightest hazard. Sammy was always ready to turn his back during the rough games they played as if he had practised cowardice in front of a mirror. Why were these living ghosts coming to visit him now, he wondered?

Cowards all... He, Ted, wasn't a coward. He just wasn't a hero either. An image of Sammy McClelland lingered in his mind, seeming to demand some attention, a further scrutiny, a reassessment of some kind and Ted found himself looking at all the evidence again, not realising that it was an involuntary mental game imposed upon him to keep one foot moving in front of the other. Sammy was bigger than most of them, probably the second biggest boy in his class. He could fight and he could throw stones with superhuman accuracy. And yet, he fought in a way which made defeat seem like the appropriate outcome and he threw stones like... like what? He threw stones like a coward, Ted decided.

Sammy's sandy coloured hair always had a springy tuft that sat out from the back of his head at right angles. Ted pictured his Mum dragging him to school by this errant lock, practically flinging him through the school gates. It was all to do with him being a coward.

'Ted', said Mig. He was at the back of their modest procession and at first Ted didn't hear him. 'Ted', he repeated urgently.

'What?'

'There's a man up there. A Frog soldier.'

Ted followed the invisible line that extended from the Londoner's pointed finger but still couldn't see anyone.

'Yeah, I can see him too, Ted', said John. 'At the junction, under a tree.'

'Right. Got 'im. Wonder why he's standin' there?', said Ted, softly. John listened with mild fascination as if hearing the Ulsterman speak for the first time. He talked as if the words he used had had some of their letters removed. It could almost be another language at times or, even more aptly, an abridged version of English. He liked that.

'Do we keep going?', asked Mig.

'Spose. He's seen us anyway. Now, if he was a German...' There was no need to finish the sentence.

The Frenchman seemed fairly nonchalant, bored even, as if waiting for a bus that would take him on a journey about which he was entirely unenthused. He looked in their direction occasionally, checking their progress, taking stock and subtly making sure they knew there was some kind of exchange required once the gap between them had been closed. They took comfort from the fact that this man did not act as if any of them were in danger. As they got closer, they realised that his uniform was actually that of a gendarme rather than a soldier.

He wore a Kepi, dark blue tunic and trousers. His neatly trimmed moustache underlined a hooked Gallic nose that added to his sophisticated face as did his powder blue eyes. He straightened as the men came to him and rested a hand on his pistol belt, as if asserting authority in a land where only a gun would do. Ted was reminded of the Wild West. He quickly scanned the man's uniform for rank badges or insignia but found none, other than brass-coloured collar patches, denoting what he thought was some kind of bird. He didn't know how to address this man, or to what extent his authority impinged upon that of the BEF.

'*Bonjour les camarades*', said the Frenchman. He spoke with the usual lyrical qualities of the French but his face betrayed no emotion, certainly nothing to indicate friendship. Perhaps that was just the man's nature, mused Ted, or simply the way in which the French police conducted their affairs. An image of his brother in the dark green uniform of the RUC flitted through his mind.

'*Bonjour*', he replied. For a moment he wondered if he might again surprise himself by pulling another helpful phrase from some rarely explored corner of his mind, but nothing came. The gendarme spoke again, pointing to his left, their right.

'*Vous devez aller dans ce direction*' He nodded in the direction he wanted them to go to dispel any confusion there might have been.

'This way?', asked Mig. He turned to look at Ted as he spoke.

'*Oui, cela est correct*', confirmed the Frenchman.

'That's away from the coast, Ted. It's the opposite direction to what we want.' A glance at John confirmed that he too shared this concern.

'That's away from the beach – *la plage* is this way', he said pointing. The gendarme looked exasperated and made a noise like a mother tutting at a child.

'*Ceux-ci sont mes ordres*', he said with a shrug. He hoped that it was clear to the men that he was trying to help. *He was giving them a safe route, could they not see?*

'We need the beach. Dunkerque', said Ted, as if their intended destination had not been obvious.

'*Pour vous obtenir à la plage, bien sûr.*'

'Maybe this part of the beach is mined or something', said John but he realised that it was a ridiculous idea. The

187

French had never feared, nor suffered a sea borne landing; mining this or any other part of the thousands of miles of coast would not have stopped a German invasion. 'Or there might be Germans that way', he added.

'God knows', said Ted, perplexed. 'We'll do what he says and see what happens.' The Frenchman looked relieved as they set off. They walked for about fifty yards, the distant sounds of battle that had become the aural backdrop to their quest seeming to diminish and then return more intensely than before, only to fade away again. John spoke.

'Ted, I'm not happy about this. I'm a bit dubious about that fella.' They had stopped and Ted turned to see the Frenchman still at his post. When he noticed that they had stopped he waved them away with his hands, ushering them forwards and shouting something that was lost in a gust of wind.

'Right let's get around the corner, so that yer man can't see us', advised Ted. Twenty further yards took them to a point where they were now invisible from the junction.

'Okay John. What's the matter?'

'None of us feel that this is the right direction to take. That's the first thing.'

'Okay, but it might be...'

'Just a minute, hear me out. He's got no rank badges on his uniform', said John. He looked directly at Ted, willing him to consider the point he was making. Ted stuck his bottom lip out and breathed deeply.

'Maybe they take them off in wartime.'

'Maybe they do, Ted. But another suspicious thing is that he was there by himself. Wouldn't you have two or more men doing that job? And he was very eager to send us off this way. He didn't really tell us why we had to go this way, did he?'

'I don't know. I don't speak French.'

'I don't speak French, either', interjected Mig. 'But it didn't sound like he was warning us off the Germans or anything like that.'

'But he *was* French', said Ted.

'He *spoke* French', corrected the pilot. 'Doesn't mean he was French.'

'So, you're saying he's a German, John? A German spy?'

'It might sound daft but he could be. A fifth columnist or something. There was something not right about him. There will be plenty of Germans who can speak good French. Why wouldn't they use one to send stragglers from the BEF into a trap?'

'It's possible, Ted. I agree with John. We need to be careful about this', said Mig.

Ted looked at the two earnest faces of his friends. He was doubtful about John's claim. Both John and Mig accepted his leadership but he was outnumbered. He recalled one of his old sergeants complaining about a new, green officer, bemoaning the fact that he didn't listen to the advice that was on offer. Ted had *de facto* advisors on tap – two men he trusted. Neither John nor Mig were naïve. Nor were they stupid, and having been responsible for leading them all to Calais instead of Dunkerque, he decided that now was a good time to take heed of their counsel.

'Right then. Here's what we'll do', he said.

Chapter Eighteen

Mig took cover on one side of the path and John on the other. Between them they could see both ways and also maintain eye contact. John had his revolver drawn and felt the dead weight of it in his hand. He dreaded having to use it – this method of dealing death was rather too immediate for his liking – but was comforted by its presence nevertheless. It was a huge, unwieldy thing, but reassuring for all its awkwardness.

He opened the weapon's bulky chamber and checked for the six rounds at his disposal, marvelling both at their size and the engineering that had gone into making the weapon as a whole. Had the medic not left it behind when he surrendered, he would be unarmed now. It felt like weeks ago. He winced in anticipation of the revolver's terrific kick, running through the simple actions required to fire the great beast.

He had drawn himself back into an emaciated hedge that formed a fringe along the ditch that ran alongside the path. The hedge was ragged like a frayed cuff but still offered him concealment. A sharp branch had plunged itself into the soft flesh at the base of his skull as he had manoeuvred into position and he rubbed at it now thinking that it must have bled. When he looked at his hand there was no blood on it, and with a grim smile he hoped that the day would continue in that way – with no blood on his hands.

Long, patchy grass projected from the soil and it was behind this that he took cover, looking through rather than over the thick blades. It was the sort of grass that country boys could put between their two thumbs and blow through to make a tuneless screech like that of an exotic bird in pain. The desire to emulate them was not strong.

John used the interregnum to make sense of his situation and thought about Ted, once again going alone to resolve what might otherwise be a crisis. He admired the soldier's obvious stoicism and yet thought he detected a tortured soul within his slim, earthly frame. Then again, he thought that this might be the wrong time to pass judgement on anybody. He didn't really know the man at all, but perhaps in better times he would like to hear his story.

He glanced over at Mig. The soldier grinned, *his* demons at least temporarily shut out. In the last few days it felt like they had shared a great deal – mainly fear – and that they really got to know each other, without actually knowing anything. What would happen in twenty years if they all got together? What would they talk about? Perhaps all they had in common was this one excruciating odyssey through northern France.

His thoughts strayed into territory that he didn't wish to explore: the world in twenty years' time. Would he still be a living, breathing part of it (he couldn't be sure that he'd be part of it in twenty minutes time) and what sort of world would it be? 1960. He couldn't conjure up any image of the world in 1960. Finally, he pulled down a shutter in his mind and forced himself to think about his current situation. He understood it little better.

***

Thirty minutes. Not very long to conduct a reconnaissance but a long time to spend sitting in a damp ditch swathed in shrubbery.

Mig tried to think about something other than the wet grass that soaked through his trouser leg. Ted was doing the right thing and his caution was sensible, but another delay, even a short one, was unbearable. For Mig it felt like they were almost there – safe. That feeling of safety triggered a string of childhood recollections. He remembered a train journey back from the coast and into the centre of London; his Mum, Dad, his sister and he returning from their day to the seaside. It was late at night and the train stopped in the middle of nowhere for what seemed like hours. He almost felt it judder to a halt as he recalled it. They were tired, pleasantly so. It was fatigue brought on by the sea air. Their day was finished and it only remained to get home to bed. But no: the train stopped and that was that. He could see the frustration on his dad's face, the resignation in his mum's face. He'd fallen asleep. When he woke, they were at the station and he had no idea how long the rest of their journey had taken.

This situation was much worse – incomparably so – but the thought of curling up and sleeping was an attractive one. He wasn't tired but he'd always felt that there was something comforting about sleep: the only escape from dreary reality that was readily available to the poor. Sleep was free. There was rarely any blame attached to it and even soldiers at war were encouraged to sleep except when they were on sentry duty, or as in this case, dumped at the side of a path and told to keep an eye out.

He thought about the cigarettes that the farmer's wife had given them and of their shared disappointment at the discovery that not one of them had a single dry match. He could still picture his last match crumbling, demolishing itself against the abrasive surface of the striker. It had been a poor, damp thing, a weedy specimen, runt of the litter.

John had joked bitterly that they would now have to rub two boy scouts together, but none of them had laughed, least of all Mig, whose relationship with tobacco was a very deep and enduring one. His sigh was correspondingly heartfelt and he sighed again now at the memory.

He was wiping an oily speck of dust from the receiver of his Thompson when he heard the first of a series of tentative footsteps. A list of possibilities ran through his mind. It might be an errant sheep making a plodding break for freedom, or a person walking a dog, but he knew that it was likely to be their suspicious gendarme. He looked over to John crouched in the thicket and tapped the butt of his weapon to attract his attention. It was an old soldier's trick; the noise just loud enough for your comrades to hear but too quiet to alert your enemies. The sound of flesh striking wood didn't jar too badly with the noise of the forest either.

John turned his head and saw Mig pointing and cupping his ear. The pilot nestled further into his hide and together they waited for the proud owner of what sounded like at least two feet to come into view. He looked again at the revolver and wondered if he would know when to fire and when to refrain from doing so. He suspected that whoever was approaching was not going to be a German soldier, and even then the decision to open fire would not be a clear cut one. He would take his lead from Mig.

The footsteps stopped, started again – just a few paces – and then stopped. It seemed as if this unseen person was pausing to let his other senses take some of the burden... or *was* it a sheep? A wary sheep. Had they even seen any sheep?

Mig swallowed and then allowed his thumb to caress the safety catch of his Thompson. He lifted his hand to touch the cocking lever situated on top of the receiver, as if to reassure himself that it was still there. He would have to operate both if he needed to open fire. He didn't want to fumble and die.

The footsteps came steadily now, crunching on the sand and gravel, surfaces that deprived their man of stealth. Both men breathed slowly and deliberately, their hearts seeming to pound away in their chests noisily. Mig hoped that John would know what to do when the moment came, then questioned his own possible actions. What would *he* do? The best thing would be to remain in cover.

A formation of Heinkel bombers rent a hole in the near silence as they passed through the air, miles above their heads, all other matters seemed to be suspended; friend and foe transfixed at the spectacle they offered. Soon they heard the whistle of falling bombs and the crump of ack-ack, explosions; a symphony of calamity. When the noise receded, the footsteps had stopped, but neither man knew the location of the unseen intruder.

Chapter Nineteen

He had no idea how long he was going to have to keep
this up. Each step seemed so laborious and noisy. Each
one reinforced his doubts. He wondered if his caution was
actually necessary. Was his enemy fifty yards away, or fifty
miles? Or simply not there at all? He couldn't creep along
with such stealth indefinitely. He paused, turning his head
to one side, letting his mouth fall open. He was listening
for sounds that had no place in the forest: the dull clank of
mess tins, speech, a cough. Any of these were giveaways
from men whose alertness was waning, whose tiredness
made them careless as hour after hour their prey failed to
appear. If the trap wasn't sprung then the spring would
weaken. Fatigue. No-one was immune. The toughest
soldiers would still succumb. To do so was human nature,
even for German soldiers, presumably.

He thought of his two friends further down the road
and wondered how they were faring. He'd given them half
an hour, and a glance at his watch showed him he used up
ten minutes already. Half an hour and they would go on
without him. Half an hour and they would assume that he
was captured. He hoped to God that it didn't happen. He
desperately wanted to go home. *Half an hour...*

He sniffed the air, feeling faintly ludicrous like a man
caught impersonating a rabbit. He was trying to pick up
scents that would provide clues about what lay ahead. The
main one would be cigarette smoke, every sentry's comfort
and a smell that could not be mistaken for anything else.
Perhaps he would smell soap or toothpaste. He might

smell *eau-de-cologne* if there were any dandified officers in the area. The air was clear, scentless, scrubbed of anything that nature hadn't put there.

He listened again and continued walking, keeping to the side of the path, looking for signs and looking too for available cover. He thought about taking to the overgrown copse that lined the right-hand side of the path but then decided against the move. It would give him cover but create too much noise if he tried to take advantage of it.

Now a glance at his watch told him he had been gone for fourteen minutes.

Fourteen minutes of slow, tentative forward movement.

When the time came to retrace his outward route, stealth would be unnecessary and he could speed up a little.

Sixteen minutes out, he calculated. *Two spent observing and twelve minutes for his return.*

He was on a bend when the formation of bombers ploughed through the clear skies above. He used them as a distraction and moved at a crouch into the ditch, from which vantage point he could see clearly up the road. Ted crawled painfully over the stones that lined the base of the ditch, the weight of his body taken on two knees and the palm of one hand. In the other hand was his rifle. He settled into a recess in a curled slump, his rifle settled against one leg. It was uncomfortable and damp. An absurd image of him lying on a *chaise longue* eating grapes leapt unaccountably into his mind. He frowned.

The sound of the bombers receded, to be replaced by the cacophony of falling bombs and explosions. For those on the ground it was a one-sided battle with no possibility of surrender. In another era it might have been deemed rather unchivalrous to have prosecuted war in such a manner.

Ted watched.

He watched the trees that bounded the right-hand side of the path, looking into the pattern of leaves and shadows for a straight line, or a colour that didn't belong. Branches moved in the gentle breeze but he looked past that, filtering it out for something else, some jerky animal movement, the spasm of a sneeze, or of cramp taking hold. He turned his head again looking but not seeing, listening with his mouth slightly agape. He had no idea why this worked except that it let the noises of his brain escape the confines of his head and left him with a clean aural palate to work upon.

A throat being cleared, a sniff, a stifled sneeze – these were the things that even the best-trained soldier sometimes couldn't avoid. As time wore on and the difficulty of remaining still became more of a burden, even the toughest soldiers might shift their position.

Of course, the phrase *it'll never happen to me,* or its German equivalent, also played a part. The initial anticipation gone, the soldier thinks that nothing is going to happen, that no enemy is going to appear. It was, as ever, human nature acting in contravention of the blurred instincts left to us by our primitive forebears.

There was nothing. No smells apart from the musty odour of the ditch. No sounds apart from the bustling rustle of starchy leaves and the melancholy melody of a distant bird. There was nothing there. He allowed his gaze to slowly traverse the scene in front of him: the trees, a section of fence, the path, the ditch, the bank, the thicket, more trees, grass… He was wasting his time now.

His watch told him that it was time to return. He had twelve minutes but he couldn't quite take himself from the area. There was something that kept him, some ill-defined doubt in his mind and he realised that he wanted to see what lay round the next corner. If *he* were setting up an ambush it would be there. His mind was a storm of possibilities and he questioned his own judgement, thinking that paranoia had hijacked his thoughts. But when the German soldier accidentally stepped into view, withdrawing a fraction of a second later, he knew he was right.

Chapter Twenty

John looked over to Mig but the soldier didn't move. He gazed intently down the path, each sense on high alert, waiting for the next sound, the next miniscule molecule of information to come his way.

Mig felt like a burglar trapped by the police or the night-watchman as they painstakingly checked the old London warehouse he'd come to rob. He was moments away from action, from some act of violence, and he knew he was ready: ready to kill or capture, ready to stifle a cry or throttle the life out of a man.

The steps began again, cautious but not so stealthy. This unseen adversary was a policeman not a soldier, more gamekeeper than poacher and his skills were not so sharp, perhaps. So Mig told himself. Or maybe this Frenchman – if that's what he was – didn't really expect to find anything.

The Frenchman stepped around the corner, made no attempt at concealment but scanned the area carefully. His revolver was drawn.

***

John watched the gendarme's eyes. He fought the impulse to press himself further into his hide when the man's gaze seemed to fall upon him. Suddenly, he felt exposed as if a gust of wind had blown away all the sundry plant life that provided him with fragile camouflage. Surely, he could see him.

Surely.

But his gaze drifted away as if he was losing interest in that indistinct shape that had originally caught his attention. Was he looking at Mig now, wondered John? Was he picking out the incongruous shape of a British soldier from the greenery, by increments piecing together the whole from assorted fragments?

Then all at once his caution disappeared, shrugged off like a cloak. The man hunched his shoulders momentarily, extracted and lit a pungent cigarette, then stood for a minute with the bored nonchalance of a man in command of his situation.

John knew then that their suspicions were unfounded. He was relieved but that relief was tempered by the knowledge that they had wasted time by waiting here and sending Ted off on a fool's errand. What they saw before them was a French gendarme, in France, with orders to provide directions to escaping British soldiers. Upon what were their suspicions founded, he wondered? He glanced over at Mig, as if to check that they shared the same emotions: relief mixed with frustration. Did Mig's assessment of the situation coincide with his own? But Mig's gaze was still fixed upon the gendarme. Perhaps the penny hadn't dropped. The gendarme had replaced his revolver. He thrust one hand into his trouser pocket then kicked idly at a stone, missing, his sole scuffing the ground. He chortled quietly to himself as if unwilling to disturb the peace of the forest.

'In den Netzen, Alois', he said with a rueful shake of his head.

The words, uttered in German, jarred like a blow to the head. John's heart leapt but before he could react, Mig had sprung from his lair and had the muzzle of his submachine gun thrust into the man's throat. The German kept his head to one side as Mig applied the pressure. His hand fumbled for the revolver at his waist.

'Don't flamin' bother', spat Mig, his lips curled like a cornered dog. The man's eyes bulged from his head as if they might pop out like two corks. John was next to him and deftly removed the revolver before flinging it into the bushes behind them.

'What now?', he asked Mig.

'We wait for Ted and then we either take this Kraut bastard with us, or we kill him.' The Kraut bastard in question obviously understood the gist of Miglorine's words and whimpered.

'A shot'll give us away.'

'A bayonet won't', said Mig. His captor seemed to understand that too and began to murmur indistinctly. John almost recoiled in horror at the suggestion and wondered if the happy-go-lucky Mig was capable of carrying out such an act. He hadn't even noticed him having a bayonet but when he took a surreptitious look at his webbing, he saw it hanging there like a stunted sword.

'What if Ted's been captured? Our friend here has obviously been sending us into a trap.' John hated the thought of abandoning the Ulsterman.

'We'll have to go without him', said Mig. 'If we wait past the half hour then we know they've got him and might come looking for us. We don't know when they were expecting to see this one again, either', said Mig jabbing the Thompson's flash suppressor into the German's throat for emphasis. The man winced and spoke in French.

'Too late for that, mate', said John.

'Let's get into some cover while we wait.'

John stood with his back to a tree. Mig lay next to him with their prisoner. The sub machine gun's muzzle was fixed to his throat as if it had grown there. John referred to his watch and saw that their time was up. He noticed Mig looking at him expectantly and nodded.

'We'll have to go', he said, sadly.

They swiftly retraced their steps, eager to get on their way yet still reluctant to leave their friend behind. John wondered if they were making a mistake, being disloyal. Did Ted really mean it when he said to move on after half an hour? Did he secretly hope that in the event they would wait for him? Would he feel betrayed? Of course he might not be coming back, and the thought of that was even worse. Ted had been their leader and had been more than equal to the job. John would miss the trust and the friendship that existed between them. Their strange odyssey would be missing the vital spark. He tried to recall a similar situation and how he had dealt with things then but he had never experienced anything even remotely comparable to this. What had he ever learned that would help him now? Obedience? Blind obedience? That made his decision both easier and harder.

The sound of running feet alerted them to the sudden need for action. In a panic they pushed the prisoner back into cover and stumbled off the path. The copse swallowed them up as if they had never existed in this darkened canopy of trees, or the uneven route which cut through it. A sort of bewildered hope registered on their prisoner's face just before he tripped over a tree root and lurched headfirst into the base of another tree. He lifted himself from the spongy soil a moment later, his features smeared with lichen like a dirty green birthmark.

'Don't bloody speak', hissed Mig. He emphasized his command with a sharp prod from the muzzle of his

Thompson, simultaneously reminding the man of his new vulnerable status. 'Make a noise and you'll never whistle Lili Marlene again', he added for good measure. His tone, if not his words, seemed to convey the appropriate message to his captive. John watched the man nod his agreement and marvelled at the menace his companion had summoned up for the purpose of intimidation.

He briefly wondered about Mig's past life. Had he been a gangster? Certainly, the quip about Lili Marlene could have been taken from a compendium of favourite gangland sayings.

The running feet continued to thump out their peculiar beat on the path, sounding hollow like a folded blanket being smacked rhythmically with a broom handle. They peered out from their hiding place and moments later a sheep, an ovine torpedo, scampered into view, charging headlong to safety. Its body arched with each stride and its legs tucked neatly to its underside like undercarriage folding away and then springing out again.

John was reminded of a riderless horse pointlessly finishing a race. He emitted a little, derisory snort of laughter and saw Mig roll his eyes. The prisoner looked from one to the other, as if hoping this funny incident had somehow altered his position and that they might now let him go with a friendly clap on the back. He opened his mouth to speak but Mig, seemingly without even looking, jabbed his tender neck with the muzzle once more and said, 'Don't.'

He didn't.

Almost at once they realised that another set of feet were following those of the sheep. As the sound of its pounding hooves receded, they heard the heavy footfalls of a human wearing boots. A second later, Ted came into sight, trotting steadily with his rifle across his chest. He looked like someone making up time and not like someone under pursuit. John stepped out of the copse. Ted skidded to halt, clearly alarmed.

'Christ!', he exclaimed. 'First that bloody sheep and then you. Where's Mig?'

'I'm here, Ted', said the Londoner. 'And I've got a little friend.' He pushed the fake gendarme out of the wood and the man tripped again as if bound and unable to maintain his balance.

'Oh aye, it's our wee policeman. There's loads of bloody Krauts up there waitin' for us', he gabbled, trying to catch his breath. 'They didn't see me so I came back. I was runnin' and that bloody sheep shot out of the ditch and ran all the way down the path ahead of me.'

'Must have thought you wanted to eat him', quipped John.

'Scared the bloody life out of me!'

'So, what now?', asked Mig.

'Get goin'. Go the way we were headin' anyway.'

'And what about him, Ted?', asked John.

Ted looked at the fake Frenchman.

'Kill him.'

The gendarme blanched began to gabble away in some patois of French, German and English, begging for his life.

'Or we might have to take him with us. Either that or kill 'im', said Ted.

'Still pretendin' 'ees French', said Mig. 'But 'ees not. 'Ees German. We 'eard him speak German.' John nodded his own confirmation.

'We could let him go but he might just go up the road and tell them where we are', said John. In truth he relished neither the prospect of taking the man with them, nor of disposing of him. It was war but this was too close, too intimate and the man was a prisoner, after all. He looked at the gendarme almost pityingly. 'We can't kill him', he said.

'He's actually a spy', reminded Ted. Even as he said these words of justification, he knew that *he* didn't particularly want to kill the man in cold blood either. He doubted if Mig or John had the stomach for it.

'Okay, he's a spy but spies get a trial and so on', said John.

'And *then* they get shot', said Mig appending the pilot's sentence for him.

For a tense moment there was silence and the four men stood there unsure of their future course of action. The hiatus didn't last long. The gendarme bolted, suddenly and shockingly. He began running up the slight incline to where the Germans lay in wait but he would have moved more quickly had he set off downhill, letting gravity help him. He sealed his fate when he started calling out in his native tongue, breathless sobs, warning, begging... Mig looked at Ted, then cocked his gun but didn't fire.

'Someone...', said John.

Mig fired a burst from the hip but the German was already sixty yards away and his bullets went wide, plucking shallow holes from the clay. Ted kneeled, cocking the Lee Enfield as he did so, adjusted the sights down to their lowest setting and drew the weapon into his shoulder in one fluid movement. But his first shot missed, smacking the dirt of the path, yards ahead of the fleeing man. It was his second shot which connected. The heavy bullet hit the man squarely in the lower back and he pitched forwards, his spine severed, his organs smashed and pulped by spinning fragments of bone.

'Go!', shouted Ted and the three of them sprinted down the path to the place where they had first met the gendarme.

Chapter Twenty-one

None of the men realised that the Luftwaffe had destroyed the port of Dunkerque. None of them realised that the town was ringed by British and French troops who would be sacrificed to help the BEF to escape to Britain. Beyond them sat huge concentrations of German troops resting, repairing equipment that had been worked almost to the point of mechanical expiration. The German Army commanders, used to decisive orders from their commander in chief, Hitler, made use of the unexpected pause to restore their formations to full fighting fitness.

Yet their relief at the respite was tempered with something approaching bewilderment. Why, with the British Army surrounded, its heavy equipment destroyed, its men demoralised, its allies in turmoil and its back to a narrow but significant stretch of water, were they being held back? The prize sat there before them, tantalizing like a wounded beast in the sights of a big game hunter, and yet they were denied their victory.

In their desperation to escape the British were destroying their heavy equipment and became more vulnerable by the hour.

These were the first men who had really fought like proper soldiers since they had crushed the Poles, a nation in arms doomed from the start because of dithering western politics. The Wehrmacht still had immense professional respect for the BEF. But this was a BEF left exposed by the dismal performance of their allies: the naïve Belgians, the contemptuous and complacent French.

Goering, that fat buffoon whose time was long past, had created a myth surrounding 'his' Luftwaffe and promised that they would finish the British off on the beaches. It simply was not happening in the manner of which he boasted. It was like using a fly swat to kill swarming microbes. And day by day more men slipped away, when a sustained ground offensive on their last redoubt would have swallowed them up and destroyed the only fighting force capable of repelling or containing the Wehrmacht.

So, they waited. They watched the Junkers dive-bombers dropping their precise loads of HE onto imprecise targets a mile beneath them. The RAF largely stayed on their bases, husbanding their resources for the next enemy offensive, which was, as everyone knew, going to be aimed at Britain.

For days the troops queued patiently, or not so patiently, alongside a wooden breakwater that became famous as the Mole.

To the south, the battle for France continued, the vast French Army, once the largest and most powerful in Europe, marshalling its resources, hoping to absorb the punishment meted out by their old adversaries. They had squandered so many advantages but fought on with greater determination than ever, whilst resenting their allies for an act of treachery. Astonishingly, a second BEF would be landed in France and then withdrawn again, having barely set their metaphorical bags down.

Some troops were evacuated from Boulogne after a confused defence of the town that left relations between the high commands of France and Britain more strained than ever. Each blamed the other for their failures, and for once Britain's stout and practical defence was tempered by gross disobedience from units of labour troops who sought escape from their plight by consuming large quantities of alcohol and beginning a drunken rampage.

As the Germans rested their men and their horses, refuelled and repaired their panzers and finalised their plans, the defenders of Dunkerque fought the Luftwaffe with rifle fire. The Royal Navy and a myriad civilian craft plucked stranded soldiers from the beaches of the shattered port. Every now and again a destroyer would be sent to the bottom, dispatched with a thousand-pounder dropped from the crank-winged JU87 Stuka. This large metal vulture came to symbolise the German assault upon the port, its appearance in the black-streaked skies a terrifying sight to those who lay defenceless in its path.

In foxholes and gun pits men waited for the onslaught, each last moment wrung of every nuance of survival and of hope that somehow their forthcoming torment was for a greater good from which some day they would benefit. *There are no atheists in a foxhole*, went the saying and they denied themselves that logic until the tanks appeared and their situation became utterly hopeless.

The rancour between the allies became something like hostility, with commanders on one side railing against the poor performance of the French Army and commanders on the other side bewailing the treachery displayed by the British. Units of the French Army fought bravely to allow what they saw as a British evacuation to take place, but units of the BEF were also sacrificed to allow French soldiers to escape. Arguments broke out between both sides as to who had precedence when it came to getting off the beaches.

For the fighting soldiers, crouched behind makeshift barricades, improvised blockhouses and hastily dug trenches, their lives were spent in hopeless torment for a greater good that seemed to have little resonance for them. The intimate allegiances that kept them fighting through the greatest adversity counted for nothing; their ultimate fate was internment at best, interment at worst. For them there would be no medals and no hero's welcome. The prospect of thanks from those whom they helped to save seemed a distant one.

For the professional soldiers here was the point where their careers stalled. For the married men, here was where their domestic lives ended.

Hanging above them, of course, like the blackest of rain clouds was a doubt. *Was it all worth it? Would the country fight on and did they stand a chance of defeating Hitler?*

Chapter Twenty-two

But for the extreme tension they felt, it might have been funny. Ted stopped so suddenly that the other men skidded into him like a human concertina. They stood for a moment like the three stooges and then stepped away, creating the gap that was necessary. John shrugged a question. *Why have we stopped?*

They were on the edge of a little seaside village, comprising dainty, whitewashed fisherman's cottages. Triangles of roof gave the bright blue sky a serrated edge and seabirds added their own wailing cliché as peace departed the confines of town. A column of German tanks lined the road, nose to tail. Crewmen clad in black busied themselves with maintenance, whilst officers pointed at maps and sentries paced slowly back and forth enjoying the sun and the quiet. Mechanics fought tiny engineering battles, hiding behind engine covers and dipping into oily holdalls bulging with tools.

It could have been any army at rest, unaware of the scrutiny, not fighting and not putting on a show.

It was a scene that would never make a propaganda film. No fake cinematic bullets flew and no one smiled defiantly for the camera. There was no victory and no defeat. The sentries thought that they had been posted simply because it hadn't occurred to anyone *not* to do so.

Ted crouched slowly and the others followed suit. They had reached an alley that gave access to the back doors of another row of houses. A few weeds grew in shallow soil in cracks and between bricks and stone. A solitary household bin sat beside a door like a forgotten child. They could retreat to the cover of the low wall they had just surmounted or they could find an escape route in the alley itself. Footsteps froze them where they sat and rendered them incapable of finding the cover they needed. The German was unarmed and unbuttoning his flies as he rounded the corner, singing softly for no one but himself to hear. His mouth formed the shape of a single word but the word never came, supplanted by an involuntary gasp.

His eyes went wide and he paused, his astonishment worse than that of a boy stumbling across lovers in a wood. A new word formed all in an instant but the bayonet was in Ted's hand and he sprang at the German. With one deft movement his left hand cupped the soldier's chin, exposing the pale skin of his neck. Ted propelled him against the rough brickwork of the house and then the point of his bayonet sliced upwards in a series of sickening jerks as it cut through cartilage and muscle before piercing bone and finally entering the brain, its journey complete. The soldier went limp, immediately lifeless and Ted lowered him gently to the ground, his expression as blank as that of the corpse.

Horror was written large across John and Mig's faces but they stood and followed Ted as he walked quietly up the alley. He tried not to shake. He wanted to think clearly but he also wanted to get the blood off his hands if he could. This was no time for panic or reproach. After fifty yards they came to another road that intersected their alley and approached this with caution. John glanced behind to see if anyone had missed the soldier who lay slumped next to the bin. The column of tanks was unbroken, the earlier scene repeated in detail.

'Bloody hell', muttered Ted. He peered around the corner again, as if to assuage his doubts. 'This is a whole regiment or something', he said. The line of grey-painted battlewagons stood between them and freedom. Each iron machine, long barrelled Panzer lIIs and short barrelled Panzer lVs, sat liked a dormant monster. They exuded menace despite their immobility.

'We need to get goin', Ted', said Mig. 'Those Krauts are goin' to notice that their friend is missin' soon enough.'

'Okay, do what I do', said Ted. He strode casually across the gap to the continuation of the alleyway, looking neither left nor right. He was a study of apparent casualness… probably too casual, in fact. On the other side he stopped and leaned against the wall. His view of the street was better from here and he watched with mute horror as a party of German MPs, recognisable from their metal chest plates, strolled towards him, chatting animatedly. They paused at the corner and one of them patted his pockets as if searching for something, realised he had it and then laughed. Another man spoke with mock anger from beneath his coal scuttle helmet.

'Dürfen wir fortfahren?'

'Ja. Ja. Ich habe gedacht dass ich meine Zigaretten vergessen hatte.'

There was laughter, a playful shove in the back when he found his cigarettes and they continued on their way. Ted looked over at his two friends and blew air from his cheeks to show his relief. With the backward tilt of his head, he urged them to cross and they did so, joining him as he once again walked up the alley to the next intersection. They walked in tandem with the *Kettenhunden*, separated by the houses, and reached the next break at roughly the same time.

They waited until the Germans had crossed over and then proceeded. Still the road was lined with tanks. On the hull of one, just in front of the turret, stood a crewman with his padded black beret firmly clamped to his head. He sang loudly in an operatic style accompanied by a gramophone upon which a crackling record lazily spun. Ted watched as he reached for a high note, plucked the beret from his head and clasped it to his chest like a rescued child, his face rent by a facsimile of torment. The note seemed to go on forever, shooting skywards like a wave of invisible energy and then the song ended with a dramatic orchestral flourish. The singer let his head fall onto his chest as if spent from the sheer effort of delivering his masterpiece and then produced a coda of pretend sobs. His audience clapped and cheered appreciatively. He shouted at them and then joined their mocking laughter.

'Oh! Sie meinen es nicht! Sie scherzen!' They don't mean it. They are joking.

Someone blew a raspberry and Ted strolled across the gap nonchalantly, unseen because he simply shouldn't have been there. He wondered how many times he could get away with it. How many times would the sheer impossibility of his presence make him invisible? From the other side John and Mig looked doubtful but he urged them to come across and this they did, mimicking his devil-may-care attitude. One of the Germans from the singer's audience caught sight of the two Britishers as they crossed. He and John exchanged glances but he didn't recognise the pilot for what he was, just as someone might look at their watch without taking note of the time.

'We can't keep this up, Ted', said John. 'We're going to get caught.'

'Well, this is the end of the alley now', said Ted pointing to a final intersection beyond which was a row of houses. 'At the end we'll go right. Or left. Whichever direction has the fewest Germans milling about.'

He looked at his blood-stained hands. The stuff of life had dried and cracked. He was disgusted and wanted more than ever to wash it off.

At the end of the alley, they crouched behind a low wall, home to various juvenile weeds and a small pile of human excrement decorated with a flower of shiny toilet paper.

'Nice spot you picked', said John, grimacing. Ted ignored him and whispered, 'wait here.' He edged forwards out of cover, placing each foot carefully and soundlessly in front of the other. Just before the corner, he got down on his belly and poked his head out, almost at ground level. To his left he saw the last of the tanks, even more monstrous in appearance from this grovelling vantage point. To his right he saw two armoured cars and a small truck with a box body. There were no sentries, no mechanics and no officers. This end of the street was in shade. Like lizards, the Germans seemed to need sunlight.

The armoured cars and the tank were pointed to the left but the little truck was pointed in the other direction and no parked vehicles blocked its exit. Where the armoured wagons had a solid grey paint scheme, it had a camouflage pattern of browns, greens and black; the lunatic daubings of an experimental artist. A similarly painted telescopic mast for a radio antenna was attached to the box body. Another antenna was wound around the edge of the roof in a great distended loop.

Ted backed away from the road.

'We might have some transport', he said. A quick inspection indicated that the vehicle was empty and that the keys were in the ignition. 'Mig, you drive. John navigate, and I'll get in the back and see what they've got we can use. Take it easy. Act natural. Just drive carefully. Look like you should be driving it.'

The box body contained two chairs fastened to the floor opposite a table that folded down from the wall to form a right angle with a map board. A map of northern France showed clearly the precarious state of the Allies' defences. German units, armoured and infantry, surrounded an enclave of British and French divisions sited around the port of Dunkerque. To the south there was still something resembling a front; French versus Germans with a few isolated British units still theoretically in existence. This was not propaganda. This was the real war, the real dispositions of the protagonists graphically displayed.

Ted shook his head in despair but had expected nothing else. He heard the engine start, feeling vibrations through the metal floor and then a crunch as the gears engaged. Mig pulled away into the road with a lurch as he struggled with the unfamiliar controls and Ted almost hugged himself, making his body small, waiting for a volley of bullets that might follow their departure. None came. The vehicle rocked as he crashed one gear and then another. He felt them turn a corner, hearing Mig's increasingly expert double de-clutching and the brief rev that got the cogs spinning at the correct speed to mesh. He smiled, thinking of the soldier driving round London with his load of women's underwear. Odd what skills were needed in wartime.

They turned a few more corners and then took to a clear road, with sweeping bends. Ted had a more detailed look at the signalling equipment in the truck, light streaming in from two small windows set high in the walls. He found a satchel containing papers, a codebook, pens and some radio logs, one of which was partially completed.

He scanned the words written in an unfamiliar language looking for meaning but finding none. Radio signals could seem incomprehensible even when written in plain English but these were largely encoded and, of course, written in German. He shrugged.

On the wall behind the cab, he found a safe. The door was locked but the key was in place and turned with a smooth, almost liquid, ease. The safe walls were half an inch thick and the lock was a masterpiece of German engineering. Inside he found three solid pistons, or cams, each an inch thick with complicated shapes milled onto their cylindrical surfaces. They looked like part of an elaborate puzzle and could have been made from gunmetal, an impression that was strengthened when he touched one and felt the oily residue that he might find on the working parts of a well-maintained weapon.

He turned his attention to the desk. There was a telephone handset, two headsets and a metal box with two lids, one on the front and one on the top. He remembered someone joking that telephone handsets were for officers because they lacked the co-ordination to put a headset on. Come to think of it, he wasn't sure if it really was a joke.

The box was firmly bolted down. He lifted the lid and looked inside. Two long recesses led down to a sump filled with metal projections made with the same care and from the same metal as the pistons in the safe. The other lid revealed a keyboard like that found on a typewriter but slightly smaller. Ted lifted down one of the pistons from its bracket and let it drop into the machine. The fit was perfect. He knew then that had found an encoding device of some description.

Suddenly, he felt the truck pulling to one side of the road and then stopping. The silence was profound after the engine had chugged to a halt. He heard John and Mig talking, then footsteps and then the door was opened and he was left blinking like a man seeing sunlight for the first time after years of dark incarceration.

Chapter Twenty-three

'What's the plan, Ted?', asked Mig. He was clearly buoyed up by their escape, the release of tension evident as he jumped from foot to foot like a child at Christmas.

Ted stepped down from the box body. He felt a wave of nausea rise from his boots to his throat and his head swam. Sweat broke on his forehead. He thought he might faint and felt foolish at the prospect.

'Just a minute', he managed and ran for the sheltered verge. John spoke to Mig as the Ulsterman emptied his digestive tract, hacking up bile with convulsive heaves that threatened to turn him inside out.

'It's a nervous reaction', explained the pilot. 'He killed that German but he hasn't had time to get over it. I used to see aircrew doing the same thing after they got back on the ground, especially if they'd had a close call or seen another plane get it. Sometimes they just puked in the plane.' They heard him heave again and then take a gulp of water, rinse his mouth and spit out.

'You okay?', asked John. He'd felt the aftershock of death himself on many occasions and had still felt repulsed by his personal proximity to the German soldier's final moments. Ted had killed before but he hadn't really been a *killer* until the moment when he had plunged the bayonet into the soldier's skull. John guessed that his new friend could do it again. The barriers to death through close combat were down now and might never be replaced. *What sort of person would he become?*

'I'm fine. It just got the better of me for a moment', he said, candour compensating for his verbal economy. 'Where are we?'

'We are here, Ted.', said John pointing to a grey line on the map. I think that we are two miles from these beaches. I just think we should do the rest of the journey on foot. We don't want to get shot up by our own lads.'

'I agree. That would be a bloody waste. There's another map you might want to look at in the back here. Shows where we are – the British that is – and where the Germans are.' He glanced over at the pall of smoke that lifted from Dunkerque as John climbed into the back. 'We might have a clear run through now', he shouted into the back of the truck.

'Some interesting stuff in the back here, Ted', said the pilot. Ted leaned against the aluminium doorframe, one foot on the step.

'That's the next thing I was going to tell you about. It's an encoding machine, or whatever you want to call it. If we can get it unbolted it might be worth taking back with us.'

'You think so? I think it's called an encryption device.'

'Could be. It looks heavy but…'

'I think we should leave it and just get ourselves back', said Mig. His apprehension was returning. He had a sense of foreboding.

'Are you getting' windy, Mig?', asked Ted, only half-jokingly.

'Windy?' He sounded as if he was going to refute the suggestion but then relented. 'Yes. Frankly, I am windy. Whatever this bloody machine is, it's not as if the old Krauts only have one of it. What difference does it make whether we take it or leave it?'

'This could mean our people being able to decipher German radio messages.'

'Right. Do what you want', said Mig, crossly. 'Let's get on with it.'

John had already found a spanner from a built-in tool chest that doubled as an additional seat. Within two minutes he had detached the device and with Ted's help loaded it, the codebook and the 'pistons' from the safe into the satchel.

'It's heavy', he said, passing the bag to Ted. 'A box of ammo', he added, making a comparison that a soldier would understand. Indeed, not only was it as heavy as John had suggested but awkwardly shaped too. The satchel did little to hold the device firmly or to cushion the various painful protrusions that would dig into Ted's side as he walked.

'Doesn't matter', said Ted, dismissively. 'Let's get on that flamin' boat.' He looked at the sky with hope. 'Nice day for a voyage.'

***

Ted had little time for introspection now, with the prize so close. Even thoughts of the way in which he had dispatched the unfortunate German back in the village could not impinge upon the relief he felt at having made it to Dunkerque at last. Images of home flitted randomly through his mind, each one vivid yet indistinct, more real and yet less realistic than anything he had ever actually experienced. His father, a man usually exhausted by a day's work at the shipyard, became a wonderful, animated figure, full of fun and life.

Ted realised that in these muted daydreams he himself had become a little boy again, small enough for his father to pick up and burl round upon his return from school. He allowed the thought to linger, dismissing the fact that in reality his father was always at work when he returned from school.

Every sense was reawakened by these phantom recollections. The house smelt of freshly baked bread and his mother would wave a floury hand at him as he came in through the front door with his battered leather satchel. *Well, that hasn't changed*, he thought wryly, looking down at the bulky bag that jostled his hip as he walked. Strange too how the smell of baking displaced the natural odours of the seaside, he thought.

His musings were an amalgam of reality and reminiscence, for now he was at the seaside of his youth on a day trip to Bangor, a resort, thirteen train miles from his home in Belfast. Their day began with a long walk to the station, his father working out how much money they would have left after paying for the train ride and his mother looking at the sky wondering how the gods of weather would treat them. He would stare directly out of the window most of the way, marvelling at the speed of the train and imagine himself running along beside it. His father would point out the cranes in the shipyard and name some of the men who operated them from their precarious glazed perches high in the air above the worker ants below. He would tell Ted of the great ships that had been built there, always omitting the name Titanic, as if it was shameful or simply old hat to mention it.

Ted remembered some of the ship's names: Olympic, Britannic and HMS Glorious. There had been hundreds of them, probably millions of tons of iron or steel forged into leviathans of the ocean, but the other names were gone, lost in the files of his personal history.

Of Bangor itself, he could remember the sea wall and the beach beneath, having an ice cream and his dad scolding him as it began to melt and run down the cone onto his hand. He recalled seeing his dad increasingly annoyed at tiny happenings and heard his mum telling him to take his jacket off because he was too hot. That always worked. Why didn't he ever think just to take the jacket off himself? Ted always held his mum's hand to cross the street as if there was a mass of traffic to avoid. In reality there was almost none, just a few vans and cars.

Periodically, an image of a dying man forced itself onto the stage upon which his memories took form. The dying man was in his arms and got heavier and heavier until Ted had to lay him down on the ground. Their eyes met, one set lifeless the other set plagued with life and its attendant horrors. The dead man had something of Ted's. He bent to pull the bayonet from the German's head, felt the resistance as tissue formed a seal round the blade. He wiped blood from the weapon... What did he wipe it on?

Belfast was an industrial monotone but Bangor was colourful and bright. Belfast stood for industry, rain and commerce eked out from nothing but the tireless efforts of the working man. Conversely, Bangor represented bustle, noise, happiness. Food tasted better in Bangor, the sun always shone, the air was fresh and no one worried about anything. Of course, none of it was true – or certainly not all of it – but that did nothing to dispel the myths that his brain had created for him.

He turned to look at his two companions and felt a strange compulsion to drag them into the better world that inhabited his head. But they had their own daydreams.

John thought of survival, an indistinct entity; something that never quite became tangible, expressing itself via an unreliable train of events that people called 'life'. Those who survived usually looked no different from those whose survival had never been in question. You couldn't necessarily pick out a survivor from a group of ordinary people. Those things that made them different were locked up in their head, captive electricity and chemicals.

A wounded man might have the scars to prove that he had been involved in an event that threatened to end his life, but a plain old survivor had nothing. There was no portal to his brain, no access to the archives. Those archives might themselves fade like the yellowing pages of a book and then one day they would be gone forever of course. He looked at his hands.

Mig thought exclusively about their immediate destination, namely the port of Dunkerque. The permanent black cloud that hung in the air stifled any thoughts he had of finding a town like Bognor Regis or Southend, but he wanted to see the English Channel. He wanted to dip his hand into the water that connected him with his own country. When he could do that there was nothing to stop him from getting home. Nothing would bar his exit from this increasingly strange land, where even their friends seemed cloaked with enmity.

As the end of their current phase of civilisation and culture drew to a close and their comfortable certainties were taken away and replaced by a harsh future under the rule of cruel new masters, the French would have to re-examine their allegiances. Mig wanted to be well away when all that happened. He wanted to go back to Britain, a place where people were solidly, unequivocally... British. Mig wanted people around him who ate sausages, pies, mashed potato. He wanted people who weren't making plans for how they would live their lives under German rule. He wanted the King and Queen in Buckingham Palace. Just to know that they were there was enough. Black cabs, London buses. He wanted the comfort of ordinary things.

'Nearly there, lads', said Ted. Ahead of them a sand dune sprinkled with scutch grass obscured their view, but they knew instinctively that their salvation lay beyond that immense grainy pile. Opportunist seabirds wheeled noisily above a long beach from which the once mighty British Expeditionary Force was being evacuated, unbowed. Each of them had their own private version of what lay ahead. Ted began to run. John and then Mig followed suit, the pilot reaching the top of the sand dune just a moment before the other two. They stopped there briefly, breathless and skylined, caution discarded like an empty cigarette packet.

Ted blinked as if to wipe an image from his mind. None of them spoke.

Jetties made from trucks cut into the sea, other trucks lay abandoned and wrecked. The distant mole formed a long arm, seemingly bent to scoop up the sunken ships whose funnels reached bluntly from the calm waters. Another wooden jetty could be seen and only at a second viewing was it possible to pick out the trucks that lay beneath the planks to make an expensive foundation. A destroyer lay on the sands, canted to one side, abandoned and useless. Ted felt as if someone had reached inside him, taken hold of his intestines and twisted them painfully and maliciously. Someone who said through gritted teeth, *I told you. I told you. Who did you think you were? I told you.*

The beach was completely deserted, devoid of human life except for a few Germans who picked over the carrion of a lost battle.

Chapter Twenty-four

The last of the men had been lifted off the previous night. A senior officer had come close inshore calling for the stragglers to make themselves known. The launch drifted up and down the coast, avoiding semi-submerged obstacles that, just days previously, had been potent weapons of war. Now they were merely sunken testimony to the power of the Stuka. The officer felt a desperate sadness for those they had taken off the beach but more so for those left behind. When would they ever see their homes again?

They had room on the neighbouring destroyer for another few hundred men but their calls had gone unanswered. It seemed as if they really had got every available soldier out of France. The end for that country seemed to be just days away. He looked down at the lamp mounted on the gun'wale and considered using it to attract attention.

'Not sure what sort of attention we might get if I switch this on', he said to the coxswain.

'Should be okay, sir. But you never know', said the seaman, cautiously. He'd spent day after day motoring back and forth from ship to shore, shore to ship. It was a relentless and dangerous merry-go-round. On one occasion he had been taking a party of soldiers back to a destroyer only to see it hit and sunk. Some of those he had deposited on his previous foray were undoubtedly killed in the carnage of that moment. The little grey ship had died before his eyes, those who were able jumping to the dubious safety of the water. He'd diverted to another ship, leaving those on board to their fate.

To lose his life now, to a German sharpshooter perhaps... it was unthinkable.

'I think we're done here, sir', he said.

'I think you're right.' The officer bent to dip his hand in the water as if patting the head of a dying pet. 'Back to the ship.'

Shortly afterwards the orders were given for the forces defending Dunkerque to surrender and the French were left to their own devices, fighting on until the situation was beyond retrieval from them. It would be four excruciating years before the British and their new allies returned.

Chapter Twenty-five

'My God. We've come all this way...' John didn't finish his sentence. There were no words that quite fitted. For a few anguished moments they stood in silence, like mourners at a graveside. Mig spoke next.

'Get down', he said and they were reminded of their situation. The beach they had striven to reach was now in enemy hands.

'They'll have patrols out looking for stragglers', suggested John.

'Maybe. Or they'll just wait until the stragglers come to them', said Ted. He felt utterly crushed.

Ted wondered if they had come to the right place, but of course they had. The trucks and jetties, the sunken ships, all of these were mute testimony to a mass exodus. He had no answers. What had he expected? That the evacuation would go on indefinitely? That they would wait on the off chance that three forgotten servicemen might turn up? That he would be reunited with his unit, maybe see Pomeroy or the CSM again, if they weren't dead?

The phrase *I told you so* resonated in his brain and yet no one had actually used these unkind words. They should never have spent that night in the farmhouse. If only they had pressed on...

'We're not in the bag yet', said John. 'We're still free and no-one is looking for us. The Krauts are just enjoying their moment of victory.'

Mig said, 'shit.' Never had his favourite word been applied to a situation with such aptness. The Londoner shook his head and spoke again. 'It's hard to see how we get back to England', he said. He could not keep the disappointment and anxiety from his voice.

'Get another boat', said Ted, simply. 'Go to the harbour and help ourselves.' The men stopped talking as a flight of Hurricanes flew in low over the beach, their arrival and subsequent disappearance over in seconds.

'A bit late, lads', said John with a hint of bitterness. Mig and Ted looked at him. Neither had expected a comment like this from him, an RAF pilot. 'Well, it's true, isn't it?', he said glumly.

'Okay Mig, what do you think we should do?', asked Ted. He felt himself rallying. Perhaps, the sight of the Hurricanes had shown him that all was not lost. They still had a country to go to. It was just a question of getting there. Mig's response was a temporary dead end, however. He shrugged, miserably.

'John?'

'The boat idea seems like a good one. I can't actually think of an alternative.'

'Where is the actual port? The dock?', asked Ted. He and John consulted the map and they saw at once that a great many Germans were likely to stand between them and freedom. 'It's going to be guarded as well. Where else are people like us going to head for?' As they talked each man became aware of a distant buzz. It grew steadily in volume until John held a hand up to silence the other men. They listened.

'Sounds like a light aircraft, that', said the pilot, eventually. The possible significance of this was lost on his companions.

'So?'

'Might be a spotter', he explained. 'I suggest we lie here and keep very still.' They lay on their backs, each one alone with his thoughts again and only a neutral sky for company. Mig wished for something to happen even if it was only capture. Once he was captured then hope was gone and without hope there could be no further disappointment. There was no happy ending that he could see, so why not give in to the Germans? They'd get food and a place to sleep and they'd get home someday he was sure. He kept his thoughts to himself.

The spotter plane seemed to get no nearer, its engine just a constant drone in the background. John listened with an accustomed ear. This was not the sound of a thousand horsepower, rather two or three hundred, and that narrowed the possibilities right down to a trainer or a spotter. He could see no reason why the Luftwaffe would fly a training mission over the recently contested Dunkerque beaches. As he listened, he heard the engine note change, or the plane alter its course.

Finally, it sounded as if it was coming nearer, but more than that it sounded like it was going to land. He frowned and looked over at Ted. The Ulsterman just stared at the sky, his face registering nothing at all.

'Wait here', he said and slithered off. He crept to the top of the dune and then crawled to its summit on his belly to a vantage point from where he could see the beach through a screen of grass. Little had changed. Groups of Germans chatted and smoked whilst others scoured the sand for souvenirs. He saw a party of medical orderlies carrying an inert lump off the beach, one man at each corner of the stretcher. Their feet sank in the soft sand of the dunes and they stumbled and cursed under the weight of their burden. John saw an arm fall from the cover of the blanket but the men were too busy to bother with the nicety of putting it back under. At the very far end of the beach he thought he saw a party of French POWs being marched under guard by Wehrmacht soldiers. Their blue uniforms were indistinct at this great distance. They could have been in the RAF, he supposed. The thought shook him. He could be joining them soon.

The little aircraft he had heard was a distant speck now. Maybe he'd got it wrong. Nevertheless, he surveyed the beach, assessing its suitability as a landing strip for a light aircraft.

The flat expanse of sand was littered with the detritus of war, mainly trucks that had been intended to form part of a jetty or breakwater but which had got stuck or been found another use. There was one stretch of clear, flat sand near the water's edge that he could imagine being hard-packed enough to support an aircraft's weight. It would take an exceptional pilot and an exceptional plane to bring this about. He was unaware of it at the time but this was precisely the sort of thing the Luftwaffe had in fair numbers.

The plane, more distinct now, seemed to turn lazily and then head back to the beach. There was no apparent urgency. He thought of the Hurricanes that had flown over earlier and how much he would like to see them return right now. The outline of the little aircraft became increasingly clear. It presented a tiny aspect head on, with a low powered in-line engine, a lot of cabin glass, long wings and an intricate, spindly-looking, fixed undercarriage. He was reminded of a daddy-long-legs.

It was maybe a mile away when he saw the nose dip, the pilot coming down close to the beach, skimming over the carcass of a truck, then dipping again. There clearly wasn't room to land and yet the wheels touched down, bounced gently and the aeroplane settled on the ground. The engine note changed again and an array of flaps appeared on the wings like a complex pattern of feathers. Moments later, the plane taxied to a halt and the prop shuddered to a standstill. They had landed in an inconceivably short distance. John was simultaneously astonished and filled with admiration at the pilot's skill. In a different time and place he might have stood and applauded. What he had just witnessed made him extremely happy nonetheless.

He looked down at Ted and urged him to come up with a backwards nod. The Ulsterman scrambled upwards through the soft sand.

'Bloody hell', he muttered. A soldier ran over to the plane. The passenger door was opened from within and another soldier stepped out. He placed his peaked cap on his head and returned the salute he had been offered. General Rommel then followed the junior officer up the beach to meet the men who had finally captured Dunkerque. The pilot followed on at a respectful distance. A single, bored soldier, his rifle slung, was left to guard the Fieseler Storch aeroplane he had arrived in.

'I can read your mind, John', said Ted. John smiled and said nothing.

Chapter Twenty-six

It was night time when they finally made their move. John had kept a look out all day, hardly daring to believe that this esteemed visitor to the front, whoever he might be, was prepared to stay as long as he did.

He watched the sentries hand over, none of them particularly enamoured by the task they'd been given and none of them bristling with alertness. As far as these soldiers were concerned the immediate danger to their lives and continued well-being was gone. They saw themselves as garrison troops now and hoped that this situation might last for a very long time – preferably until their demob. If the rest of the Wehrmacht could roll up the remaining French forces as quickly as they had done there was no reason to think that they would have to fight again. Or not for some time, anyway.

John's stomach knotted over and over again with a mix of anxiety and frustration. The days were long now, the sun reluctant to dip below the horizon, but only darkness could give them the cover they needed to make their escape. The non-return of the VIP passenger was just the first in a short series of things that they required to get off this beach. If they managed that – and it was of course out of their control – they still had to get to the plane.

That achieved, they had to hope that John could fly it.

He hadn't even mentioned his concerns that the strange little plane might actually be just a two-seater. He assumed that his seat was guaranteed but who got the other one? Of course, the plane might easily fly with three men on board and none of them were particular heavyweights, but he was conscious of the short take off run that he had. He would be lucky to get more than one attempt. In fact, he was certain that he would not.

There were other problems. John wasn't experienced at flying at night. He had done so, of course, but the Fairey Battle was purely a day bomber and his flying practice had centred around that important fact. More pertinently he had no experience of flying a short take-off and landing aircraft. He had seen the unorthodox arrangement of flaps and wondered if he would get the hang of them in the short moments available to him when he first climbed in. Sitting at the controls of an unfamiliar aircraft in the dark would be bad enough. Waiting for a hail of bullets to end his life made that particular proposition even less attractive. He didn't share his doubts with the two men who now relied upon him.

To counterbalance his doubts, he had this one thought, *it's this or nothing*. He hadn't said so to Ted and Mig but he didn't have to. The truth was self-evident; they weren't going home on a ship. There was no brief pleasure cruise across the channel for them and they certainly couldn't walk home. Mig had suggested going back to Geneviève's house but they all knew that it was hardly a practical idea. Besides which it would only be short-term solution and it would put her in mortal danger. If the Germans turned her house over to find the three men, her outlook would be bleak indeed, and they would be no closer to getting home even if the Germans didn't put in an appearance.

He felt the sand beneath him move, falling away from his elbow in tiny rivulets. John looked over to see Ted squirming up next to him.

'How are we doin'? Is that wee plane still there?'

'It is. Just sitting there waiting for us', confirmed John. His mouth was dry. His stomach rattled with hunger and fear.

'Well, let's hope yer man has brought his toothbrush and pyjamas.'

John laughed. A companionable silence followed.

'And you're sure you can fly it?'

'Of course. I can fly anything with wings and a propellor.' A look passed between the two men and they both knew its meaning. He wasn't sure that he could fly it at all. However, it was tacitly understood that they would all take their chances with no recriminations – even if they survived. They had discussed their plan in scant detail simply because there was precious little of that commodity to be had. They would strip their outlines of anything obviously British in origin – their tin hats were the first thing to go – and walk up to the plane with an air of disregard. Nonchalance was the key. Furtiveness would be the ultimate give away.

They had to appear like men who belonged there, whose business it was to approach this plane and...

Well, that was the tricky part, where it all got a bit messy. None of them spoke German and none of them was, upon close inspection, a high-ranking Wehrmacht officer like the one who had arrived in the plane. John might pass muster as a Luftwaffe pilot but that was about it. Darkness helped. In fact, it was essential but it would do nothing to disguise an inability to converse in German.

'Let's hope he's got himself smashed on champagne and is holing up in a nice French chateau somewhere', said John.

'In bed with the countess, maybe? That might be too hard to leave.'

'Once it's dark of course, we've cracked it. He won't be going anywhere in that aeroplane once it's dark.'

'Couple of hours', said Ted. 'Until it's dark.'

John nodded.

They watched as an artillery crew set up a little anti-aircraft gun, removing trailer wheels, splaying its legs to form a base and loading ammunition. A party of pioneers or sappers filled sandbags nearby and these were passed up the short sea wall to form a protective ring around the gun. It was an army at work. The Germans were good soldiers but they were still just men who smoked, drank and whored like any others. They were entirely oblivious to the fact that they were being observed. They worked efficiently with a smooth rhythm that would get the job done with relative ease.

Further down the beach he saw a convoy of six heavy trucks pull onto the firm sand. For an hour they watched as the trucks methodically hitched themselves to the stranded British vehicles on the beach and towed them onto some hard standing. Elsewhere, a few men in dark overalls went from truck to truck examining their engine bays and then trying to start them up, clearly trying to salvage anything that might be useful to the new rulers of France. Their foraging seemed to bring them little success and occasionally they would call out to each other, verbally comparing notes and inevitably sharing a shrug of disgust.

'They're not letting the grass grow under their feet, are they?', said John.

Ted thought of the little soldier who had stayed behind to disable the vast truck graveyard and who had shared his rations with them. He couldn't remember his name. He wondered if he had managed to get away but it seemed unlikely.

Near the plane, a few soldiers played with a stray dog that barked and yelped, with its tail beating out a silent percussion in the air.

'That dog is a collaborator', said Ted with grim humour.

'Probably the first of many', agreed John.

One of the soldiers, taller than the rest, stamped his foot and growled theatrically at the excited animal. The dog crouched in response and barked even more while the Germans split their sides laughing at its antics. The same soldier picked up a discarded boot and threw it, just missing the hapless sentry next to the Fieseler. He shouted something at them, a reprimand and pointed at the aircraft. One of the soldiers shouted back and then they all moved on with the dog yapping at their feet.

'I felt like shouting something at them myself', said John.

'Aye. *Get off my bloody aeroplane*', suggested the Ulsterman.

Finally, the sun began to sink below the horizon and the air took on a chill.

'Nearly time', said Ted. John looked at him, searching his face for nerves, some sign of the tension that he must surely be feeling. There seemed to be nothing beyond an implacable stare.

'Are we waiting for pitch black or just dusk?'

'For the purposes of flying, I think dusk might be better.'

'I'll get Mig', said Ted.

***

'No webbing, no helmet, weapons slung. Casual. We're Germans now. Just for the next few minutes. We take it easy, no jerky movements, or trying to hide. We just bluff the whole thing out. No one is expecting three Britishers to turn up.'

'Fine, Ted', said Mig.

'We'll be home in twenty minutes', said John.

'Twenty minutes?', queried Mig.

'It's not far', confirmed the pilot. Ted imagined that it might seem like a rather long twenty minutes but said nothing to this effect.

'What about the sentry?', said Mig.

'I'll take care of him', replied Ted. '*Guten abend* and a bayonet in his throat.'

'You're getting a taste for this, Ted', said John with feigned reproach.

'If you've got a better idea let me know. Maybe he'll swap the aeroplane for a packet of French fags.'

'I didn't know you spoke German', said Mig, vaguely.

'Nor did I', said Ted.

***

The outline grew in size, framed against the last rays of the sun glinting off the calm sea. They had skirted round a tiny group of Germans who sat on the beach playing cards and drinking spirits by the light of a campfire like a gang of renegade boy scouts. These fallen angels all had mothers just like Ted and Mig and John. Some of them may have had fathers too. At their feet or next to them, within arm's reach at all times, lay the paraphernalia of their trade, grenades, rifles and sub-machine guns.

The sentry moved from foot to foot, stamping more out of boredom than to stave off the cold. Occasionally, he completed a little circuit of the plane. He whistled tunelessly but stopped to peer into the near blackness ahead of him. Three men approached. One looked like a pilot but neither of the others had the appearance of a Wehrmacht general, that is to say the familiar outline of jackboots, peaked cap and sidearm. They were ten metres away, walking in silence, when he issued the password, feeling faintly ridiculous as he did so. There was no response at first and then one of the men said good evening to him. He replied falteringly. They should have given him the other part of the password. *Pissed*, he thought.

They weren't going to fly in that state, were they?

The man on the left, he might have been the one who spoke, increased his pace.

'*Sie haben nicht richtig geantwortet*', he said desperately. You did not respond correctly. He wondered if he had got *his* portion of the password wrong. If this was an NCO or sergeant major approaching he would be for the high jump. He was about to speak again when the man was upon him and he felt the bayonet on his throat and then slicing through his flesh. Speech was impossible, the pain incredible… He felt warm blood cascading down his tunic front.

Then he felt nothing.

***

John climbed into the cramped front seat, at once feeling more at home than he had expected. The plane somehow *felt* flimsier, less powerful than the sturdy but ponderous bomber he was used to. The control panel was in darkness, no hint as to how to bring it to life. One never lost the knack of flying, of course, but stepping into an unfamiliar aircraft was daunting at any time, much more so at night.

Normally, no one would ever expect a pilot to take his first flight in a new type without any form of instruction and it went without saying that one's first flight would take place during the day and in favourable weather conditions. Pilots cost too much to train to throw their lives away.

However, there was nothing normal about this situation. The Fieseler rocked in the breeze and the rocked again as the other two men clambered aboard behind him. He heard the cabin door being pulled shut as he groped in the darkness for the starter button.

'We're in, John', said Mig, wrongly interpreting the reason for their delayed departure.

'Good', he replied, running an ungloved hand over the instrument panel feeling for a button or switch that would breathe life into the complex machine that had consumed them. His index finger dipped into the tiny watchglass of a gauge, then into another. He blindly flicked switches until he found the battery master. He flicked it and the central instrument panel illuminated. Behind him his two passengers discussed their surroundings like excited schoolboys.

'Never flown before, Ted', said Mig, still astonished that they had actually made it to the plane. His elation was clear. Escape seemed unbearably close after their recent disappointment.

'Me neither', replied Ted, anxiously. His anxiety stemmed not from the necessity of killing yet another German, nor from his ambivalence at having done so. Nor was he unduly worried about his forthcoming first flight. Rather, he wondered how long they would remain earthbound and, more importantly, undiscovered.

'It's a bit cramped in here', said Mig. 'It's this bloody suitcase', he said invisibly kicking the luggage at his feet.

'Just think yourself lucky you were allowed inside the plane. John wanted you to sit on the wing.' The humour was forced.

John found another Bakelite switch and flicked it, illuminating the rest of the controls.

'Aha', he muttered with restrained triumphalism. An orange button was now apparent. Underneath the button was the word *Windshutzscheibenwischer*. John smiled and pressed down with a flourish.

Chapter Twenty-seven

A tiny wiper scudded lazily across the bone-dry windscreen with a noise like a bicycle brake. Disappointment and fear hit John like a thump in the chest and he swallowed forcefully, swore and scanned the metal fascia for a button that might aid their escape to better purpose. Already they had been cocooned in the little plane for five seconds and made no progress whatsoever. From the corner of his eye, John saw lights from a torch or a distant vehicle. His stomach seemed to knot just a little bit more. He imagined his intestine looking like a cat's cradle.

Another button caught his eye. It was red, round, illuminated. *Red for stop? Red for go?* His finger hovered, ready to press. He'd finally made progress, improved their lot by a tiny increment. The aircraft was no longer an inanimate concoction of wire, fabric, metal struts and genius; it was a living thing, ready to take them home.

Red for go? Red for stop?

Did he really want to undo all that he had achieved so far? The pumps continued to hum and he could smell oil as it warmed up nearby. Did he want to close down their last hope of salvation? *Red for stop?* It was this or indefinite internment. Or was it? *Red for go?* That wasn't right. He looked for other buttons to push, found none that he liked.

His attention was drawn to this one button, either because it glowed like an evil eye or because he was short of alternatives.

Red for stop? Red for go? What would Ted do? He didn't know. What would Mig do? He overheard the little Londoner swearing in the back. Mig would say, 'shit' and press the button.

Red for stop? He looked at the button again. Underneath it was the word, *Maschinenanfang*. What the hell did that mean? What was the German word for stop? *Halt*.

'Shit', he said as he pressed the button. There was silence but only for a moment. The little Argus engine spluttered asthmatically and the prop turned over once like someone reluctantly waking from a deep sleep. It turned over again as the engine came to life, now a cacophony of sounds reaching into the grateful fibre of their souls. Mig and Ted sat up, nervous and alert. Was that the hard bit over, they wondered? Did it get more difficult? When was someone going to start shooting at them?

At once John felt at home, back where he belonged, with pedals at his feet and a control column in his hand. No more sneaking through France, ducking behind walls, lying in ditches, at least not for a while, he hoped. He moved the controls and felt the flaps respond with precision. He scanned the instruments gathering information about the aircraft's status, notably fuel, and then began to manoeuvre blindly.

Mig could just see the outline of Ted's face and smiled. This was it! Or it should be, he thought. He felt the suitcase beneath his feet and kicked it to clear more space. The case burst open and Mig reached inside to find treasure of sorts. The case was full of silk underwear.

'Knickers!', he said, his voice lost in the din. At that point the little plane lurched forward and then span through one hundred and eighty degrees. The movement was a violent wrench from immobility and no sooner had the aircraft settled on its suspension than they felt it drive forward under power. Ted thought he saw a figure running through the darkness to intercept them and braced himself for the impact of a bullet, but none came and after an impossibly short run he felt himself being pitched out of his rearward facing seat as the Fieseler unstuck itself from the sandy runway below. He had the sensation of being plucked from gravity's greedy grasp and flipped into space as John drew away from the Earth. He felt no impression of great forward motion, rather that he was a puppet, only loosely connected to his controller. He craned his neck to see out of the window, caught a glimpse of a campfire and then nothing more.

'Still there?', shouted John.

'Think so', replied Ted. He could just see the flash of Mig's smile in the blackness. Conversation was virtually impossible so they settled down for the short hop to Kent, Ted holding onto his rifle and Mig up to his ankles in French lady's underwear. He couldn't have been happier.

***

They flew without incident for fifteen minutes. John knew that they were heading for the coast of England but had little idea where he would put down. Britain was blacked out but the moon at least illuminated the islands sufficiently for him to have confidence that they were still where he'd left them. He glanced downwards and then to his front, picking up the ragged white line of waves hitting the coast. His two companions said nothing, or certainly nothing that he could hear. Mig saw the pilot, picked out by the gentle glow of the instrument panel, twisting his head from side to side, looking for landmarks.

He smiled to himself and marvelled at their good fortune. They had stumbled upon one of the few people with the ability to get them home from the country so recently abandoned by their army. The odds against it were

245

huge. He reached down for a pair of knickers hoping to examine them in the moonlight. He couldn't see much but they felt like good quality items and he was an expert, after all.

Ted closed his eyes. The satchel and its uncomfortable cargo dug into his thigh. The aircraft lurched as if it were suspended from elastic. He didn't even feel as if they were moving forwards, only that they were being thrown about like a storm-tossed dinghy. He'd never been in a storm-tossed dinghy.

They were safe now. So long as John could find somewhere to land they were safe. The darkness shielded them from the attentions of the British ack-ack. He shuddered at the thought of the reception they might have received had they crept into British airspace in this ponderous little aeroplane in daylight.

John sighed. How many times had he breathed that deep, profound sigh at just making it back, at surviving? Seven at least, he thought grimly, seven sorties and he hadn't had to land in the dark before. Nor was there much chance of him finding an airfield.

He shelved those thoughts for a moment. Ahead of them – directly ahead, in fact on a collision course – was a fireball. A disembodied meteor describing a course that ran parallel to the Earth's surface, was closing in at an alarming rate. He wondered whether to dive or climb but his brain froze and he did neither. A second later the fireball, which he now recognised as a burning bomber, sped past, missing them by feet. The little Fieseler rocked and bucked in the turbulence caused by the passage of the big Heinkel 111. John held the controls tightly and rode out the brief storm they had passed through, his thoughts with the crew of that stricken plane. Just for that moment they weren't the enemy, they were fellow flyers, terrified by the prospect of a horrible death.

Faces of the dead appeared in his mind and were gone again. He sensed the discomfort of his two passengers. Each of them was aware that *something* had happened but he doubted if they realised how close they had come to death. Had they collided, John, Ted and Mig would have ceased to exist in an instant. No one would ever have known what happened to them and would never have guessed that they had ever met each other or shared a common death. He could explain all this later when they were safely on the ground.

The little aeroplane swept overland, leaving the sea behind after another minute had passed. They were only a few hundred feet up and John gently lowered their altitude still further.

At last they had solid land beneath the aeroplane – the fields of Kent – and it only remained for him to unite the two in such a way that none of them was hurt or killed. He could discern fields and hedges. Sleepy cows looked at them, wonderingly. From this perspective and with only moonlight he couldn't judge the lie of the land. Were these fields as flat as they seemed and did he have enough skill to bring the plane to a halt in the tiny distance afforded to him? He circled at three hundred feet giving himself time to think, looking for a place to land. Dark shadows clawed at the corners of the fields as his perspective changed, as round and round he went.

His mouth felt quite dry. To throw it all away now was unthinkable. A pilot who couldn't land was worse than useless. Better never to take off if you couldn't subsequently land. The fuel gauge looked to be a quarter full so he knew that he had time and he increased the size of the lazy loop he flew. Below, he saw dark squares and rectangles, each barely visible in the gloom and he knew that he had found buildings. Whether their presence helped him or not was another matter.

He flew lower, two and fifty hundred feet and then down to two hundred. He was looking at a village, nothing more than a few scattered houses either side of a road. They flew so slowly that in any other aircraft they would have stalled and crashed but the little Fieseler clung tenaciously to the air that kept them invisibly afloat.

As he watched he saw a skewed diamond of light appear, become a rectangle, a figure briefly framed, then a diamond once more before disappearing altogether; a door opened and shut, a crack in the blackout. Running parallel to the road was a field, longer than the others perhaps but with two great banks of trees along either edge and a herd of cows that had packed themselves into an invisible corral. Maybe they would scatter when he came into to land. He flew past and executed a slow turn keeping the field in view as best as he could. He would buzz the cows first, frighten them and create his own runway from the most unpromising material.

The little plane came in low, the wings close to, but thankfully not hitting, the trees. The engine noise was enough to scatter the animals as he had hoped and he pulled up again, trying to turn again before they regrouped into an immoveable bovine knot. To hit a cow during landing would be disastrous for all concerned, not least the animal. An image of cuts of beef describing elegant arcs through the night sky flitted unwanted through his mind and then was gone.

The German plane handled beautifully he had to admit. It wasn't the fastest thing in the sky – probably about the slowest – but it turned on a sixpence and could fly at speeds at which any other plane would plunge to the ground like a lead weight. He knew it could land in impossibly short distances – he'd seen it do so, just hours before – but wasn't sure if he personally possessed the ability to fully exploit this facet of its handling. He skimmed the treeline now and needed the Fieseler to drop to the ground suddenly but not crash. He held his breath and fought with the aeroplane until he felt he was only feet above the grass. Still, he couldn't quite bring her down, as if a mental barrier prevented him from taking that final step. He pulled back on the control column and the plane lifted again, beginning to stall as the nose lifted too high. He corrected and took them round again.

'Okay back there?', he called. Silence. 'Technical hitch', he explained, with enforced cheer. He had never doubted his own ability as much as he did now.

Mig held on to a metal spar and wondered if his life was going to end with him wrapped round a tree, women's underwear strewn everywhere like soft leaves. It wasn't the heroic end he had envisaged.

Ted said nothing.

This time John thought he felt the left wheel of the undercarriage clip a branch but they were still on course and they dipped suddenly downwards like a department store lift. He scratched off more speed, coaxed them down another few feet, saw the end of the field looming like a darkened auditorium of trees. The left wheel touched – it was still there, thankfully – then the right. He cut the engine, plunging them into an eerie, rustling silence and the Fieseler bumped along the grass like a huge unwieldy go-cart, slowing as it hit a gentle incline. When they stopped, John breathed out again. The three of them sat in silence for a few long, delicious moments and then Mig said,

'Right. I'm gettin' out.' It almost sounded ungrateful.

Chapter Twenty-eight

He might have been stepping off a bus to hear him talk but when his feet touched the ground his legs collapsed beneath him as if devoid of bone.

'Shit', he said. John heard Ted climbing out into the dark-shrouded field and regained his feet with difficulty.

'Can't believe we're here. The Germans are so close now.'

'Thank God for the Channel', said John who had just joined them. 'Let's get to that village', he said and waited for the men to collect their meagre belongings. Ted emerged from the cabin with his awkward satchel.

'I'm ready', he said. He almost felt the need to whisper – they'd done little else for days. He could just make out the figure of Mig hauling the captured suitcase from the plane. 'What do you want with that?', he asked.

'Listen. You've got your code thingy', he said pointing to Ted. 'You've got your aeroplane and I've got me knickers. Okay?' The other men nodded in the gloom. 'Right, then.' They set off, but after a few paces Ted paused.

'What's up, Ted?', asked John turning to face the soldier in the gloom. Mig looked on silently.

'Are you sure this is England? You definitely flew over the Channel?'

In the darkness he heard Mig chortle. 'I wondered the same thing', he said.

John smiled. 'Definitely England, Ted. Come on.'

The grass was dry, the surface more uneven than they could ever have imagined from John's landing. They barely spoke as they neared the road. There was too much to say, or was it too little? Ted held a wooden gate open for them and they stepped onto the road like men setting foot in a newly discovered country for the first time. Just for a moment each of them was lost in his own thoughts until Mig began to laugh.

'What's so funny?', asked Ted, smiling.

'I don't really know. Just glad to be home, I suppose. When we got to that beach and everyone else 'ad buggered off I thought we'd 'ad it.'

'We all thought that', agreed Ted.

'If we 'adn't picked up this man from the gutter we still be there', said Mig, pointing at John. His words carried with them a mixture of awe, gratitude, relief, disbelief and unutterable happiness, as if he were speaking on behalf of several different people at once. John stood looking up the road, just a few feet from his new friends. Ted and Mig looked at him, knowing that he had saved them and knowing too that he had done so in a quite spectacular way. Whilst recognising that they had little expertise in the area, neither of them doubted that he had flown brilliantly.

He would later play his part down, claiming that his success was due to luck and trial and error, but for now they looked on in awe and left him to his own complex thoughts. For much of the time in France he had been a passenger of sorts, relying on the two soldiers to get him through, but now he had taken on a heroic aspect which made him stand apart from his earthbound comrades.

Ted wondered if the dexterity and intelligence needed to fly a plane, which John so clearly possessed, would now become a barrier to their friendship. Maybe the status quo had been re-established. They were men whose paths should never have crossed and would never do so again. Perhaps he was a superman and they were peasants. What went on in his brain, he wondered? That question was answered moments later.

'I think that's a pub up there', he said, without turning around. He began walking with purpose.

***

The pub was called the Stonemason's Arms and was populated by men from all walks of life other than stonemasonry. For instance, the bank manager was there, seeking respite from his wife, or, as he sometimes wondered, was that respite from his life? He was a veteran of the Great War, had won a Military Medal at Mons, been wounded on the Somme, been commissioned and then ended the war as a captain. He had tried to rejoin the army in 1939 but the combination of a back injury and his forty-five years had made this impossible.

He had sought solace in the ranks of the Local Defence Volunteers, in which he now served with the rank of corporal. Now that they were finally being supplied with uniforms and weapons, he felt new life and new hope in his veins. He actually wanted to kill some Germans. It surprised him to discover how much he wanted to add to his tally from the previous war.

How much more satisfying would that be than interviewing farmers who wanted more money to buy more cows to make more milk, to make more money and so on? Next to him, one of those farmers, Ron Sheriden, sat nursing a pint of ale, paid for from his bank loan no doubt. Ron was a private in the LDV and had been just too young to take part in the last war and slightly too old to stand much chance of taking part in this one. Besides which, his was a reserved occupation. If the Germans came, as seemed increasingly likely, they would all get their chance and their names would probably be added to the war memorial along with all the others without anyone saying, *well, they were only the LDV.*

That's precisely what some unkind souls were saying now. He'd already heard it once tonight and the man responsible was just getting into his drink-fuelled stride.

'If the army gets kicked out of France without a fight then I don't see what point there is in having a flamin' LDV', said Tommy Bartlett. 'Not done much of a job, 'ave they? First sign of trouble and they get on their boats and run like hell. Don't know what that Froggies must think of 'em.'

Tommy was a thickset man, a labourer, and never one to shy away from sharing his opinions. Many villagers wished that Tommy would do the decent thing and volunteer for the army – show them how it should be done – or at least be conscripted. Beyond that, their interest in his fate was somewhat less than kindly intended. The bank manager knew that the sleight was aimed at him but remained quiet. Perhaps, the day would come when Bartlett would be glad of the army and the LDV, but for now he remained what he had always been – a malicious malcontent and a thug.

The bank manager imagined that Britain's prisons were stocked almost exclusively with people like Tommy Bartlett. There was simply nothing that could be done for them, or with them. He, the bank manager, was an informed man and had once read an article in a newspaper in which a journalist talked in apocalyptic terms of an increasing number of people who, as he saw it, 'lived on the edges of society.' Bartlett was undoubtedly one of those, although most local people might have wished for him to move further away than merely the edge. The next town would have been good, or across the Channel perhaps.

The bank manager whispered to Ron Sheriden, conspiratorially.

'The trouble with that bastard Bartlett is that no one tells him to shut up', he said. Sheriden thought about this and nodded. 'Including me, I'm sorry to say', added the bank manager, regretfully.

'He's a big lad. That's why. Certainly, no patriot, is he?', said Sheriden. He noticed that Bartlett was looking in their direction as if he could hear what they said about him.

'We should get him into the platoon, you know. Take him on manoeuvres, accidentally shoot him', said the bank manager. Sheriden looked at his companion, shock written across his face. This was the bank manager talking! He drank deeply from his pint, his eyes just visible above the rim of his glass as if he were hiding behind it.

'I'm just joking, Ron', said the bank manager. But he wasn't. Ron seemed to regain his composure. He spoke quietly to the bank manager, trying not to look in Bartlett's direction as he did so.

'It's alright him saying that stuff about the army and so on when it's just you and me here. He wouldn't be saying it for long if a few of those boys from the BEF walked in right now.'

'No indeed', chuckled his companion, suddenly cheered by the thought. He remembered the men of the previous BEF – he had been in their number – they wouldn't have stood for it. He was about to say something else in the same general vein when the door to the pub opened. Moments later there was absolute silence.

Chapter Twenty-nine

'Bloody quiet in 'ere', said Mig from the corner of his mouth. 'Is it a wake?' Eight pairs of eyes looked at them and a couple of mouths fell damply open and stayed that way. Mig spotted a large man with a beard, sitting slightly apart from the rest of the customers. The man stared, then screwed up his eyes and stood. He was like a pantomime villain but the sense of menace he communicated was real enough. His stool scraped across the floor noisily.

'What's ee starin' at?', asked Mig, defensively.

'You've got a pair of lady's knickers sticking to you collar', said Ted, pulling the offending item off and stuffing it into the Londoner's pocket. Mig giggled.

'Thanks, Mum', he said. He turned to John, who looked on, smiling broadly for the first time in weeks. 'I'm always doin' that', he explained. Still, none of the bar's customers spoke. Each was frozen, like people captured in a photograph. This bizarre tableau continued for what, to the three new arrivals, seemed like minutes but was really only seconds, and not very many of those.

'Why're they starin'?', repeated Mig.

'Look at us', replied Ted. 'They were hardly expectin' three dirty-lookin' reprobates like us to walk in, were they?'

'Fresh from the battlefield, so to speak', added John. Mig looked down at his uniform and then at his two companions. They were military vagabonds: unwashed, unshaven and more to the point, still armed. On the rare occasions in which the army had passed through this Kentish backwater, they had looked somewhat more pristine than the three wraiths who now stood guard just inside the pub door. Predictably it was Tommy Bartlett who spoke first.

'My God. No wonder we're losin'', he said. The bank manager shot a look at the landlord, Bernard Graves, which said, *do something.*

'Now, now Tommy. Just keep your opinions to yourself.' He looked over to the three new arrivals and smiled, hiding his confusion. 'A drink for you gents?', he asked.

'Only got French money', said Ted.

'Yeah, we just got in', joked John. 'Haven't been to the bank yet.' There was a general murmur from the customers as their initial shock subsided and then one smartly dressed man spoke up.

'I'll get these, Bernard', said the bank manager. 'What's your poison, gentlemen?'

'I wouldn't waste my money on 'em', said Tommy loudly. He sneered theatrically revealing a rotten gap in his front teeth. Ron Sheriden looked from Tommy to the bank manager and back again. A dozen possible questions raced through his mind but he narrowed this down to one.

'*How had he known?*' How had the bank manager known that these three men were about to walk in?

The bank manager was talking again, clearly enjoying himself, eager to make an effort, to show his loyalty and his appreciation.

'Just ignore Tommy', he said. 'He's a fat blowhard. Scared to do his bit', he said, glancing Tommy's way. 'So, what are you having?'

'Uh, a pint, I suppose', said Ted looking warily. 'We all havin' a pint?', he said looking at John and Mig. They nodded.

Tommy spoke again.

'Germans on your tail, are they?', Bartlett said, taunting the new arrivals. He was spoiling for a fight, partly because that was what he was expected to do. He was the everyman critic of everything and had to keep up appearances. No one usually bothered to argue. On this occasion, however, he began to wonder if he had miscalculated, although he felt he had no option but to keep going with his hurtful diatribe. This was different though. Unusually, the objects upon which his ire was focussed were actually in the bar with him. Normally, he complained about those who couldn't defend themselves, mostly because they were absent but sometimes because he knew they were scared of him. These three men were armed, of course. That was different as well and the one with the funny accent had the indefinable look of a man who could kill.

'Three pints of ale, Bernard', ordered the bank manager. The effort required to ignore Bartlett almost seemed to take on a physical presence as big as the man himself. The concentration needed to filter out his insults required energy enough to stun an elephant and yet that's what they did: they ignored him. But still he kept on goading, because to have backed down would have required more courage than to keep going.

'I can't imagine how you got here, chaps', said the bank manager, gamely. Their drinks arrived at that moment. 'Cheers', he said. Their glasses clashed dully and Ted suddenly felt himself not in need of a drink so much as a bed. He looked at John and Mig, saw the same thing in their eyes. That over-riding depletion of energy, of will, the need to rest, to just be something *other* than hunted men. But the drink was good. It hit the mark. They drank deeply and the bank manager signalled that replacements would be needed shortly.

'Won't be getting' a drink off me', said Tommy loudly. He belched and wiped froth from his beard. His stare was fixed on Ted. The Ulsterman was aware of this but studiously ignored Tommy. Conflict was not on his mind. Not right now.

'So where have you been?', said the bank manager. 'France obviously but you haven't come in with the others – the rest of the BEF – I take it.'

'Flew in', said John. There was no trace of boastfulness in his voice. He wanted to downplay their escape.

'Flew in?', queried the bank manager. The beginnings of an incredulous smile came to his lips. John wasn't surprised.

'The plane is in the field across the road. You can check if you like.'

'No, no. It's fine. I…' He had been about to say *I believe you* but the words wouldn't quite come. John shrugged and turned back to his pint. 'Must be a while since you had a drink?', said the bank manager. 'I think you'll probably get a few more bought for you before the night's out.'

'Not from me 'ee won't', shouted Tommy. The landlord, exasperated, remonstrated with him once more.

'Bugger off', said Tommy, a nasty mood getting nastier.

Ted enjoyed the slight blurring of reality caused by the beer. It came on quickly. He had never been a big drinker but for the moment the beer was a good substitute for sleep. Or perhaps it was a good precursor to sleep, although he had no idea where they were going to spend the night. He felt the incipient light-headedness that comes with alcohol just leaching into the blood, starting its journey round the body, making stops to ease the tensions of a nervous system at full stretch.

He gradually began to realise that he was free and safe. He didn't have to look over his shoulder, or duck behind walls, or crawl through fields, at least not for a while. He did need the toilet though.

The hubbub of conversation continued, having picked up after the brief hiatus caused by their unexpected entry to the pub. He had two more drinks lined up on the bar and he had heard one of the other men order each of them a whisky. The pressure on his bladder would brook no argument. Ted stood, looked down at his rifle and the bag with the so-called 'encryption device' and decided that he could leave them on the floor.

Then he decided that he couldn't.

He'd leave the bag – he didn't really care about it or its contents, but the rifle? It had been in his hand or within arm's reach constantly for several months now. It had become like a part of his body. To go somewhere, even to the toilet, without it would be like going on parade without your trousers. No, he decided, that wasn't right. That connection wasn't strong enough – it would be like going on parade without your head.

'Just off to the bog', he said. No-one answered. He reached down and scooped the rifle from the floor, slung it on his shoulder and made his way to the gents. The door opened soundlessly then gave a slight bang as it shut. Ted propped his rifle against the wall and made his way to the urinal, feeling slightly foolish. He was home – well, back in England, anyway – he didn't need take his rifle everywhere with him but old habits died hard.

He had just finished nature's business when the door of the toilets banged shut again and a man spoke. Immediately, he knew which man.

'Back home safe and sound, eh?', said the man. Ted fastened his flies.

'Looks that way', he said, turning. It was no great surprise to see the large, bearded man blocking the door.

'Bet you thought you didn't have to keep looking over your shoulder anymore, didn't ya?'

'Funny enough, but that's exactly what I was thinkin'.'

'You lot can't be much good at fightin'. I mean you all just run away from the nasty Germans, didn't ya?'

'It must seem that way but we did our best', said Ted with a weary sigh in his voice. He smiled and made a move towards the door, collecting his rifle on the way. He held it loosely in one hand. The big man still blocked his way. 'Excuse me', Ted said politely.

Ted detected a change in his own mood. It was nothing more than a dip in his good humour, but profound enough in its own way. Perhaps his patience was running out, or the drink was starting to take control. Either way, he felt that it would be best if the large figure barring his exit stepped aside.

'Am I in your way?' asked Tommy. He gave Ted a menacing smile. Ted shrugged and pretended to look over the man's shoulder at someone on the other side of the door's opaque glass window. Duped, Tommy half turned his head and as he did so, Ted jerked the foresight of the Lee Enfield into his opponent's crotch. Tommy howled in pain and reached for the soldier like a blinded bear but Ted had stepped to one side, reversed his hold on the rifle and now connected the brass butt plate with the big man's face. He heard a crunch.

Blood splattered onto the floor and Ted looked at his hands for traces of the same stuff which had come from the German he had killed. When was it? Today? Yesterday? He couldn't remember now. The blood had gone.

Tommy staggered back into the door, hitting it with a thump that resounded through the pub.

John and Mig reacted first, sprinting for the door which refused to open.

'It's jammed shut', they heard Ted shout. 'This big bastard's fallen against it.'

'Shit', said John, borrowing one of Mig's favourite words. An image of two dead Germans flashed through his mind. He knew that Ted was a killer…

Chapter Thirty

There wasn't much to see or to do in the cell. He looked at the four walls from the discomfort of his hard bed and then scanned the ceiling for cracks. There were none. His cell was spotless. Not one speck of dust had been allowed to settle, not one smudge had been allowed to form on the pristine paintwork. What did he expect? It was an army cell after all, scrubbed clean.

This wasn't quite the reception he had expected having completed his perilous journey through northern France. He allowed himself a bitter smile and waited for someone to enter the cell, to berate him and threaten him with some dire punishment. That was how the army worked. It was not, in his experience, the most compassionate of organisations, and the truth was he didn't expect it to be anything other than what it was: a legally sanctioned open prison with brutality and occasional hard labour. What else could it be? How else could the army make men do the most appalling of deeds, witness man at his most base, put their lives in mortal peril and yet still function as human beings.

The casual brutality of the NCOs at St Patrick's Barracks, where his basic training had been carried out, had shocked him far more than the hardships they endured. He got used to the early mornings, the runs, endless weapon training and drill, the meals that were bolted down in a way that would have appalled their mothers. He got used to the cold and the fatigue, the apparent senselessness of the some of the tasks they routinely performed. They had once stood on parade in the rain for an hour while their NCOs drank tea inside their billet, but they got used to it and were ready for it next time.

All of these things had been a shock – despite his father's warnings about army life – but it was the violence that had stunned him into a feeling of almost doomed submission. He had seen men routinely kicked and thumped. He knew of another recruit who had been thrown down some stairs by the men in his section at the behest of their corporal.

Almost unnoticeable uniform infringements were rewarded with routine acts of brutality. The NCOs wielded canes or blackthorn sticks to enforce discipline and they did so with impunity. It became a fact of life and Ted had realised that none of the recruits could ever do anything right for either the beatings or the beastings, the punishment PT that was part of the process of turning them into soldiers.

Had they been presented with a bunch of young men who had understood exactly what was expected of them from the start and who had followed every order in the manner of a trained soldier, they would still have found themselves standing in the rain, nursing bruised knuckles, struck in the chest or head with a blackthorn stick, made to run up and down hills in full kit until they felt close to death. It was just part of the conditioning process but had it made them into good soldiers?

Yes, was the answer. Ted smiled, revelling in the memory of those times and glad that he was no longer a recruit. They had become men who followed orders when every sinew and nerve was telling them to run. Did it help him now as he lay abandoned and filthy in a cell? Again, the answer was yes. The worst was over. They trained hard in the hope that anything that followed would seem easy. It didn't always work out that way – war certainly was hell – but they never expected anything to be straightforward, comfortable or even safe. And in that respect, they were rarely disappointed.

He sat up, his arms behind him, and appraised his situation. It wasn't all bad. For one thing he didn't have a hangover, simply because the fight had happened before he had had the chance to drink too much.

But against that, he was a prisoner.

Of course, he could so easily have been a prisoner of the Germans instead. Just the previous day that had seemed like a real possibility, maybe a certainty. However, there was no escape from the fact that this was hardly fitting treatment for a man who had just fought for his country. He had killed at close quarters. Was it patriotism or self-preservation? Some mixture of the two that had no discrete name? There were no easy answers.

The distinction – the line between heroism and cowardice or that which lay between self-preservation and selfless bravery – was one that was rarely explored. He could have been indignant had he wanted to be but, as with everything, what was the point? He could protest…and make his situation worse. He even had a notion that he could ask to speak to an officer. He imagined a meeting with the unsympathetic Captain Pomeroy, could see his loathsome smirk, and decided against that course of action. Instead, he would lie here and accept his fate, or more accurately wait to see what his fate was going to be.

He hoped that someone would realise the importance of his escape, the sheer daring of it and the fact that they'd brough home an invaluable code machine…

He sighed and continued to stare at the ceiling, thinking of the time when he could leave the army forever. Ted often looked forward to his demob, that distant event when he would leave the army and its strictures behind and restart his stalled life. All soldiers thought the same way, except those who were criminally barmy.

He imagined mornings in bed with nowhere to go and nothing to do. His mind carefully filtered out unpleasant realities such as the need to earn money. Men with more experience of civilian life warned him that civvy street could be tough in its own way but he refused to believe.

Ted sniffed and ran a hand through his hair. It was stiff and matted like... well, unwashed hair. He needed some of that shampoo stuff of Geneviève's. He smelt his hand. It smelled of unwashed hair. He had felt coarse grains of sand on his scalp, a little reminder of the beach at Dunkerque. His thoughts strayed to that strange time so recently ended and he found himself worrying about John and Mig, his two steadfast companions of late. He wondered if he would have made it home without them, certainly not without John.

Mig had been a tonic for his spirits and a means of countering his isolation. He had been another pair of eyes and ears, another trigger finger, but more than that he had been a redoubtable friend, a source of humour and, in a sense, another reason to get home. He'd felt a responsibility to help the Londoner regain the shores of England. Mig had thrown his lot in with Ted, trusted him implicitly. Now he and John lay in their own cells, having done absolutely nothing wrong.

His reverie was about to be interrupted. He heard footsteps in the corridor and a door being unlocked. He heard voices, those of Miglorine and an officer. The same process was repeated a moment later but this time with

John. Then his own cell door was opened. Ted stood as an MP corporal followed by a colonel entered the cell. He straightened himself out, standing shambolically to attention.

'Lance Corporal Edward Dexter?', asked the officer.

'Yes sir.'

'Come with me.'

Chapter Thirty-one

The house was a sprawling red brick mansion with at least two obvious façades. It looked different from every angle, no section of its structure looking contiguous with any other, as if it had been designed by a committee whose members worked in complete isolation. Ahead he saw John and Mig stepping out of a black Wolseley car similar to the one in which he himself rode. Both men looked distinctly uncomfortable, like peasants invited to entertain the nobility with their rough ways and agricultural humour. He saw the pilot speaking and Mig shrug a reply. They still looked unkempt, men plucked from the battlefield and dumped in the homeland of the aristocracy.

'Pull up to the main door, corporal', said the colonel. The driver said, 'yes sir'. Neither man had spoken on the way here, not to each other or to Ted. It suited him fine. A moment later he stepped out of the car and joined his two friends. Mig pulled a face that somehow expressed the doubts they all felt.

'This way please, gents', said the colonel as he strode past the sentries on the door. They snapped out a disconcerting salute, and Ted almost responded with a salute of his own as if he was the revered visitor.

The hall was high-ceilinged and decked out with ornate plaster mouldings and pictures of great but forgotten men from history. These were, without exception, men who had made Britain great. The nature of their achievement was often unclear or forgotten. In some cases, their reputations were undeserved. They were scions of industry and the military, empire builders or those who had created or provided the means to build an empire. Ted looked around him in awe. A flight of stairs that would not have looked out of place on MGM's soundstage both dominated the entrance hall and diminished the warrant officer clerk who sat at the ubiquitous folding table. He stood but did not salute as the colonel approached.

'They're ready to see you, sir', he said, enigmatically. The officer thanked him and they made their way upstairs under the canvas scrutiny of the great men who provided a mute honour guard. None of the visitors spoke. Ted, a man brought up in a terraced house and therefore used to confined spaces, felt humbled by his new surroundings, and ever more aware of his temporary hygiene problems. He hoped that whoever it was who wanted to see them had a limited sense of smell. No sense of smell would be better.

They reached the top of the stairs, following in the wake of the colonel, who had still not introduced himself or told them the purpose of their visit to this magnificent pile. They turned right and carried on down a short corridor, their footsteps muffled by a deep crimson carpet.

'Wait here, gentlemen', said the colonel, knocking on the door and peering inside. The three men looked at each other like naughty school children summoned to the head's office, wondering if they had got their story straight. John raised an eyebrow. There was a brief exchange and then they were ushered inside.

Both General Brooke and the Prime Minister stood as the three men entered.

'Welcome, gentlemen', said Churchill. 'It would seem that you have had quite a journey and brought us some lovely gifts from the continent. Please take a seat. We have a lot to discuss.' They all sat and a mess orderly came in with tea and delicate little biscuits that looked like they had been assembled by a talented mouse. The tea was poured into china cups and Ted felt faintly ridiculous drinking from bone china whilst dressed like a soldier and smelling like a vagrant. To be doing so in the presence of the Prime Minister added another layer of incredulity to that which he already felt. Ted only just remembered to close his mouth again after his initial surprise.

'You have brought us what I am told is an extremely interesting aeroplane, a Fieseler. I imagine that was your doing, Sergeant Guy', said Churchill with a mischievous smile. John nodded, unsure what to say. 'You are, of course, well aware of this aeroplane's capabilities and we will have some fellows from the Air Ministry examining it in some detail. Brilliant piece of flying by all accounts. The RAF were quite astonished that you managed to land it in that field in the dark.'

'Thank you, sir', said John, quietly.

'The equipment that came with you in the satchel is an OKW encryption device. OKW is the German High Command and they may not even realise that this machine is missing. It will enable us to decode Wehrmacht radio signals. We will be fully aware of German intentions, just so long as they keep using radios for communication. I am sure that you will realise we believe a German invasion to be, if not imminent, then certainly a strong possibility. Hopefully, now we can keep track of their intentions.' There was a pause and the general spoke for the first time.

'Which of you brought that?', he said. John and Mig looked at Ted. He muttered from behind his teacup.

'I think I found it, sir', he said, bashfully. He looked at the plate of biscuits, so far untouched and wished that someone would take the first one. Churchill intercepted his glance and reached for the plate. He took a biscuit and then offered the plate to Ted.

'Have a biscuit, Corporal Dexter. Lastly, we seem to have found ourselves in possession of the personal effects of one General Erwin Rommel, including his pyjamas, his diary and a large amount of ladies' underwear from a boutique in Lille. We assume that the underwear was for his wife or mistress, if he has one. His diary is currently being translated and the underwear is going to be sewn together to make parachutes', said Churchill, poker faced. He caught Mig's look of shock.

'Unless of course you can find some other use for them Private Miglorine?'

The men laughed. Even the invariably taciturn Brooke cracked a smile.

They continued to chat for a few minutes, Churchill eager to share his ideas with them. He told them of the battles that he thought lay ahead and of the difficulties he foresaw. Throughout he remained optimistic, bullish.

'In time of war we must accept the role that is allocated to us by fate; to do otherwise is to live that part of our lives as a lie. Having done so we are then judged by how we perform that role and how much closer to victory we came as a result… and let us not forget that it is the victors who write the history books.' The three men nodded, feeling as if they had been temporarily drawn into a privileged and secretive world.

'You can all expect a summons to the palace for medals and a promotion. So, Lance Corporal Miglorine, a Military Medal has been proposed. Corporal Dexter we thought that a Distinguished Conduct Medal might be appropriate for your leadership and courage. Bringing us the encryption machine might change the course of the war at this critical stage.' Mig and Ted both beamed despite their nerves and fatigue.

'As for you Sergeant Guy, we rather thought that a Distinguished Flying Medal would be appropriate. You stole a German aeroplane from a French beach and despite your unfamiliarity with it, managed to fly it back to Britain at night with two valuable men on board. A quite incredible feat. But then we heard about your exploits with your squadron. When we take into account that you seem to be the only surviving pilot and that you are then able to bring about this amazing escape it would seem that a Victoria Cross would be the most appropriate decoration.'

John's mouth almost fell open but before the news could sink in Churchill was talking again.

'We have very important things to discuss with each of you. You will be debriefed separately. I hope that we meet again gentlemen but if we don't, I would like you to know that your country owes you a great deal for what you have achieved. I personally am very proud of you and of the spirit you have shown in getting back to continue the fight.' The meeting was obviously at an end and they followed General Brooke's lead as he stood.

Ted was led to another office just down the hall and ushered into the presence of another senior officer who introduced himself as Brigadier Murray. Murray shook his hand and invited him to sit.

'I'm sure you'd be glad of a bath and some new uniform, Corporal Dexter', he said, smiling.

'I would, sir. And something to eat and some leave', added Ted. He thought that the officer's smile diminished ever so slightly as if he had been over familiar or committed some classic *faux pas* of the class to which he belonged. He was unaccountably disappointed at the man's reaction, just as he wasn't quite sure that there had been any reaction at all. *They were giving him a medal but no leave? Could that be true?*

'We'll see what we can do', said the brigadier, non-commitally. 'The PM is very keen to make use of your talents and it is my job to debrief you and to assess exactly what talents you have.' Ted, who considered himself to be rather without talent, pulled a face. 'You look confused and I am not surprised, but if I tell you a little bit more about my job then things might make more sense. When I have finished you will have a decision to make and you won't have very much time in which to make it. Not everything that you are about to hear will be to your liking and *all* of it is top secret.' The brigadier smiled again as he spoke. 'If you talk about it, you'll be shot', he said. His eyes held those of Ted. Ted waited for him to explain that it was a joke. 'Do you understand that, corporal?'

Ted nodded. It wasn't a joke after all.

'Sir', he said.

'Good. The biggest challenge that we face as a nation is the possibility of an invasion by the Germans. Hitler has virtually overrun Western Europe – we expect France to surrender soon – and that makes it highly unlikely, in our view, that he will leave the United Kingdom sitting unmolested, unconquered, just twenty miles from the edge of his new empire. Being brutal about the state of things, Corporal Dexter, it is only the English Channel keeping us in the fight.' He paused and looked at the young NCO in front of him. He liked what he saw. Dexter was bright and clearly resourceful if his recent actions were anything to go by. He wished that he'd been given the opportunity to get washed and changed into a new uniform but he understood the pressure of time.

'You may have figured all this out for yourself – I suspect that you have – and you may be wondering why we are sitting here now.' He glanced behind him at a world map on the plain wall of his office. 'Britain, that tiny nation, that speck which makes hardly an impression on a map of the world, is the last thing that stands between Hitler and domination of Europe. Once he has conquered Europe he can do more or less whatever he likes. The only other people in a position to stand up to Hitler are the Russians, and he has signed a non-aggression pact with them.

'Germany and Russia are ideologically opposed but for the moment there will be peace between them. The fight back against Hitler will have to start from here, from Britain, but before that can happen we need to protect ourselves from invasion. If we can defeat an invasion then we will hopefully prevent the Germans from making another attempt for years to come. We will have bought ourselves time.' He looked at Dexter again. The NCO nodded.

'We are building our defences, training soldiers, producing tanks and aeroplanes, preparing the people for invasion. But the PM wants more. He wants us to fight back now in whatever way we can. He wants people to go into Europe and cause chaos.' Ted said nothing. He felt his stomach knot. None of this was what he wanted to hear. He wanted to be told that he had done enough killing, had risked his life enough times, had made his outstanding contribution to the war effort and that his service was over. Instead, this man was telling him that he would be required to do more of the same.

'The PM wants you to be his personal agent. I don't know what exactly that might entail and, I suspect, nor does he, but that's the job. That's why you are here.' The brigadier smiled again. Ted couldn't tell if it was a cold smile or a warm one. 'So, what is your answer?'

Ted looked into his lap. He said, 'can I have leave and then think about it, sir?'

For a moment, a split second only, the brigadier looked uncomfortable. He sucked on his teeth and then spoke.

'No', he said. 'For this to work you would have to be declared dead or missing in action. In other words, you would cease to exist. Much easier that way.'

'But my mum and dad...'

'Already think you are dead. Don't forget the rest of your battalion got home days ago and you weren't with them. In time the Germans will inform us of their prisoners of war. They do this through the Red Cross but your name will never appear in those lists.'

'But I could go on leave and then they would know...'

'Yes. We are only asking you to volunteer. You can go on leave, get your medal from the King, rejoin your battalion and never mention this again. The choice is yours but I need your answer now, before you leave this room.'

Ted looked at the officer and at his medal ribbons from the Great War. His mind was a swirl of painful emotions and contradictory hopes. He knew little about Churchill, other than that he was the new Prime Minister.

Ted sighed. Would he, Ted Dexter, succumb to some hastily assembled words of flattery tacked onto his life like an afterthought, he wondered? The officer spoke again.

'Your parents have already grieved for you. Churchill believes that he needs you.'

Ted gave a tiny nod of understanding. This was too dangerous for him. He had no special gifts to offer. He was too tired to even contemplate giving up his current life for one of danger and discomfort.

'Okay. I'll do it.'

The Avenger's Apprentice

Ted's adventures continue in the next book in the Lost Man series, 'The Avenger's Apprentice', which sees Ted return to France on his first mission for Brigadier Murray.

'What can you see?'

'Nothing.'

'Keep looking.'

Ted strained his eyes to see better in the dark... but it was the dark which was the problem; impenetrable, complete. Not one ray of light made it into the room and Ted just shook his head at the sheer impossibility of his task. They had practically admitted they didn't know what they were doing; now he knew for sure that they hadn't been lying. If anything, they had underplayed their lack of... what was it... competence? Experience, maybe? He wondered if they actually knew anything more than he did.

'Just keep looking', said the voice. 'Let me know when you see something.'

Ted could still see nothing. He had never known such unadulterated blackness as that in which he now stood. But he could smell something. Burning? Smouldering perhaps, like a dry cloth carelessly fallen onto a light bulb or dust on a seldom used heater. Whatever produced the smell emitted no light. But he could hear something; a low hum from somewhere, like the sound of an electrical transformer. He connected the smell to the sound, which achieved nothing of course; they wanted him to see.

'Can you see anything?', asked the voice. Did he detect a trace of despair displacing the quiet optimism of only a few minutes ago?

'Nothing. Just blackness.'

'Can you see the outline of any shapes? Even slightly?'

'Nothing', said Ted. His small reserves of patience suddenly ran out like the last grains of sand in an egg-timer. 'Why don't you just put the bloody light on?', he asked facetiously. There was no reply but a moment later the light did indeed come on. Ted shielded his eyes. 'I think I can see something now', he said.

The voice on the other side of the plywood wall was muffled but still audible. 'Cheeky bastard.'